Jazmin Lister

The Heart of the Beast Prince

A Beauty and the Beast Tale

First Edition March 2026
EPUB ISBN: 978-1-972125-00-7
Paperback ISBN: 978-1-972125-01-4
Hardback ISBN: 978-1-972125-02-1
Cover Art by MIBLART

Published by JB Legacy Publishing, LLC
Enterprise, USA

A BEAUTY AND THE BEAST TALE

THE HEART OF THE BEAST PRINCE

JAZMIN LISTER

Table of Contents

Prologue-Icen: 4

Chapter 1-Axen 14

Chapter 2-Icen: 25

Chapter 3-Axen: 37

Chapter 4-Icen: 54

Chapter 5-Axen: 65

Chapter 6-Axen: 74

Icen 84

Chapter 7-Icen: 89

Chapter 8-Axen: 98

Chapter 9-Axen: 114

Chapter 10-Icen: 129

Chapter 11-Axen: 135

Chapter 12-Axen: 147

Chapter 13-Axen: 154

Chapter 14-Icen: 164

Chapter 15-Axen: 170

Chapter 16-Icen: 178

Chapter 17-Axen: 180

Chapter 18-Axen: 190
Chapter 19-Axen:.. 200
Chapter 20-Axen:.. 211
Chapter 21-Icen:.. 220
Chapter 22-Axen:.. 222
Chapter 23-Axen 234
Chapter 24-Icen: 246
Chapter 25-Axen: 257
Chapter 26-Axen:.. 266
Chapter 27-Axen: 276
Chapter 28-Axen:.. 283
Chapter 29-Axen:.. 294
Chapter 30-Icen: 302
Chapter 31-Axen:.. 307
Chapter 32-Axen: 322
Icen 333
Chapter 33-Icen: 334
Acknowledgements: 346
About the Author: 347
Sneak Peak: Depth of the Ocean.. 348

Pronunciation Guide:

Icen—Eye-sen

Xahamen—Zaw-a-men

Caissidde—Kai-sid-he

Jaque mate—haw kay maw tay

Ajed—A head

Maps

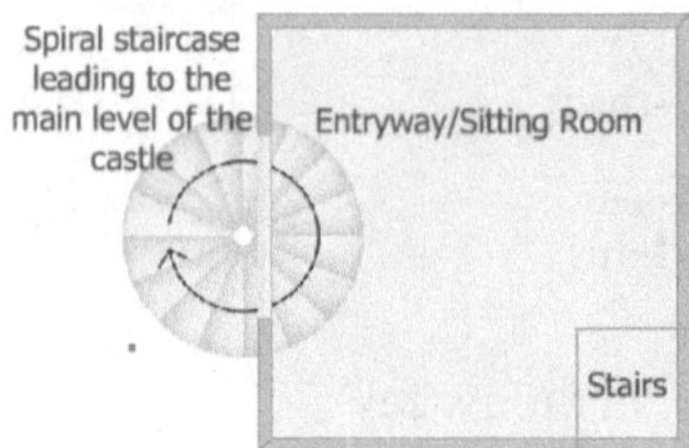

First Floor

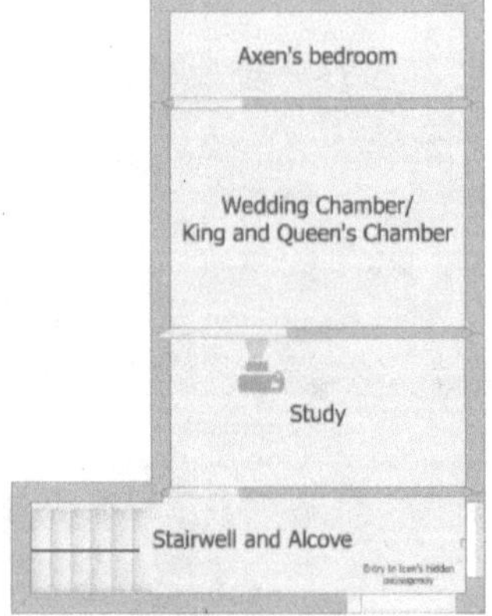

Second Floor

This book is dedicated to:

Danielle, my guardian angel.

My mom and sisters, who suffered through the early drafts.

And my Ben. Thank you for suffering through the long hours, endless drafts, and hard days with me. I will always pursue my dreams because of you.

Prologue-Icen:

"This was folly," Icen hissed. Shifting his weight to free his limbs from beneath his body, he tried to stem the bleeding from several serious wounds. His slippery hands were no match for the free-flowing blood. He moved a fist to his eye, the wound he feared the most.

They were too far from the castle for immediate help, and everything had gone wrong. He had come to end the war he waged against the Tersinian kingdom with a final, powerful strike. And he had failed.

"Kidnapping, foiled. Ambush, foiled. Invasion, foiled." Icen could hear his best friend, Regan, complaining in his deep voice, somewhere in the darkness off to his right. "Who knew the Tersinian prince would show up and turn the tide?"

Breathless, Icen wanted to lift his voice in response, but he was exhausted. Maga flowers bowed above him, glaring down at him. The ocean lapped at his legs, and the salt water burned the wounds gifted him by his Tersinian equal. Prince Kole had flowed from weapon to weapon as though each were an extension of his arm: bow, javelin, sword, dagger. Kole, the son of a traitor, had bested Icen.

"Prince Icen, where are you?" Regan called. "Dead yet?"

"You only wish." He reached up to smooth back his mane of textured black hair from his face. The ocean dragged the curls past his shoulders with its greedy, heavy hands.

Regan knelt at Icen's side, spitting blood into the rising tide. "I almost couldn't see you here in that black tunic." The prince looked at the deep brown of Regan's skin, nearly hidden in the dark. Regan could have passed for Icen's brother, with similar long, curly black hair and dark skin. The fresh, disfiguring wounds across their faces would forever remind them of their failure tonight. "I tried to bandage myself. I'll get your worst wounds tied up and head for help."

The strips of cloth did nothing to stop Icen's pain, especially as they soaked up the ocean. Soon, he was more bandage than flesh. "I hope I do not lose this eye," he growled, using his good arm to feel the bandaging.

"I will go for horses, my lord," Regan said. "I remember seeing a farm not too far from here."

"Yes, go," Icen urged. He knew that Regan would have to steal them. Any blow they could strike against the Tersinian Queen Nari, no matter how petty, was worth it. "If you run, you will return within the hour, and we can ride for the capital."

"Do you think you are safe here for that long?" Regan asked, rising to his feet. He looked first to the ocean's horizon and then back to the thick jungle behind them.

"They'll take the prisoners back to somewhere more defensible. We should have time."

Regan towered over the weakened Prince. Like Icen, Regan's face wound was frightening, splitting his mouth wider into an inhuman maw. "I'll run."

Grunting, Icen managed to pull himself up. Bracing himself against a root, he watched with his one good eye as Regan sneaked away into the foreign jungle.

A cold chill of realization shot through Icen's heart. Perhaps Regan would not return from the darkness that consumed his departure. Deep in Tersine, enemies were everywhere, and neither he, the warmonger Xahamenian prince, nor his soldiers would be welcomed with palm fronds. If Regan were discovered, he would be killed.

Icen waited, slipping in and out of consciousness. The tide came in like a fish slipping into the waves, slapping ever closer until the stinging warmth began soaking through Icen's bandages. Willing himself to move, Icen gripped another root with his good arm and pulled himself into a sitting position. Lights sprang before his eyes. He continued blinking frantically, his concern growing as the lights did not disappear. Raising his good hand, he scrubbed at his good eye, dislodging clots of blood, but the lights drew closer and hovered above the ground like torchlight.Icen shuddered. *Tersinians*. They must be looking for him. He paused. The approaching enemy was too silent—no boots splashed through ocean water. No footsteps thundered on the shore. No armor clanked. Digging his heels into the grinding sand, he attempted to shove his heavy body deeper into the shadows of the mangrove roots. He knew the incoming tide could be loud, but there was no way it would be loud enough to cover the sounds of many people approaching.

What is coming after me?

The lights clarified from one large light into two and then three hanging orbs. Icen couldn't look away, nor could he make sense of what he was seeing. There was no flight left in his muscles. His world began to spin.

Are these torches of the enemy?

His ragged breathing was loud. He tried to hold it, to silence it, but unconsciousness threatened. Flashing colors, pink, black, and blue, filled his vision. The lights encircled him, and he knew he couldn't get away. He was surrounded. Captured.

His good hand gripped the only weapon he had left—a six-inch ice-crystal dagger, endowed with ancient magic. He would go down fighting if he had to, but his mind couldn't make sense of what he was seeing. One of the lights lengthened and took form, slowly shaping itself into a human-like body. The angular face of Queen Jozefina of Xahamen—his deceased mother—appeared.

He whimpered. "Am I dead?"

Smiling, the relucent figure stepped closer, placing her hand on his head, pushing it back so he could meet her gaze. His chin trembled. Two almond-shaped eyes with red irises crinkled with joy. Her rich, warm skin stood out against the pale sand. The orbs of light danced and bobbed around her as she stood before him.

"No, my most precious son." Her voice a quiver. "You cannot die today." She gestured to the lights around her. "That is why we are here." She took her son's hand, holding his fingers tenderly. "I want you to know that there was nothing Nari could have done for me."

Nari. The Queen of Tersine. The woman who betrayed my mother to death.

Icen's face contorted in disgust at the woman who had abandoned his mother in her time of need.

Jozefina squeezed Icen's hand, noticing his sneer. "She was the best friend I could have ever asked for, and she gave me everything she could when she left Xahamen."

"But Mother—"

Jozefina smiled. "I know she went on to have four children. Her body was much stronger than mine."

"She could have—"

"She gave me more strength than she should have. You don't understand. You cannot. Not without asking."

Shaking her head, Jozefina continued, "The strength of her body comes from the strength of her will and her endless kindness."

"But Mother, is that why you are here? To tell me I blame the wrong person?" Icen nearly pulled from his mother's grip, betrayed. "That I am warring with Tersine for nothing?"

"I came to tell you that there is no one to blame for my death. My body was weak. Now my spirit is free." Jozefina stroked her son's face, her eyes soft, the touch of her fingertips light but insistent. "And I am here now to help you become strong. To help you become the man you are supposed to be."

She stepped away as the other lights pressed into him. Each struck his body, though he did not feel their touch—his pain vanished. One by one, his wounds ceased throbbing, and the saltwater's burning caress ebbed. Pulling off the bandage that had bound his eye, he clearly saw his mother now. The edges of her smile pulled down.

"There is a woman who is so true, her goodness can see through this curse. The very princess you sought to kidnap today," she said. "This is justice."

The lights beside his mother faded into the night, leaving Icen and Jozefina alone in the pensive starlight.

"The woman of Tersine can give you the mercy to end this curse which will carry you into your joint destiny."

Jozefina looked up at the three moons. “Through your efforts, you can heal your bodily curse. Until the curse is broken, you will be unable to move forward to fulfill the prophecy together.”

“What curse, Mother?” Icen asked, anxiously rising to his feet. He flexed his sword hand with renewed mobility. “What are you talking about?” A feeling of strength filled his previously trembling thighs, a strength that scant minutes ago had abandoned him.

With a wave of her hand, Jozefina directed Icen’s gaze to the water around his calves. It pooled in unnatural stillness. He looked and cowered at his beastly reflection. Unbidden tears of horror desecrated Icen’s eyes.

“You did this to me?” he asked, his voice and hands shaking. The skin on his face was lost under the shiny, black scales. In desperation, he looked to his mother. He refused to look at his own reflection again or even look down at his physical form.

“You did this to yourself, Icen.” Jozefina choked back grief. “What you see on your face—on your skin—is the canker you allowed to infest your body. This curse is a gift if you will let it be. Fight the darkness, and you will win. Succumb, and this will be your face and form forever. All hope of healing this world’s magic will be lost.”

“But you said the woman can undo this.”

“No. Only you can undo this. Once you have, her mercy will finish its work. You are responsible for healing the black blight of hatred you let fester in your soul. The princess in turn, is responsible for her destiny. I only pray that she will let you retain your part in it."

A long descending note of despair ripped from Icen's throat. "How can I do that? How can I earn her mercy? I cannot forgive her mother for abandoning you in your weakness. She won't give me mercy when I have tried to kill her father, brother, and people." Apprehension filled his soul.

"You must or remain a beast forever."

Icen winced. *I must do something. But admit I was wrong?* Another groan tightened his chest. "The princess couldn't possibly let go what I have done to her and her people."

"She has a willing heart." Jozefina smiled and took Icen's trembling hands in hers. "It is your job to win not only her mercy, but her love."

"Love?" Icen scoffed. "But you have turned me into a beast."

"Dear son, you have made yourself into this monster. The mark you see on your skin is a direct reflection of the darkness in your heart."

Icen's shaking began in earnest. His muscles, recently strengthened, betrayed his inner turmoil. "Mother, I . . . I . . ."

"You must remember that you cannot *make* the princess love you. It is entirely up to her."

"Then what do I do?"

Jozefina began to fade before Icen's eyes, and he snatched at her in desperation.

"You must heal, Icen, my most precious child." Jozefina melted into the darkness.

Icen's ears perked up—he heard horses, a fading whisper of his name, and Regan's approach. His knees quivered in fear. Regan could not see him as he was now. No one could. He wouldn't allow it. Regan would surely kill him.

"Icen!" a muffled call came.

"I am here, Regan." His slithering voice was no longer his own. Reaching up, there was a rasp of scale on scale as he grabbed at his throat. "Do not come any closer."

"But I have horses," Regan called back, though his forward progress stalled.

"Ride home, Regan. I will do what I can for myself. Leave me the horse, and do not come back."

A long pause stretched between the men, but finally, Regan departed. The pounding of hooves echoed against the roots and packed sand until there was no sound left but a quiet nickering from the horse waiting in the dark.

Stepping carefully in his approach, Icen moved to where the nickering animal was. His newly enhanced eyes shirked the darkness to look through the trees and ensure Regan was gone. The horse panicked when Icen touched it, kicking up sand and shooting off through the mangroves back in the direction from which it had come.

The beast prince steeled himself and ran home.

Chapter 1-Axen

Axen shifted her youngest brother behind her as she drew her bow string. Little Matteus clung to the leather strap of the quiver, ducking behind his sister's shoulder. With an arrow notched at the ready, the two stood in the attitude of stillness and silence, waiting for Axen's prey to move into position.

She grinned. Through the dense jungle undergrowth, Princess Axen watched as their eldest brother, heir to the throne and target, Kole, reached into the sack resting on the ground at his side and withdrew a bright red pomarrosa fruit to lift to his mouth. As his teeth closed for a bite, she released the arrow, striking the fruit from between his teeth before he could sink them into the juicy flesh.

Matteus and Axen high-fived as the pomarrosa tumbled to the ground. Little bits of the juice flew into the air and splashed their brother's astonished face. In the next heartbeat, Kole flew to his feet, fists up, head whipping around to find his opponent. A grin split Axen's face. He couldn't find them. They were too well-hidden and far enough away to make discovery impossible.

Axen tossed her bow back over her shoulder and gripped tiny, eight-year-old Matteus tightly to her side.

She meandered along, bouncing her brother playfully with her hip, zigzagging along the game path through the jungle until they came upon the tall grasses and endemic Tersinian maga flowers. The princess drew her sword. The shiny silver flashed as she cut her way through the grasses, shrubs, and then the dangling air roots that made an impassable wall beneath the canopy of umbrella-shaped trees. Axen stopped. The foliage-concealed rocks and roots were often slick with moisture and could send her sprawling or break her ankle easily if she didn't have secure footing. Helping her brother, she lumbered along awkwardly until they came upon their special tree. As the tallest tree around, with its dense cluster of soft pine needles on each branch, it afforded the best view of the surrounding valley while providing a comfortable place to rest.

Matteus scrambled up first, jumping from branch to branch, searching out the small platform Axen had built in the topmost branches. She pulled her body up from vine to vine and bough to bough until she caught up with Matteus. He wrapped his arms and legs around her from the back, a well-practiced pose for both. At the top, they lowered themselves to the platform.

Matteus grinned. A breathy laugh escaped his mouth. "We got him," he said, pumping a fist up and down. "Do you think he knew it was us?"

Smiling back, Axen reclined into their hidden haven. "Probably. I mean, who else would it be?"

"Do you think he saw where we went?" Matteus took up his position, belly flat on the platform, fingers and eyes peeking over the side to the jungle floor far below.

Axen's eyes twinkled with mirth. "Not a chance." But she knew Kole would find them eventually. All her brothers knew this was where she would go, especially if she had Matteus with her. The siblings looped their arms over each other's shoulders. They watched the afternoon sky grow more dynamic in its coloring, lighting the jungled hills with celestial fire, until little Matteus nodded off beneath Axen's encircling arm.

A great, suffocating, and swelling embrace rose and tightened across Axen's chest as she looked at the cherubic face in the dimming light. His skin tone paled next to her sun-kissed hue—he was a sickly child. But their dark brown, copper-tinged haloes of hair exposed them as siblings. Thoughts she had tried to avoid came in a torrent. Terror. Indignation. Hope. Heartbreak. The contents of the letter she had received that morning lowered on her like the twilight.

In her memory, she recoiled at the blood red wax of the fanged lizard stamp outlined by traditional Xahamenian roses that had sealed the letter shut. The horrifying seal of the beast prince. As a child he had chosen the ferocious creature for his personal crest, and it left no doubt of the originator. The proposal was from the land of Xahamen. Unrolling the parchment had revealed her likely future and set her mood into a hurricane of anxiety. The neatly written words from the king and prince of the northlands declared a desire for a truce.

The beast prince wanted to trade her freedom for his surrender.

A darkness filled her mind. Since her birth, she had known that her marriage had been prophesied to be important for the future of the world's magic—the enchantments that governed the way the world changed and grew. Tersine had been cut off from the magical source long before Axen had been born, and magic was foreign to the princess, merely a fairytale her parents had spun for their nighttime stories.

So many outcomes hinged on this marriage: a treaty, the spreading of the magicless curse on the world, and her future happiness. Axen took in Matteus' features. His dark eyelashes and brows rested on cheeks that sagged beneath their cherubic weight.

Three brothers, one father, and her future. Could she trade potential happiness for their lives and prospects? Even if her marriage was prophesied to save the world from magical collapse. Her love for them surged in a sudden tide, choking her. Human flesh for a treaty. Her life for theirs.

A sound broke her trance of concentration. Despite not being able to get an immediate visual, Axen knew it wasn't Kole. With his direct inheritance to the throne and the ongoing war with Xahamen, Kole wouldn't dare go into the forest alone. Prince Icen had marked him repeatedly as a target.

Holding her breath, she withdrew Matteus's sleeping form as far from sight as she could. The same pressure that bound her to stabilize magic for the Five Lands now sharpened her vigilance–fear once again driving her duty. Long moments of tranquility and the lowering sun set Axen into suspicion. She needed to go down for a look before moonrise, or whoever, or *whatever*, was down there may have set a trap for those who would come to collect her.

Tucking her sword and bow close to her sides to eliminate their sharp edges from sight, she flipped her hood and lowered herself down a few rows of branches. Her eyes roved the area. Her ears perked to receive any sound of anything that approached. She held her body perfectly still. Her clenched muscles screamed and trembled.

Axen saw nothing, but the hushed bugs and frogs made her uneasy. The world was windless and noiseless with what her mother called 'the magicless void.' While the princess had never known the existence of magic, her mother had, and so had the rest of the Five Lands.

Matteus, having grown cold from the darkening of the day, whispered something down to his sister. Looking up, she brusquely held a fist to her lips and shook her head. He retreated obediently into the hidden space of the platform. She knew her other brothers would be coming soon. The recognition brought a surge of relief and a wave of grief. Her brothers. Her home.

She didn't know if her parents would expect her to marry Prince Icen, but she knew without a doubt they wouldn't force her. Neither would her brothers, despite their lives being wrapped up in the treaty. It was her decision alone. She didn't know if she could sacrifice her own future for the futures of those she loved—especially for a lifetime with a beast.

A soft groan from below reignited her vigil, followed by a sharp bugle cry. Axen's brothers converged on their platform in the tree. She still searched the ground below, lowering herself a few more branches.

After her earlier teasing attack, Kole certainly believed they were playing a game, but the fact that he brought a guard eased Axen's anxiety. The darkness grew heavy, making it harder to see. She stiffened. Not ten feet below her, at the base of a tree, a man was sprawled unconscious on the jungle floor. His tunic bore the colors of Xahamen: a pale blue and a vibrant rose red. Yet something was odd. While his nearly comatose eyes stared up, he didn't see her. He wasn't really looking through his eyes. They remained open out of habit.

She whistled, drawing her sword and dropping to the ground. The shrill noise jolted the Xahamenian to consciousness. His eyes focused and found hers as her brothers whistled back.

The sound of metal on sheath caused the disoriented man beneath her to draw his sword, but before it was even halfway out of its scabbard, he released it, turning his palms up and reaching them toward Axen—a sign he meant no harm. Then his hands fell, and he slumped back against the tree, head lolling to the side. The tip of Axen's sword drooped as she approached the enemy.

"Axen?" Kole yelled. Matteus dropped to the ground beside her.

"Here, brothers!" Axen hollered. "Please hurry."

Panicked voices broke through the noise of the jungle around them. Axen looked at Matteus and chuckled when the rushed steps stopped and were punctuated with a solid thwack and a loud curse.

"Can't see a branch at face height, huh?" Kole's lilting voice came through the trees. "Hopefully, there are no enemies nearby, or they will simply wait until you take us all out, brother."

Axen pushed Matteus behind her, keeping the Xahamenian at swordpoint until Kole and Sunder flanked her. Kole's guards surrounded them. The man didn't stir with the new company.

"What did you do, sis, tree a Xahamenian soldier?" Kole teased, elbowing his sister in jest. She caught his lowered eyebrows and narrowed eyes. He, too, was suspicious of trickery. When Kole had made it to the unknown man's side, he placed an ear to the motionless chest. "You beat him senseless?" he asked with a note of pride in his voice.

"If he was senseless, Zen, why didn't you haul him in?" Sunder asked, rubbing the branch-shaped bruise already blossoming on his face. "It's dark, and I'm hungry."

"He's a spy!" Matteus declared, chest puffed out. "And Axen captured him first."

The soldiers, dragged along by Kole and Sunder's need for armed chaperones, still wielded weapons. Some faced inward toward the siblings and the intruder; others faced outward.

Axen, now secure that the battered human before her was indeed not a current threat, sheathed her weapon. The man was older, perhaps twice her age, with graying hair, wrinkles, and black moles covering his dark skin—skin a shade darker than hers. Beaten badly, the Xahamenian soldier's face took on a purple, bruised hue.

She noticed the man's listlessness and moved to take him into her arms. "If we lay him down, I am sure he will be more comfortable," she said, her voice strained as she staggered under his weight.

"I've got him," Kole interjected. He and Sunder stepped up to assist the staggering Axen with the man's weight. The four siblings looked at the man. Axen trembled from adrenaline and fear.

"Use my cloak to make a stretcher," Kole barked, one arm gesturing to the guards.

The crown prince's guard each took up a corner and bore the man back through the undergrowth toward the castle. Once the soldiers were gone with the potential spy, the four siblings followed, ducking their way through the plants.

"What did you think you were doing, shooting me like that?" Kole asked.

Axen cast a sidelong glance at him and smiled sadly. The resistance of the branch bending against her lift squared her shoulders and set her jaw. She stared at the ground as her thoughts were once again captured by her impending future. Her tears would have been a dead giveaway that something was wrong. Earlier in the day, she had sought relief—the reason she had bothered antagonizing him in the first place. But now, she shook her head. Life felt much too real with a Xahamenian in Tersine.

"You could have hurt me—" Kole started.

"Yeah, she could have," Sunder countered, stumbling into a shrub, "but she didn't. She doesn't make mistakes."

Axen made no reply as he dusted the bits of broken branch and leaf debris from his hair and shoulders. The three brothers looked at her, concern evident in their faces.

"I am competent," she said reluctantly. Her stomach twisted in knots. "I wouldn't have hurt you, Kole. But that man?" she said, trying to unclench her jaw. "And that letter today? It's becoming too real." She fell silent. Matteus' little hand slipped into hers, causing the cage around her heart to relax its chokehold.

Kole caught on to her trepidation and spoke first, extending a maga flower for her to take. "Because he's from Xahamen, and their beast prince wants to marry you?"

"You always outsmart and outwit anyone, Zen," Sunder said. "You will find a way out of the terms of the treaty unless you would rather outrank all of us except Kole."

"The senseless violence will end. Dad and Kole have fought for that," Axen whispered into her footsteps, tucking the maga flower behind her ear, but her brothers still heard. "And maybe I can fulfill the prophecy of healing the magic and stopping the decay? What if I can keep the people from starving? What if I can actually stop the rivers from drying up, the children from crying to their mothers in hunger?"

"I hate that it has to be you," Matteus pitched in.

A gust of guilt blew through Axen as she reached for her baby brother, tucking him into her side once again. "Matty, do you know I love you?" She had directed her words at Matteus, but hoped all three brothers knew she spoke these words to them individually. Matteus' little face looked up at her, round and trusting in the moonlight. Axen looked to each of her brothers in turn. The golden light softened their set jaws and hid wrinkles of consternation, wiping away time and harsh experience. *This is my safe world. The only world I have ever known.*

"Matty?" she asked, softly but firmly. "Cross your heart and promise me that you know."

Each of her brothers took their pointer fingers and solemnly crossed their hearts. Little Matteus paused a moment to gather his words. "I cross my heart and promise you that I know." His words carried years of memories.

Chapter 2-Icen:

The returning Xahamenian prisoners of war marched along the main thoroughfare toward the capital. Mediation with Tersine had been successful. Hundreds of soldiers had been released after a series of successful negotiations—the last remaining men from the battle at Tersine. Icen shuddered at the memory of the night he had been cursed. He tried to keep his chin up and his back erect, even though no one could see him within the dark shelter of his carriage's interior.

"Are you sure you want him up there?" Nic hissed through the window, breaking Icen's brooding. An excellent swordsman, brown-black-haired, short-tempered, solidly stout, honorable, Nic was Icen's only guard. Icen's gaze followed Nic's pointing finger to the man on the raised dais in front of them. Clouds of frost puffed around the passionate orator as he spoke. He wore a traditional wreath of roses around his neck.

"Who else do you think should be up there?" the prince snapped back. "Regan is my best friend and second in command. No one else would have been an acceptable substitute." Icen wanted to strike him, but the smirking Nic stepped sideways out of Icen's reach. The elite sentry knew Icen wouldn't leave the carriage.

Icen hissed in a breath, wishing he could dismiss Nic as his armed escort, but he couldn't. His father, King Caissidde, held the highest power in this instance, and Icen's shame at his unwillingness to stand before his people made him testy.

From where Icen sat, he could see Regan standing on the podium, arms set in a stately manner behind his back. The troops marched past and disappeared from the prince's line of sight. Once all were past, only Regan's rallying voice and form reached Icen.

Flicking a finger, Icen used his fae—invisible creatures of wind and mischief—to draw the curtains closed over the carriage windows. The crimson velvet rippled as the breezy energy danced around the fabric, hesitant. His fae swirled around him, settling into their invisible, but undeniable, position around him.

Sonorous tones from Regan's speech reached Icen's ears, though the distinct words were indecipherable from this angle. The anger-filled prince didn't need to hear the discourse.

I wrote it. The words spoke of his regret for the war and his gratitude for the sacrifice of the men loyal to him and the crown. While the regret was an outright lie, the gratitude tugged at his heart.

"No mention of the treaty yet, I see," Nic commented, breaking Icen's trance. The sentry stood, facing the crowd.

"I don't want to give the country false hope. It will take a miracle to get the king to agree to the terms," Icen responded coolly. "Not that it is any of your business."

"Does Regan know?"

Icen bit back his retort. It really should have been him, the prince, on the podium delivering the eulogy to the fallen warriors, but at the last moment, he had balked. Regan had been all too willing to step up.

"Ah. I guessed not," Nic continued. "Are you ready to marry the Tersinian princess?"

Icen turned to hear his guard better. "I hope the royal family received my father's treaty proposal, yes. If all goes well, she will accept the proposal of marriage."

"Is this an alternate kidnapping attempt?" Nic asked. His eyes never stopped scanning the narrow street around them. It was the guard's job to keep Icen alive—even if, in his current cursed, invincible, and lizard-like state, Icen didn't need any help.

"No," Icen ground his teeth. "I already told you that."

"So, what *is your purpose*? Why are you forcing her here?"

"I don't like your tone, Nic."

"I don't like your deceit, Majesty. Answer directly, or I will send an envoy myself. Do you still intend to imprison her?"

Icen's conscience burned him at Nic's words. Most would not dare address him in such a familiar manner, but Nic was special. Icen hadn't picked Nic for the guard—he wouldn't have picked anyone so young—the choice had been out of his hands and placed in Maarten's, the king's advisor and head of the royal guard.

"I intend to bring peace to both of our people. There is no ulterior motive," Icen lied. "The rebel activity at the border has been concerning too. It will be beneficial for both our countries.

Nic scoffed, "Are you going to let your people see you?"

"I dare not."

"It would honor the soldiers who lost their lives and assure these men that you still hold the power and not Regan."

Regret for his selfishness pinched Icen's heart. "I know you want me to," he muttered. "I wish you would mind your own business."

Nic's lighthearted chuckle rumbled in his throat. "I care about the soldiers who are loyal to you."

"As do I." No defensiveness tinged Icen's tone, just dejection. He didn't know how much more rejection he could take. He hadn't even been able to muster the courage to show Regan his transfigured face. "I don't think their living families would want to see . . . this." Icen looked down at himself.

“I am sorry I didn’t take it well,” Nic murmured.

He spoke of the night Icen returned, when his transfiguration had taken both him and Maarten by surprise. Nic’s reaction had stung. So had Icen’s father, Caissidde. The older men had cried. Nic had turned away in fear and disgust. Hours had passed before Nic returned to Icen’s company.

“I don’t want to frighten them,” Icen said. If only he believed he could let people see his face without them turning to run. The rejection he had felt—still felt—shook him.

“I understand, Prince. I do. Maarten was right, I think. If you show them your face sooner, it will give them time to get used to it.”

Growling, Icen wanted to reply, but Nic asked, “Have you shown Regan your face yet?”

Icen’s anger cooled instantaneously, and he pulled the curtain back a fraction of an inch to peek out. Regan gestured grandly to the soldiers below him as he spoke.

“No.”

Nic hummed thoughtfully. “I don’t like him. I never have. Has he convinced you to hide your face?”

Icen laughed a mirthless laugh. “Regan is like my brother.”

“What a brother he is. I don’t think he will stop fighting in some way or another until he rules Tersine.”

Irritation at the implied disloyalty almost made Icen open the carriage door, but the thought of being seen held him back. “You don’t know him. Or me.”

“He was my commander for a long time, my prince. I know that I don’t like him. Even if he ends up ruling Tersine, I don’t think he will stop until he takes over Xahamen too.”

“Regan would never do anything to hurt me,” Icen said. He wanted to believe in his best friend, but the words Nic had said worried the edges of the prince’s anxiety.

“Sure, sure. In the same way he wouldn’t hurt Maarten?” Anger filled Nic’s voice.

“He didn’t hurt Maarten.”

“Then why isn’t Maarten here?”

Icen fell silent. He couldn’t betray a confidence, even if Maarten was missing by design.

“He didn’t tell you?” If Maarten hadn’t said anything, there was no way Nic would believe that Maarten’s absence came of his own volition.

“No?”

Loud drums broke up their conversation. Together, they watched as the remembrance ceremony began.

Every battalion captain raised his ceremonial gourd. Light flashed and enchanted knives sliced shallow notches into the peels, one for each man who had been lost in battle. The notches transfigured the fruits into an instrument symbolizing that the lives of the fallen now contributed to the magic and music of the world.

Too many notches rested on Icen's conscience. Regan read each name of the fallen as the marks were made. *The reading should have been my job.*

"I wish I hadn't sworn to serve you. I am a man of honor, and serving a prince of deceit wasn't how I planned to spend my life," Nic muttered.

"I wish you hadn't either," Icen agreed, his temper taking control of him. But when a hush fell on the crowd outside, Icen's anger cooled.

He didn't speak, and neither did Nic. Their mutual silence honored their fallen men, who had died for Icen's revenge and Regan's ambition.

At the conclusion of the moment of silence, Nic asked, "Do you think the Tersinian king will allow you to marry his daughter?"

"I don't care if the king consents or not," Icen growled. Regan had finished the speech and walked toward the carriage. "I am more worried about letting my people down."

"Because you refuse to rule your country? Or because you have waged war for years with no good reason?"

Icen swallowed a retort, and Nic straightened as Regan stepped to the carriage door.

"The prince requests that no one enter," Nic relayed. The rise of his shoulder indicated that his hand had moved to his sword.

"I have no desire to enter. I will ride my horse." The snarky tone in Regan's voice took Icen by surprise. *Has Regan always behaved this way toward Nic?*

Icen surveyed his best friend. Regan's dark eyes grieved, making the prince certain his snappish words came from the heavy loss they both carried.

"We need to proceed to the memorial. Is that agreeable, Icen?" Regan addressed the carriage door with a bow, his tone cordial.

"Yes, Regan. Please lead the procession. I would like my carriage to follow you in line."

Regan sized up the guard, his eyes running the length of Nic's form. He sneered. The men squared off before Regan thought better, whipped around, and stepped into the stirrup of his horse. Something tainted his friend's behavior a dark gray. *Why is Regan so defensive, so aggressive? Has he always been this way?* Icen remembered them play-fighting as children. Regan had frequently utilized Icen's shielding fae to block his blows, but it had all been in fun. *Hadn't it?*

"You won't even play the ceremonial güiro with the other men?" Nic asked with an unmistakable plea in his voice. It should have been Icen's privilege to lead the song of mourning. Icen felt the sting of shirking this responsibility.

Icen had given Regan the royal güiro to play at the head of the funeral procession, preferring that the tradition be upheld in a more visual manner. On the bench beside him rested the one usually played by the queen. "I will play as well, Nic."

"No one will know."

"They will if you tell them."

Icen lifted his own instrument as Regan, every general, commander, and captain lifted their respective güiros in a melody of remembrance. The soldiers raised their voices in the song of mourning, chanting along with the scratching rhythms. They marched along slowly in well-practiced unity. Icen's carriage rocked into motion, Nic stepped to his position on the side, and they rolled along with the procession.

Shame accompanied Icen's playing. Each scratching beat drummed against his heart. Because he hadn't forgiven Nari, the Tersinian queen, he had the blood of his countrymen on his hands. Even more, he was also responsible for the blood of Princess Axen's people. The Tersinians hadn't wanted the war.

In contrast, his country, his people, his responsibility and power, had stood behind him, even in his misguided anger to settle a personal score. They died for him with honor, and greedily he had taken their sacrifices. The greed he now wore on his visage, once seen, couldn't be easily forgotten.

A keening forced Icen to open his minuscule window triangle a few inches more. He needed to see their faces. The faces of those who had lost loved ones due to Icen's foolishness. A woman with a halo of black curls caught his eye. Tears streamed down her crumpled face.

While he didn't think showing his deformed face to the people was the best way to earn back their trust, he knew he needed to do something. Chagrin stung Icen's eyes. The canker on his skin would be fixed by intentional repentance, but even that couldn't stop the dying magic. It was changing in a way that couldn't easily be undone. Once, wild fae had been free for bonding, but now only fae inherited by the royal families remained in Xahamen. The blight from the arrival of the Star People was spreading and had limited his future to a destiny. He wiped his face. If Princess Axen refused the marriage that would allow the magic cycle to heal, it would be another way he let his people down.

Nic had drawn close to the side of the carriage while Icen had been lost in remorse. "Look at the man you have chosen to represent you," he hissed.

Regan climbed the steps to the funeral pyre in the city center. The look on his face betrayed a rapturous cruelty in the quirked set of the lips and the güiro held nonchalantly under his arm.

"He should still be playing," Icen lamented. His own hands raked the machete along his instrument, punctuating the memories of his failures with its raspy tune.

"Regan does whatever he wants," Nic snarled. "He leads you around like a puppet. Everyone knows it. You do not stand up to him, and he slowly takes the power you wield into his own hands. Every moment you hide away is dangerous."

Icen tried to ignore the censure in Nic's voice. "I am trying to do what I feel is best for our country," he said the moment all music faded away. "You wouldn't understand."

"I understand far more than you think, Prince." Nic's shoulders slumped. The carriage came to a standstill. "Look again."

Icen's eyes darted to Regan, who, against protocol, had ignited the funeral pyre. Then the naked, red blade lashed at Regan's hip caught his attention. A dark mirage burned around it.

The sword? Is fae coming from it?

"Where did he get that sword?" Icen asked Nic, concern etching his words. As far as the prince knew, only five enchanted swords were forged at the founding of the world: one for each of Jeony, Palameru, Dazmorn,

Xahamen, and Tersine. These swords were guarded jealously, worn proudly, and passed only to direct heirs. Regan was not an heir. If this sword were endowed with fae, Regan was up to something.

"You'll have to ask him, My Lord," Nic responded, "before something happens. There is something wrong with it, and wrong with him."

Chapter 3-Axen:

Axen's heart ached. The graying of his rich dark skin made the purple bruises on the Xahamenian's face more prominent.

"Has anything happened with the spy?" King Stet asked.

Axen's head popped up. Her cheek twitched. Rolling her head from side to side, she dusted her hands across her dirty apron and stood. She noticed her father surveying her clothes.

"You know, the doctor's assistants are paid to clean the surgical messes." He lifted Axen's face to look into her eyes. She knew he could see the tears of exhaustion and discomfort she held back.

"Whoever inflicted this barbaric torment on this man has no heart," Stet grunted under his beard. He placed a heavy hand on Axen's stooped shoulder. "And yet I still want him gone. I don't like a man from Xahamen here without a signed treaty."

"He would die if we kicked him out," Axen reminded.

"And that is why we keep him until he can speak to defend his choices," Stet said, nodding.

"Do all people of Xahamen look like this?" she asked, her eyes never leaving the spy. With her father's protection near, she stepped forward to study the unconscious form.

Around the bruises, Axen noted that there were deep lines etched into the still face. The unconscious Xahamenian appeared old, yet his skin did not sag in his relaxed state. His warrior's physique stood out beneath the blanket. Axen guessed he was no ordinary regimental soldier. The flaccidness that held him now couldn't hide the broad shoulders and sinewy muscles in his arms and thighs.

"They do look quite a bit alike," Stet confirmed, coming to stand next to Axen. The contrast between the soldier's skin and hers caught her attention. The Xahamenian's skin was darker than the well-tanned hand she placed on his forehead. "Why do you ask?"

"I don't remember seeing Xahamenians before. First, the king came, and now . . ."

Stet brushed a dark, coppery brown lock of disheveled hair from Axen's forehead. "You haven't seen many since you were a tot." Father and daughter shared similar thick, wildly curly, nearly black hair. The only difference was the coppery sheen in Axen's hair, inherited from her mother. "If we had preserved relationships after Queen Jozefina died, that might have been different."

"I have never seen hair so dark," she remarked. The man's hair was blacker than night, dark like the soil they worked in the gardens—the best kind of loam full of nutrients—and tangled in tight curls like the tendrils of the vining plants that clung to the ceiba trees. She wanted to touch his hair, but she didn't dare. It seemed so foreign, so new. "Do you think his hair would look like this?" Momentary intrigue caused her to suck in her lips. Axen stepped away, still scrutinized by her father.

"Yes. His mother kept it short, but I have heard he has grown it out the last several years." Stet referred to Icen, seemingly aware of his daughter's stream of thought.

Axen examined the soldier's wide nose, the bridge set broadly between closed eyes, waiting for her father to speak more.

"Icen was a handsome lad the last time I saw him. He strongly favors his mother, but he is large like his father," Stet said, scratching his hairy neck. "This man would be considered handsome, but I would daresay that Icen is far superior-featured according to his people. And more importantly, unlike the prince, this soldier is old."

Short black lashes rested against the Xahamenian's high cheekbones. His feet dangled over the edge of the bed and were supported by a makeshift table. Axen had heard rumors that Xahamenians were exceptionally tall, dark, and violent. The last Xahamenian she had seen, their king, hadn't interested her much. If she had foreseen the outcome of the visit, she would have paid better attention.

"I think I will need to feed him soon," Axen said, turning to her father.

Stet's green eyes crinkled at the edges. "You don't let the doctors see to that?"

"No."

"Because one day, he will be one of your subjects?"

Both Axen's hands went to her mouth. Her eyes welled with tears. "Oh, Dad," she whimpered. "Do you think this is my destiny?"

Stet pulled her tight against his chest. His fatherly arms firmly wrapped around her torso. Axen's heart thudded in her ears, and the burning of her cheeks lessened. "I can't help but wonder if this offer will satisfy the demands of Cohesion?" Her words were muffled by the linen across Stet's chest.

The rumble beneath her ear sounded a definite, "I hope it could, but I would never make you marry that monster."

Deep down, she knew he wouldn't, no matter the outcome her choice afforded: good or bad. But that didn't change the fact that Axen's future felt tied inextricably to the unconscious form. While the man was far too old to be the prince, his presence indicated to Axen, by the lack of numbers and reaction of the soldier at her discovery, that Xahamen truly wanted a treaty. Perhaps they were as worried about the magic in Xahamen as the Tersinians were.

"Go ahead and feed him, Daughter," Stet coughed to cover the emotion in his voice before stepping away from their embrace. "I have a few things I need to do, but I will be back later."

When Stet left, Axen rang for the guards, who shuffled off to collect the specially formulated liquid from the kitchens. Axen hunted out the long, narrow funnel and feeding tube. As soon as the liquid arrived, she moved to sit by the man. Using the spoon, she pried his teeth apart, inserting a rubber block to keep his mouth open while she guided the tube carefully down his throat. Once satisfied with the positioning of the funnel and tube, Axen slowly poured the broth into the funnel. As with her former patients, Axen sang to calm her nerves and hopefully to ease the discomfort.

It didn't occur to her to watch for signs of the unconscious patient's waking until his brilliant purple eyes locked with hers. She dropped the bowl and stifled a yelp, hand going to her racing heart. The surprise left her dumbfounded, vulnerable with the knowledge that, if he wanted to, even in his weakened state, this man could cast her aside and flee. Or worse.

Gagging noises alarmed her. Reflexively, Axen reached up and slipped the feeding tube as quickly as she could from his throat.

"Am I in Tersine?" he asked in Xahamenian, looking around. His voice rasped harshly. His blunt words, loud in the stillness, startled her.

"Yes. You are in the palace," Axen whispered back, wondering if she had formed her words correctly. The Xahamenian words were foreign on her tongue. She unwittingly participated in the staring contest of wills until the man spoke first.

"I am very hungry," he said, switching to Tersinian, Axen's language. "May I please have something more to eat?"

Jumping into action, Axen picked up the remaining broth. "Who are you?"

"I am Maarten, loyal servant and trusted advisor to Lord Prince Icen of Xahamen." To Axen's ears, his voice sounded strained and weak, yet a note of determination startled her to curiosity.

"Welcome, Maarten. Did the Lord Prince send you?"

"He did," Maarten said. "My Lord Prince Icen commanded me to come here no matter what. Though we were doubtful I could sneak past the rebel men scattered along the border, we both believed the message I came to deliver to be of the utmost importance."

"Aren't we at war with Xahamen?"

Closing his mouth against another bite, Maarten coughed. "Miss, the prince has declared a ceasefire for the moment, pending the outcome of the treaty. But we don't have to be. Not for much longer. I came to bring word to the Princess of Tersine from my Lord Prince and hopefully to smooth the way, even, for an alliance."

Axen bit her lip and turned to leave.

"The king must know of this. I must go and tell him." She paused when his insistent voice tugged at her shoulder.

"Please, Miss. Let the king know that I must return to my Lord Prince. He needs to know of the kindness of your country. Please tell the princess I must speak to her as well," Maarten called out desperately as she stepped through the door. It swung heavily shut behind her.

She leaped up the stairs to her father. "The spy woke up! He said Icen sent him here, Dad! The prince trusts us. He thinks we are going to create an alliance too."

King Stet's glittering emerald eyes pierced Axen's armor of hope as he spoke. "That is what he wants us to hear. Daughter, you are innocent of the ways of men. Until a treaty is signed, there is no truce. Only war." He grabbed Axen's shoulders and searched her clear, multi-colored eyes with his rich green ones. Axen could see his concern for her safety plainly on his face. "Go get your mother, and I will interrogate the spy."

Axen found Nari, ringed by children and adorned with a maga flower crown, sitting on the wall surrounding the village's central well, outside the castle grounds. Sliding past the happy children, Axen covered her mouth with her hand and leaned in to speak to Nari only.

"The spy? His name is Maarten, and he's awake. Dad made me come get you," Axen explained to her mother. She tried to keep petulance from her tone, though the way her mother's eyes crinkled at the edges, Axen suspected she was unsuccessful.

Chuckling softly, Nari spoke as she and Axen made their way back to the castle, "The man–Maarten–did he give you your intended message?"

Axen shook her head. "He didn't have any idea who I was. I am pretty sure he thought me to be a maidservant, and I didn't correct him."

Nari gave a firm, grim smile and nodded her approval. "Wise, my dear. Perhaps we should present him with the princess and see what he does from there. Maybe then we can determine the stuff of his character, and perhaps the character of he who sent him." She winked at her daughter.

Axen frowned in bemusement. She suspected her mother had her own ideas about why the Xahamenian man was in Tersine.

Yelling greeted mother and daughter long before they reached the infirmary. The king, the doctor, and the man from Xahamen shouted at each other. Nari's entrance effectively silenced everyone as she stepped into their midst. The maga flower petals drifted from her crown to the floor.

In awe of her mother's influence, Axen lingered in the doorway, watching as Nari moved to the king and spoke in muted tones to prevent being overheard.

"Maarten asked to speak to the princess," the king said aloud.

Maarten waited. His eyes darted calculatingly around the room. Even lying in bed at a clear disadvantage, Axen realized he still looked threatening.

"Come, Axen," Nari cooed to assuage her daughter's fears. Despite her mother's attempt, Axen shivered with a sudden chill. Slowly, every pair of eyes in the room turned to her. The look of wonderment crossing Maarten's face alerted her that he knew who she was.

"Princess," he breathed. His face paled.

The doctor's louder-than-necessary voice demanded, "Everyone, get out."

Stet held his ground until Nari made a small noise in her throat to dismiss the group. Axen turned to leave, but Nari stopped her with a quick shake of the head.

Father, mother, and daughter shared a long look until Stet nodded and consented.

"We will be outside," he said. Hesitant glances over his shoulder punctuated his departing steps.

"I will be careful, Dad," she said to comfort him. Her father's caution shivered through her as she moved farther into the room. The doctor glared a warning at her while ducking into his chamber.

The moment they were alone, Maarten jerkily rose. His body trembled to combat the intense pain he surely suffered through. Seeing his struggle, Axen's compassion and vulnerable state choked her with tears.

"Please," she commanded, her voice breaking, "do not get up for me. This is why I did not tell you earlier. Please, Maarten. Rest!"

Ignoring her plea, Maarten made it to his knees, bowing low to the floor. His weakness forced him to sit on his feet, and Axen's heart ached for him. The power it must have taken him to position himself thusly awed and frightened Axen.

"Maarten," she said with a deep pause. Sighing, she crouched. "Rise and tell me your tidings."

The skin around his eyes wrinkled with shame as he lifted his head to look up at her. "My Lord would shudder at my earlier familiar treatment of you, My Lady." He dropped his head again, inclining it enough that Axen could hear the faint shadow of the words. "I am to tell you, and none other, that my Lord Prince has a great desire to meet you. He is not opposed to marrying you. Yet, he will not enforce that clause of the treaty if you have any reservations."

As Maarten paused to catch his breath, Axen stood transfixed, confused.

"What?" She neared. Her curiosity suspended her hesitation at getting too close and risking attack.

"You need to know that he is a beastly-looking prince." Maarten's pleading eyes darted between the door and the guard to the doctor with the tip of his nose inside the room, before settling on Axen. She was too stunned to move, and she did not know what to think.

Icen sent this man to ask for my consent rather than leave it up to our parents or force his own desire. On one hand, she was flattered. On the other, she was suspicious.

Maarten caught her scattered attention with his words. "He has done some wicked things, Milady. He has hurt many people. But I, myself, know that he is repentant." The ends of his hair brushed the polished floor. "He will become the man he used to be before he lost his mother. Before he lost his mind. He is hideous. Frightening now. But his heart—he is being forced to confront the chaos within it and finally heal." His breath came in quick, shallow gasps, and he threw a glance toward the doctor's door. The doctor's observant head broke the light shining from the chamber beyond.

The Xahamenian bowed his head lower. His nose almost brushed the hard stone floor. "He worries that you will reject him because of how he looks," Maarten admitted, and Axen angled her ear to hear him better. "I believe he wants to know if you would be willing to love him anyway, if he can prove that his heart, if not his face, is worthy of love."

Axen swayed on her haunches. "Sir," she breathed, "that is a lot to take in." She motioned the now-distraught doctor to help her lift him back into the bed, taking the time provided to think through all the things she heard.

When the doctor retreated, Axen said, "I don't care how he looks. But there is much you say that confuses me. Is he a beast or not a beast?"

Maarten stared at her evenly, respectfully inclining his head. "He is a beast in form. But not a true beast in heart."

She couldn't restrain a mirthless laugh. "He has killed my people. He hates my family."

"He has, and he did. Neither he nor I can deny it."

"With how he has tried to kill my father and brother, am I to fear dying at his hand or in his bed?" Her political training asserted itself in a tone of voice devoid of the disgust she felt inside.

"No," he said. His lavender eyes twinkled with hope. His countenance was so clear, so honest. "I vow it." A strong feeling of surprising acceptance overtook her as he continued. "He believed he was honoring his mother by starting the war and wouldn't listen to reason. But also by his hand that it will end. He sent me here to ask for your hand. He needs to know your true feelings about the situation and refuses to accept your hand as part of the treaty unless you are willing." His voice faded.

"He has told me he will not personally lead an attack on your country, and the magic of this world is decaying further. We have reason to fear what will happen if Xahamen falls."

"You imply that Tersine's complete destruction is next." Axen clenched her fists. The magic failing was a sensitive topic. She saw children starve, rivers dry up, and crops fail every day due to its declining effects. Her choice in the matter of marrying the beast prince was waning fast.

Maarten's voice continued to grow weaker. "I am not implying anything. Because of the imbalance, the lack of Cohesion, magic is hemorrhaging into Tersine, keeping it alive, but barely. Xahamen is next on the path to destruction."

"We don't have functioning magic here in Tersine." Axen squinted, examining the face before her.

"That's true. The Harmony line was damaged and broken long ago."

"So why does Xahamen's fall concern us?"

"Entropy is increasing in strength. While the war with Xahamen is soon to be over, the war to save the magic has just begun. Cohesion has not been appeased since your mother and Icen's mother made sacrifices to weaken Entropy, Cohesion's chaotic half," Maarten explained.

Two concerns tugged at Axen's desires. The man needed to rest, but she was curious. "Chaotic half, what do you mean?"

Maarten managed a weak smile. "Entropy and Harmony are opposing forces. The two halves that, when perfectly balanced, create Cohesion."

Axen nodded him on. Some of this was familiar, and some was not. It was the broken bonds of Cohesion's magic source that had placed her homeland on the edge of death's door. An alliance with Xahamen would help on more than one front.

"Once Cohesion is achieved, it cannot be undone. Its influence can weaken when Entropy or Harmony are out of balance, but neither one nor the other can overcome what has been sealed." Sweat dripped from his brow onto the stone floor below as he leaned toward her from where he lay on his side. "While Cohesion will always govern the land, some laws are unchangeable. If the magic in Xahamen fails, chaos gains another ally. Harmony loses one more foothold—we don't know if that will then be the end of your country, where all weather ceases to occur, and all sources of food, progress, and happiness will disappear."

Axen crossed her arms.

I will have to see if Mom agrees.

"What makes you think magic is tipping in Entropy's favor again?" Her compassion was winning out, and she would not ask for any more answers after this.

"A sword was forged that may hold its influence, allowing its wielder to deal in chaos. I have seen it in action, and it nearly killed me. This blade worked much like the enchanted swords forged in olden days, but with a deadly end."

"My father needs to know about this." Axen looked over her shoulder to where her father waited beyond the door. She went to stand, but Maarten weakly took her sleeve in his hand.

"Yes. But please, let me finish." His eyes were wide and desperate. "Icen and the world are losing. Without this treaty, without an alliance, the war will rage on with unseen, but powerful, desires guiding it. There will be no way to stop the famine if we lose any magic we have left. Two of the Five Lands will be lost to destruction. I am sure your mother has told you that your marriage, just like hers, could also lend strength to Harmony—the tendency for things to work together to create strength?"

"I . . . I . . .Yes."

"Queen Jozefina believed that too, of Icen. That is why you two were betrothed as children," Maarten explained. "Icen refuses to force that contract on you, and so he has sent me here to inquire how you feel about it before he commits to upholding a treaty with your honor bound in it."

"That's enough," the doctor's voice cut in from where he rebelliously stepped through the door. "The man is losing his color."

At the doctor's barking reprimand, the main door swung open, and the king entered. Axen slowly rose to her feet, blinking. Maarten's eyes rolled back into his head. His mission was complete, and he willingly released himself to exhaustion.

The room's occupants waited for the Xahamenian soldier to reawaken, but the time stretched until Stet lost his patience.

"What did he say to you, my daughter?" Stet demanded.

"He said," she rubbed a hand across her face. "He said that I am already betrothed to Icen. Is he the other half of the prophecy? I thought. . . I thought I had a choice?"

Stet blanched. “Leave now, Axen,” he commanded. “We will speak of this later.”

Despite her father’s command, Axen’s mental wheels began turning. Maarten’s revelations left so many things to process. The concern at the forefront of her mind was whether or not she could and should accept Icen’s proposal, or if, for the sake of the world, refusal was even an option.

Chapter 4-Icen:

Two thoughts swirled through Icen's turbulent mind as he sat alone in the freezing alcove hidden in his tower: to hope for an acceptance of the marriage clause between him and the Tersinian princess, or to turn his back on the world entirely and resign himself to his fate. He twirled a Xahamenian rose from his secret garden in his hand. The reality he had lived a month ago, when he and Regan connived to kidnap Princess Axen and hold her hostage until King Stet turned Tersine over to Regan's rule, felt like a terrible, fever-induced dream.

The soft swishing of a cloak tickled Icen's sensitive lizard ears. He turned and leapt abruptly when he saw Regan.

"You're back?" Icen asked in disbelief. He set the rose on his wooden workbench, placing it by the small toy sword he had been carving from enchanted ice. The rose appeared out of place among his half-finished projects. Until Regan's stealthy arrival, the prince had sulked in solitude.

"Why wouldn't I have come back?"

Their last encounter played through Icen's mind. That fateful night after the funeral procession, Icen had foolishly allowed Regan to look upon his changed face. The look of horror and disgust that Regan had given him broke his heart. Of everyone in the world, outside his family, Icen believed that Regan had loved him truly, and nothing would have changed that love. The disgust and fear in Regan's eyes betraying Icen as a monster, and a forsakable friend.

After Regan's hasty departure, Icen had never expected to see his friend again. But here he stood, dressed in the forest livery of the Xahamenian army, with a lopsided grin and a strange mix of fear and haughtiness in his posture.

"You heard we called a truce? I don't want to fight anymore," Icen said. With trepidation, Icen noticed a concerning light flicker to life behind Regan's expression as he picked up the ice-crystal dagger Icen had been customizing.

"If we don't fight anymore, how do I get Tersine?" Regan asked, his voice laced with hurt. He traced his fingers along the dagger's grip.

"I'm tired," Icen said in defense. "We have been fighting the Tersinians for so long. And with this change, I feel the need to approach Tersine in a different way."

"Marry their princess, you mean." Regan rolled his eyes. Placing one hand on the desk, the other pointing the dagger to the sky, he leaned toward and loomed over Icen. "I am sure that is appealing to you, but if you have no other ulterior motive, I remain as second to you? We are supposed to be equal."

A chill of shame played in Icen's heart. He didn't want to let Regan down, but if he truly wanted to break the curse, outright war was off the table.

Looking up, he opened his mouth to speak those words. No sound came out. The curse didn't allow him to share his story's details. When Icen pressed himself further, to his surprise, his vision went black with pain. He had never before tried this hard to speak about his curse.

He hit the floor and came to in seconds, rubbing his forehead. To his front, Regan held the ice dagger tight in his fist.

Regan, mouth open in surprise, swung the dagger at Icen's head, scraping it along the blanket of fae that was Icen's constant shield and companion.

"Hey, stop! You know you can't hurt me, but give me a second," Icen demanded, struggling to his feet, hand on his hilt. Regan dropped the small weapon to reach for his own sword. As he drew the blade, Icen saw the glowing red metal as it peeked over the scabbard.

A rush of fae that had no form or mind of their own outside the desires of the person who wielded them flowed from the sword, paralyzing Icen. The unexpected magic poured over him, swirling in a vortex before they were intercepted by Icen's own wind-like power, forcing the offending fae into surrender, binding them and holding them captive like prisoners.

Had the fae, the magic, come from Regan or the sword? Icen's eyes narrowed. Only those from ruling families could wield fae in Xahamen, and only bloodline royal heirs can wield enchanted blades. He asserted his fae once again, driving Regan's evil sword back into the sheath.

"Stand down, Regan," Icen commanded. He coughed, trying to clear the tremor from his voice. His suspicions had been confirmed. Regan's blade was enchanted, and it should not be. The spiraling tornadoes of his power trapping Regan's magic testified to this truth. Regan had somehow gained access to fae and had set his own power equal to Icen's magic.

"You frightened me," Regan said. His hands spread out before him, blocking his face from view. "I'm sure glad I didn't hurt you."

Icen flicked his fingers toward the raging gale, and the wind ceased blowing. The threat was subdued. He stepped toward Regan, who angled his body away, keeping the sword from view.

"The last we spoke, you were saying you only needed a break from war," Regan hedged.

"A break won't be enough." Icen's confused mind pulled together a coherent thought, and he remembered in a rush what he had actually said to Regan before he blacked out. "I wish I could explain more to you why I can't go forward with our old plans, but . . ."

Please try to understand my change.

The annoyed look that Regan gave the crystal dagger enticed Icen to go on the defensive. His legs spread wide, and his fae surrounded him in a zephyr as he prepared. "Why are you so different in more than that ugly body?" Regan snarled. But when Icen opened his mouth to speak, Regan held up a hand to stop the explanation in its tracks.

"Don't tell me. Tell your men. They suspect you have abandoned them." Regan's voice had lost any semblance of patience or kindness, and his disdain was evident. "You have led them in war since you convinced your father to give you power over them, and now, without warning, you have dropped them."

"For peace," Icen replied. His hope for Regan's understanding evaporated under the heat of his best friend's penetrating gaze.

"What did you do?" Icen said, shivering. His toes curled in apprehension as he wondered if Regan had uncovered the plot he and Maarten, the captain of the royal family's elite guard, had executed covertly.

"Your father announced to the entire kingdom that you and he were in negotiations with the Tersinians for peace, requiring the hand of the princess Axen as collateral." Regan pointed an accusing finger at the prince. "Why didn't you tell me you moved to the backup plan since the kidnapping and ransom failed?"

Icen lifted a flat palm to stop Regan's questioning. "I have my reasons."

Regan withdrew the waving finger, and his tone flipped rapidly to something more agreeable. "I think it's a great idea. This is far easier than any simple kidnapping. When will she come?"

"I don't know if King Stet will acquiesce," Icen said as shame trickled through him. If she did come, Princess Axen would be coming to Xahamen on false terms.

"He will. If he won't, I will go to enforce your wishes." Regan pounded one fist into the palm of his other hand.

"It is no longer about vengeance, Regan," Icen corrected. With a dismissive gesture, the prince indicated that Regan should precede him up the stairs into the main part of the castle. He wasn't sure why, but he wanted to make sure he had access to his guard, just in case.

They entered the study.

Regan moved to shut the heavy door behind him, but Icen waved a gust of fae in the way. The door whistled and blew away from Regan's hand.

"There is so much more going on." Icen inclined his head in Regan's direction, eyes pleading. He cupped his claws around his throat. "I need you to try to understand."

Regan's eyes narrowed at the gesture, but he dropped into the cushioned, enchanted-ice-carved chair across the desk from Icen. The prince sat in straight-backed observance, and Regan slouched, one hand on his magic-infused sword. "I will listen if you speak."

"I can't tell you, Regan. You have to trust me," Icen pleaded. "I would tell you if I could."

"I'm sure whatever it is holding you back, you'll get over it." Regan's close-lipped response indicated his disinterest in puzzling out Icen's clues.

Huffing in frustration. Icen's eyes went to where Regan's restless fingers pattered on the pommel. "Where did your new sword come from?"

Regan's fingers continued to tickle the jeweled grip. "It was a gift."

When Regan said no more, Icen didn't press. Dragging his eyes to his friend's face, he reluctantly changed the subject. "We will need to call off our forces from Tersine. Even our secret forces."

The casual posture Regan espoused didn't change, igniting Icen's curiosity. "I have already done so," Regan said. Unease grew in Icen's belly.

"I don't want to seek vengeance any longer, Regan," Icen said. He studied Regan. His friend was placidly drumming his fingers on his sword. "I trust you to do my bidding as you lead my army."

"Oh yes," Regan snickered and kicked one booted foot up on Icen's desk.

"I am in earnest."

"As am I." Regan rocked forward, setting his hands on the desk. "I have not forgiven that woman for murdering your mother."

"I . . . I . . ."

"And neither should you. I don't think you can—not really. While you may be trying to convince yourself that you will marry this woman in good faith, I am sure you will see I deserve to rule Tersine."

"How do you plan to obtain this end?"

"My plans are my own," Regan said.

"If it involves my country, I deserve to know."

"You have given up what control you had, Icen."

An echo of Nic's warning chilled Icen's heart at Regan's words. Shaking his head, he tried to remember his dead mother's wishes when she had visited and cursed him. Before his change, his single-minded mission had been to fight for his mother's honor, but now he must fight for peace between the lands and within himself, even if it meant angering Regan.

The anger inside Icen screamed. He wanted to hurt Regan, to shame him for the embarrassment his last words had provoked. Icen had trusted Regan to support his need to focus on healing his curse, but his friend had stepped too far over the line into usurpation. Against the rising fury, Icen grumbled out, "I think I have exacted enough Tersinian blood and fear to avenge anyone, even my mother." The words felt bitter on his forked tongue. His self-control had won, even if he felt a fraud. "I cannot put you on the throne of Tersine," he said.

"You plan to give me Xahamen, then?"

Used to Regan's tricks, Icen rehearsed, "I'm not the only ruler of Xahamen. As Prince Regent, Regan, you know I only control the army. Any other power I wield is after my father approves."

Regan's eyes narrowed. His fingers thrummed this weapon faster. "We could easily overthrow your father. He trusts you."

Icen's mouth fell open. His own hand went to the sword at his waist as Regan gripped his, too. "Why would I betray my father? Why would we? I thought you loved him."

A hand went over Regan's heart as his face elongated in offense. "No. I know. I'm sorry, I shouldn't have suggested that. Caissidde is like a father to me. And since he is like my father, I have always thought I would rule something, somewhere." The offense he affected melted. "If you marry the princess, she will give you an heir, and where will I be in the line of succession?"

"You will always be my right-hand man, no matter what."

The curled lip of disgust that passed Regan's face chilled Icen once again. "But not your equal." Regan whipped the sword out. Icen's fae stopped the blade inches away from his face.

Accustomed to Regan's brash actions, the prince casually reached up to nudge away the threatening steel. He hissed. His fingers lit with a searing pain.

"Don't touch it, fool," Regan reprimanded, though the lopsided grin of pleasure on his face indicated he may have enjoyed Icen's discomfort. "It's enchanted."

"Tell me where you got it?"

"Make me your equal."

"I can't."

"Then I won't."

There was no two ways about his statement, and it was true. Icen covered his mouth. "Do you plan to stay in the castle, or will you stay with the men?"

"I have plans I need to see to first, and then I will return to do your bidding," Regan sneered.

The prince stood but felt helpless. "Please do," he said.

Regan's ferocious footfalls rang in slapping staccato as he made his way out of Icen's chambers.

A single thought played in Icen's mind.

I hope Maarten's plan will work.

Chapter 5-Axen:

Axen awoke to the embers of the hearth's light, nearly smothered by the weight of their own ashes. Faintly, the light of the three moons danced with the ember light, brightening the room enough to see. Stealing to the hearth, Axen held a new torch to the coals and waited for it to ignite.

The warm new flames sent flickering shadows across the room. Axen moved to the window to pull back the maga-flower-embroidered curtain. The moons glowed blue, silver, and red on the horizon, dominating the night sky. Beneath the hushed darkness of midnight, the only noise in the castle came from the chorus of frogs and insects outside. Their melody enlivened the breeze until Axen drew the curtains tightly over the window, ready.

Donning a black cloak, leggings, and slippers, Axen whispered into the hallway. The torch remained in the sconce just inside her door. There were no guards. Guards were for entries and exits and prisoners, so making her way back to the infirmary proved no feat.

Nearly a week had passed since she had last seen Maarten and heard Icen's plea and proposal from the grizzled soldier's lips.

She didn't understand why her father wouldn't release him, although she was sure it had to do with the fact that they had recently been at war with Maarten's country. Running a hand through her hair, Axen had to focus on the deep, abiding certainty that convinced her the soldier needed to return to Xahamen, and soon.

Her mother hadn't stepped in to defend Axen's unrest to the king. The princess's decision to go behind their backs sent her heart racing, but the desire to satiate the hunger of the decaying magic led her feet.

Two men stood on guard at the infirmary door, laughing. Axen waited anxiously until one waved to his companion and set off on his next assignment. Taking a quieting breath, Axen wielded her dart gun and shot the remaining man. She knelt beside him, dragging him into a more upright position, checking his breathing, and removing the dart carefully so as not to prick herself. With luck, this man, and any others she might tranquilize, would simply believe they had accidentally nodded off.

Inside the infirmary, a single candle burned to mark the hour. The doctor was nowhere to be seen. Axen swept to Maarten's side like a shadow. She clamped her forearm over his mouth, using her other arm hooked through her elbow, as he woke to her touch. To Maarten's credit, he didn't struggle or make a noise as Axen centered her face in front of his and whispered, "It is I, Axen." When recognition dawned in his eyes, she released him, wordlessly placing a bundle of clothes in his hands. She turned to give him privacy. When she heard his boots settle heavily on the stone floor, she waved him forward but didn't look back.

The guard outside stirred as they passed. Axen looked the incapacitated man up and down, noting he would wake soon. Stealing around the next corner, she motioned with her head to Maarten to stay close. She intended to disorient the Xahamenian with a circuitous route through the castle. While she didn't believe the soldier posed a threat, her father's fears guided her caution, and if he asked, she could honestly tell him that despite betraying his desires, she had done all she could to keep their family safe.

"You know where we are, don't you?" she whispered. The keen look in Maarten's eye gave him away. Axen sedated the solitary guard as they exited the castle. They paused in a shadowy doorway to get Maarten's heavy breath under control. Her mind spun, running through all the layers of security they still needed to get through.

By design, the outside night watch was nearly impenetrable. Axen worried even at the thumping sounds of Maarten's boots, muffled as the steps were by the moss-and-grass-covered ground. As they moved toward the stable and the last dash across an open patch of moonlit earth, Axen hissed, "Quiet but quick."

Despite his exhaustion, Maarten managed a burst of speed, and they successfully eluded the eyes of the next guard who passed by. They made their way across the open courtyard. Maarten's teeth glinted white at the challenge, and although she was quick, Maarten kept up with her as they ducked into the shadows of the stable.

"Stay here," she commanded. Dropping her hood, she moved to the next step of her plan and approached the men on duty. Speaking fervently, Axen convinced one to help her with a midnight ride. Beloved as she was, Axen wasn't surprised that these men did her bidding without question. With a nod, the men walked around the corner with Axen, giving Maarten the opening he needed to slip inside the stable.

"You can use this torch to saddle your mount," one said, bowing slightly as he lifted a torch from the wall to give to her.

"Thank you," she said to the guard, entering the structure. She shook out her taut arm muscles. The doors swung shut behind her, bouncing once before barricading their actions from the guards' watching eyes.

As Maarten rested in the sweet hay to recover his strength, Axen saddled the horse on her own. When she cinched the last buckle tight, she took Maarten's forearm and drew him to the horse, shoving him into the saddle.

"They won't suspect anything," she hissed through her teeth. "I ride out to the city all the time when someone needs my help."

Maarten's haggard face hid in the shadows, but he nodded, leaning forward against the horse's neck.

Axen fastened his weakened frame to the horse's back with two ropes cinched around his waist. He didn't resist. The journey would be long, and though he was a warrior with an endurance beyond that of any normal person, he still hadn't fully healed from his injuries.

Bowing his head in gratitude and respect, Maarten asked before he disappeared into the dark, "He will want to know if you are willing to accept his hand and fulfill your part of the treaty. What shall I say, My Lady Princess?"

Despite all the confidence she had in her answer, Axen's breast seized as she looked into the tired eyes of her new friend. "Tell him I consent willingly," she said. Breathing in through her nose, she wondered briefly if she should have waited until her father had released Maarten, but she steeled her nerves. Something in her said that waiting could have drastic negative consequences. Her father would understand in the end.

Maarten's ears took in the tightness of her response. "He is a good man," he said gently, almost fatherly. "He will not hurt you. The prince will treat you better than any other man ever would."

Sure, sure. Axen tucked a single maga flower into Maarten's pocket. "Please give it to him," she said.

Maarten patted the stem grimly. "I will."

Managing a grimace, Axen repeated herself more firmly. "I consent." Then, checking to make sure his way was clear, she whispered a final goodbye. "Go now, Maarten. Safe journey." A resounding slap followed the crash of Axen throwing the stable door open. Maarten leaned low over the horse's neck as it raced into the dark thoroughfare. He wouldn't have long until the doctor reported him missing, but Axen knew every minute would give him a head start at making it to the Xahamenian border and safety before her father set men in pursuit.

"Our princess," one of the guards sighed, "had better come back soon. Sometimes she is too independent."

"She's probably out to help another sick woman or child," the other replied. "But I'm sure glad the king already knows she does what she wants, because then we don't have to bear the punishment if something happens."

Relief filled Axen at his words, and she slinked away into the darkness, avoiding everyone as she made her way back to her quarters.

The first alarm sounded over an hour later. The loud clanging found Axen sitting in her window seat, her bright eyes searching the horizon. Before the second one rang, Axen slid down the servants' stairs to the war chamber where she believed she would find her father. Crossing from the entrance to the armory, she snuck into the war room. Her slippered feet came in handy as she sidled up behind the war leaders, her father and brothers among them.

"Thirty cavalrymen. No infantry. No archers. I can't make it out, but this force looks like no more than foot soldiers with rusty farm equipment." The commander relayed, one hand pounding a fist into the other. "None of our scouts can see any commander, except for a dirty-looking man next to the standard bearer. Though even at that, the standard of Xahamen had so many holes it could have been nearly any flag. If this is a coordinated attack, their commanders are throwing these men to the wolves."

At these words, Axen's shoulders relaxed slightly away from her ears.

"Some men wear the royal soldier livery of crimson and blue, but their garments are nearly rags. If this force wasn't so good at disappearing into the trees, this would have been an outright massacre," the commander continued.

"If only we had a captive from Xahamen who might know what was going on," Sunder said with petulance. Taking that moment as her cue, Axen migrated from the shadows so that her presence would be acknowledged. First her brother's and then her father's faces melted into outright anger. She was sure they felt her betrayal keenly.

Trying to remain courageous, Axen turned to the commander with a question. "Was Maarten with them?"

"Not that I saw, m'lady."

"Has anyone seen him?" she continued.

"No," the commander said.

"Maarten told us about these rebels." She rounded on her father. "Are they not the ones who left him for dead?"

Stet gave a faint nod, his eyes still hard.

"As Maarten said, there is more at play here. These men could be driven by Entropy."

"Or by Icen." While Stet's eyes were more guarded, Kole and Sunder wore their sadness plainly. "They aren't attacking, but when we sent out our spies to find your Maarten, we found this band," either Kole or Sunder grunted their annoyance. Axen couldn't tell which.

Her mouth widened in surprise, then narrowed. "Then it is a good thing I released him, isn't it?"

When her father held his tongue and head proudly, indicating that he would not yield, she turned on her heels and left. She passed her mother on the way out. Nari paused to speak with her daughter.

"Did you make them angry, dear?" Nari asked, looking at the princess's dark expression.

"Fools, each one," Axen said in a soft tone. "In their search for Maarten, they found a band of renegades, and I'm still in trouble for releasing the supposed spy."

Chapter 6-Axen:

Axen positioned herself at the dungeon's entrance, setting her sights on the closed door, waiting to intercept her father. He had been interrogating members of the rag-tag band, and Axen was covetous of any information he had gleaned. The door groggily swung open, revealing Stet with dark circles under his eyes. Father and daughter shared a glare until Stet shook his thick, copper beard and slipped his arm around her shoulder with a relenting sigh.

"The men are not producing any valuable information and likely weren't sent by the crown of Xahamen. Only one of the fifteen men spoke of the prince, calling him a coward and a poor-acting regent over the army.".

"Maybe Maarten was telling the truth about the rebels?" Axen asked, looping her arm in her father's. With a tug, she set them both moving toward the infirmary.

"I don't know, Axen. Lies are meant to be convincing."

"But you just said none of the men named their commander."

"That just makes Icen a good general. I would be surprised if he doesn't know where his men are."

"And if he doesn't, then?" Axen prodded her father for further comment with her eyebrows.

"This band and the spy are not the same issue." He lowered his voice to persuade her to see it his way. "Maarten could be bringing an army on our heads right now, and we have this potential pseudo-army to contend with as a distraction."

"Aren't we prepared in that case?" Axen asked. Already her mind had gone to disclosing Icen's proposal, leaving this conversation behind.

Stet coughed out a strangled laugh. "Of course we are, that isn't the issue either!" His eyes narrowed. "What did the spy say to you?" His gaze grew intense; the anger faded and curiosity took its place.

Axen scrunched up her nose in defeat. Something in her face had given her away. Stet's scrutiny seared her with its intensity.

After a pause, he lifted his arm and in a subdued voice said, "Will you tell me if it is something I need to know?"

She stopped walking and turned toward her father. Trust shone in his green eyes, stabbing Axen straight to the conscience, coaxing from her the words that crushed all other thoughts from her mind. "Dad, Maarten was sent by the prince to ask me, personally, if I would be willing to be included as a party to the treaty. That's why he came."

Stet made a strangled noise. "And you didn't think to tell me this before?" Stet's hands grabbed Axen's shoulders firmly.

Axen showed her teeth in embarrassment. "You know you didn't give me a chance."

She could see Stet's agitated hand motions as they returned to his sides. He measured out his response. "I still don't trust that spy, but with this information, I can see why you don't think he was one." Axen waited as her father mulled over the information. His steps were heavy and slow. Tentatively, Stet turned his head toward her. "What did you tell him?

Her father's breath tickled the curls at the top of her head as she replied, "I told him that I am willing to be included as part of the treaty." A crushing hug stole Axen's breath away.

"You need to tell your mother," King Stet encouraged gently. "I think it will ease her mind."

The wrinkles between Nari's eyes relaxed as Axen repeated her decision as she stood before her parents in their receiving room. "Why didn't you come talk to me about it?" Nari asked. Axen was too busy wringing her hands to notice much about her mother's reaction, but she could hear her father sigh.

"I wanted to make my own decision. Now, I think it makes sense to marry him with haste." She bit her lip and peered through her eyelashes.

"I do too," Nari replied, taking Stet's hand and leaning into her husband with a familiar motion. The strain in her voice was gone. "But I need you to understand something."

"About the betrothal?"

"Yes."

Nari patted the chaise cushion next to her. Sitting, Axen tucked her knees under her as she angled her body to give her a good view of her mother's reaction.

Once Axen relaxed, Nari began. "I hope to help you understand why I betrothed you to Icen." Her eyes pierced Axen's mental cloud of fear. "Do you remember the history of the Star People, my people, that crashed onto our planet almost fifty years ago?"

Axen nodded, taking her mother's hand. She listened intently as her mother spoke. "In Grandfather's day, the Star People fell from the sky into Tersine's boundaries. The magic they brought with them disrupted Cohesion throughout all the Five Lands, but especially here, severing the reciprocation of magic from Tersine into Jeony."

"Yes. And you know my parents were the leaders of that community."

None of this was new information to Axen, but her heartbeat increased as furrows of lines forming on her mother's forehead deepened.

"My people." Nari closed her eyes and bowed her head in what Axen knew to be regret for her ancestor's actions. "My people's presence, and their invading magic, snapped the line of Harmony that kept Tersine thriving, leaving Tersinians struggling to live all over the country. There have been some protective surges of magic in parts of the land." She gestured vaguely north in the general direction of a small provincial town that had thrived on its own despite Tersine's overall struggle. "Otherwise, Tersinians have fought to live. We receive life-giving fae, but with no way for the fae to return to their source, all magic comes here to spend its energy and die, keeping our land alive, but only just."

Stet began rumbling with snores. Both Axen and Nari chuckled, sharing a twinkling look. This was a common bedtime story that Nari had shared over the years, and it had lulled the king into rest.

"I think I know where you are going with this, Mom," Axen said, her hands beginning to shake as their joviality ceased.

Nari raised her hand to place a finger against Axen's mouth to hush her words. "Let me tell you, so there is no confusion."

Pressing her lips together, Axen agreed to listen.

"Cohesion, the oldest, most powerful magic, fractured into two parts: Harmony, the tendency for things to work together and become stronger, and Entropy, the tendency for things to fall apart." Nari held up two fingers for emphasis. "What once had kept the world healthy and progressing now pulls the world in two directions, precariously maintaining magic and the health of the Five Lands. But my people knew, from their own history, that one type of magic will always grow stronger than the other without a balancing force, and so when I was young, I was sent to study the fountain of magic in Jeony."

"That's where you met Jozefina."

Nari's eyes softened into memory. "Yes. The best friend I have ever had. She was endowed with exorbitant amounts of fae by Cohesion's fountain--many Jeonians are, but even among them, she was special. Everyone from the Five Lands, and my people too, believed she was the key to reuniting Entropy and Harmony."

"Has Cohesion ceased to exist then?" Axen asked, biting her lip.

"Cohesion is without beginning or end. It is the strongest, most ancient type of magic. We know it as the parent of the fae, and it is the delicate balance between Entropy and Harmony that keeps the world functioning."

Axen made a face, thinking back to Maarten's explanation. Nari cocked her head, but continued.

"Cohesion still exists and will always do so. As far as I know, Xahamen, Dazmorn, Jeony, and Palameru's magic fountains all exist under Cohesion. It is stronger than any force, because it governs all forces. So when it is achieved, it endures. Not even the Star People's magic could destroy all Cohesion. It threw Tersine's magical ecosystem into chaos, leaving an opening for chaos to enter."

"Is that why you and Dad married? To restore some level of Cohesion?"

"Yes. And when our children were born, more was restored."

"And when you befriended Jozefina? But she wasn't the solution, despite the fae she bonded with?"

"She wasn't," Stet's rumbling voice came as a surprise, bringing mother and daughter back to the point and adding his perspective into the story. "The only one who has come close is your mother. The only child ever born in and to the Star People." His eyes fell on Nari with an intensity that settled Axen's anxiety.

"The prophets in our country noticed that first, when I befriended Jozefina, and again, when I married your father, Entropy and Harmony were closest to equilibrium since they had split. Jeony's prophets noticed as well.

"The shift was significant enough for both Jeonians and the refugees from the stars to continue researching the effect I was having on the world. Other major shifts occurred when you and your brothers were born, hinting that my children will have as much of an effect on the magic as I have, if not more."

"It's speculation," Stet growled.

"It's the best chance we have to save Tersine," Nari reminded, placing a hand on Stet's cheek. "We both know that without Cohesion in the other lands, Tersine will slowly decay to the point of death. The hunger of our land is satiated on the scraps of others' magic."

Stet lowered his head, leaning into his wife's touch.

"You have always known that your life and future marriage were intertwined with the magic," Nari reminded her daughter. "We have never concealed that from you."

"But this you did conceal. Why did you betroth me to Prince Icen? Are my brothers also secretly betrothed?"

The king and queen shared a look. "I promised Jozefina before you were born that I would do everything I could to protect Xahamen, her husband and son specifically. She was my best friend." Nari's dark eyes pleaded with Axen to understand.

"Every kingdom must be bloodline connected back to your people—to you—to finally heal Tersine's broken line," Axen breathed, chest tightening as she put the pieces together. "So when you promised Jozefina to protect her country . . ."

"She unwittingly betrothed you to Icen," Stet confirmed.

"Such sacrifices have preserved the Cohesion that remains in the Five Lands today, but with every passing year, the unequal balance toward Entropy weakens our country more. Our love is no longer enough to sustain the magic the way it once did, especially with Jozefina gone and both Caissidde and Icen grieving."

Stet rumbled softly, clenching his hand into a fist. "If not for your mother's promise to Jozefina, you could have married into any ruling bloodline from any of the five kingdoms. Even now, Icen isn't the only viable option." To Axen, his words sounded tired and well-rehearsed. Nari's threadbare sigh informed Axen that her parents had argued over this many times.

"I have long regretted not having another daughter, not that we didn't try." Nari's voice was hollow. Axen knew of the many babies her parents had lost. "I hadn't meant it to be a betrothal, but with you our only daughter . . . but I couldn't deny her anything. I gave her all my fae, my magic, and promised you away."

Axen's eyes blossomed wide in understanding. "What if I had said no?"

"I would have honored your decision, but I would have done everything in my power to protect Icen and Caissidde anyway," Nari answered vehemently and without apology.

“I understand, Mama.” Axen wrapped her arms around her middle. “I am not angry.”

“I am,” Stet barked, his hand slapping a loud staccato on his thigh. “Your mother did not blast a hole into Tersine, and yet she has had to carry the burden of healing what its appearance broke. And now, she is passing the responsibility on to you—there are other refugees who could step in and try something.”

“They are all aged or dead,” Nari reminded. Her hand stroked Stet’s arm, smoothing the thick hair down. “And you know as well as I that nothing has worked so well as our marriage and our children’s births in healing Cohesion.”

“But . . .”

“I wouldn’t ask Axen to do this if I didn’t think her sacrifice would change the world,” Nari said. Deep inside, Axen knew her mother’s words to be true.

“Icen is a monster,” Stet argued, throwing his hands up in exasperation.

“That has me worried less,” Nari countered. “I trust Cohesion will promptly solve that problem. But now I rest easy, knowing Axen didn’t refuse the marriage. For now, Tersine will not collapse.”

This is it, then, Axen realized. I have been prophesied to heal the magic by marrying the beast prince. I must leave my country, save my brothers, and possibly save the world.

The responsibility weighed her down.

Icen

A lone rider entered the courtyard of the castle. The body atop the horse toppled to the icy ground as the gates shut behind him. Icen stood, curious, and moved toward his lonely window. His hands caressed the glass that fogged up with the whispered word: "Maarten."

He turned and raced down the hall to the top of the stairs, then froze, one foot dangling midair. Two guards stood a few steps down. They both trembled, hands white-knuckling their swords.

"I won't come any closer," Icen assured. Turning back around, he stepped inside and shut the door behind him. Maarten would have to come to him. The only thing Icen could do was send his fae to hurry and help Maarten along. This he did with a direct command, "Get him up here as fast as you can, please." The wind thundered from around him, blowing through the doorway and down the tower stairs, leaving Icen magicless.

Inaction pushed him into pacing. Pounding up and down the stairs of his suite did little to assuage the fears swirling in his head. Maarten had been hurt, but Icen didn't know what to do to help him. When he heard the knock at the door, Icen tried not to appear too eager, but he slid down the stairs in a rhythmic thud, grabbing Maarten by the hand and dragging the wind-bedraggled man into the room.

"Maarten," Icen breathed. His eyes roved up and down Maarten's broken body. "You look like death."

"I feel like I have been minced, but I knew you would want to speak to me as soon as possible." The grizzled commander waved his hand into the spinning vortex that surrounded him.

"Come, lie down," Icen encouraged. "Pull up the couch for Maarten to rest," he said to his fae. Then, back to Maarten, he added, "You have been gone for nearly three weeks. What happened? The rebels?"

Maarten nodded, groaned, and relaxed into the cushions. The persistent fae blustered around, blowing a blanket over the soldier's body.

"I was afraid you were dead," Icen said, perching himself on the arm of the chair. He didn't remark on Maarten's trembling legs.

"I would have been if your princess hadn't found me."

"So, you made it. You spoke to her?" Icen leaned over his reclining friend.

"I am doing better now, thank you, my lord. Princess Axen and the doctors of Tersine, while more primitive due to their lack of magic, were adequate caregivers. I appreciate your concern."

"I see that you are—I'm sorry." Icen withdrew a little, his fingers gripping his black pants at the knee. His eagerness to know the princess's answer took precedence over his concern for Maarten.

"I spoke to her. She gave her consent."

Whipping his head to stare at Maarten, Icen caved in on himself a little more. "Only consent? Was she not eager?"

"I am sure she is curious to meet you, Prince." Maarten smiled, eyes closed as he patted Icen's knotted, clawed hands. "I didn't know what to tell her about your curse, but she said she would agree to marry you." The rasp of his inhale worried Icen now that his biggest question had been answered.

Icen's concave posture eased as his rigid muscles relaxed. "Did she say when she was coming?" Icen anticipated Maarten's response. His leg bounced as his advisor took a moment to rest and catch his breath.

"She didn't say." A delighted glow lit Maarten's face. "Your princess is a gem. She helped me escape from Tersine. The king was very open about his distrust, but she knew the importance of answering your plea."

Icen smirked. "She has spunk. I should go and retrieve her."

"She has integrity." Maarten shook his head. "And no. You cannot go. I am afraid of what Regan would do to you both."

"Not go? That would be an affront," Icen snapped in disbelief. Seeing Maarten flinch, he calmed his tone. "Regan wouldn't do anything to me."

"I don't know why you trust him. Did you ever find out where he got the sword?"

"I asked, but he didn't say," Icen replied. "He did let me touch it, though." Wincing, Icen held up his sword hand that bore a few small blisters.

"I thought nothing could hurt you in your current state?" Maarten was aghast. His shaking hands clutched Icen's wrist.

"That sword could," Icen replied, looking at his palm.

"And that doesn't worry you?"

Icen examined his wounds with consternation. He was worried, but despite all common sense, Icen had always wanted to love Regan and believed, beneath his friend's ambitious exterior, Regan had loved him in return. Regan wouldn't betray me, would he?

"Maybe I should stay. I think it would keep Axen safe if I could convince Regan I am indifferent toward her." Icen leaped to his feet and whirled toward the creaking door in one swift motion.

"Maarten, you're back?" Regan's voice joined them. Maarten tried to jump to his feet and nearly failed. Sweeping into the room, Regan slapped the teetering Maarten on the back, keeping the weakened man unstable. "Where did you go?"

"I could ask the same of you," Icen interjected. "You have never kept me blind to your whereabouts. It is becoming a habit," he chastised.

Regan only had eyes for the grizzled soldier. Icen felt a shift.

"I plan to go romance the princess," Regan replied, addressing Icen without looking at him. "I know you won't mind. If I don't, you'll get both kingdoms and greater magic and power."

"I should be the one to get greater power, Regan. I am the heir," Icen thundered his irritation.

"We both know you shouldn't get her country, too," Regan defended.

Icen shrugged. "If you can get her to love you, then all the better for you. I am not sure how you plan to acquire her country."

"I am sure you can imagine how," Regan shot back.

"I will not let you hurt the princess," Maarten snarled, his hand going to his sword.

In a flash, Regan yanked his sword out. Its red glow blinded Icen. "Don't you dare raise your sword at me," he snarled, swinging.

Chapter 7-Icen:

Icen jumped in front of Maarten, blocking the blow from striking his friend's weakened body. The force Regan had put behind the swing was so much that Regan himself couldn't completely stop the strike. Hissing with pain, Icen caught the glowing steel in his hands, yanking it away from its target.

"How dare you!" Icen roared, tossing the sword away from him. His skin sizzled and popped. Burning flesh filled the room with its noxious smell. Regan looked from his empty hands to Icen. An affronted grimace revealed Regan's front teeth.

"How dare I?" Regan reared back. "You are the one who turned on me. You promised me you would help me take the Tersinian throne. Instead, you sent Maarten to spy on me?"

Icen stood between Regan and the cursed sword, and Icen's wind-like fae whipped around, bandaging Icen's burning hands. Relief accompanied the breezy ministrations, and Icen gave his full attention to Regan. But it was Maarten who spoke next.

"Tell the prince how you have turned parts of his army against him. Tell him how you sold your soul for that blade. Tell him how you still plan to make war with Tersine," Maarten interjected. He discreetly stepped his way toward the entrance, likely going for backup. "Tell him how you tried to kill me."

"What?" The revelation flew at Icen in a cutting torrent, and he felt the wind rise around him, whipping the hem of his coat. "You sold your soul?"

Regan sneered in disgust. "Sold. Traded. I need power, Icen. You are the one who denied me authority and prestige. I had to find it somewhere else."

A breathy laugh of disbelief escaped Icen's gaping mouth. "Where?"

"You know, Entropy has its ways of endowing people."

Icen hadn't known. "You can't." His chest heaved as he tried to rein in his fae from destroying the room around them. "Regan, what does this mean?"

Regan's laugh, once frequently shared with Icen, was now no longer recognizable. "It means that you aren't the only one wielding fae anymore, Icen. It means I am as powerful as you."

Looking at the sword again, Icen's brain swam in circles. "Why would you try to kill Maarten? He is loyal to me."

A softening of Regan's posture reminded Icen of the man, the friend he remembered. "We talked about trying to trick the princess with a betrothal and a treaty, which would end the war. But then, you decided to back out of the war and leave me empty-handed. That left me needing an army to usurp power in Tersine. Maarten mistakenly discovered my secret on his way to visit the princess."

"You created the rebellion?" Icen looked between Maarten and Regan. Of these two men he had loved and admired, one had morphed into someone he hardly recognized.

"You forced me." Regan shrugged and extended his arm. His enchanted sword flew into his fingers.

Icen's jaw ticked. Life was simpler when only royalty from Jeony or one of the refugees from the stars could control thc fae.

"And when I rule Tersine, you will thank me for ignoring your order and continuing with our plans. Even if you refuse to help me, I still plan on cutting you a share of any other country I conquer," Regan said. The smell of burning flesh continued to permeate the room, and Icen didn't know if his eyes were watering because of that or because the person he thought was his best friend had deliberately thwarted him. With a small dismissive shake of the head, Regan turned to leave. "I came to give you one more chance, Icen. I am doing what is best. For both of us. I know you still want this."

Confused, Icen stared at Regan's back. "You don't know what I want, Regan. You won't take the time to . . ." Icen's hands opened and shut at his sides as he tried to muscle his way past the pain that rose in his throat. "I want to trust you, Regan. I want to help you get what you desire. But you have to trust me in return. This plan, destroying the Tersinian royal line, cannot work any longer. We'll do something else. Perhaps we can conquer one of the other kingdoms . . . ?" Icen pleaded, but Regan wagged his head in disbelief.

"I know you plan to take Tersine for yourself, as if Xahamen isn't enough. I am sick of being second in power to you. I'm doing it my way now. You said you trust me. Stop spying on me." He turned and walked from the room.

Maarten, standing at the door now, dropped his hands to his sides. "I will get a healer up here," he said. "Neither of us is in great condition." The grizzled soldier stayed.

Icen stared after Regan.

"You shouldn't trust him, Icen. While I am sure he believes he has affection for you, a relationship should work both ways and to the advantage of both."

They stood across the room from each other. The enchanted-ice settees they had sat peaceably on were at sharp angles. One burgundy-velvet armchair had been knocked over in Icen's haste to preserve Maarten's life.

"I know Maarten, but how does one walk away from their longest friendship?"

"No, Icen. He is no longer a friend. Regan must have made a deal with Entropy, the magic trying to destroy us. You have to take this seriously." Maarten argued despite his exhaustion.

"I'm trying, Maarten." But his heart resisted.

"If he truly has banded with Entropy, your marriage is the main goal right now. Without healing the magic, we can't stop the rebellion. We can't stop Regan."

Struggling under the shock wave, Icen tried to focus as his world spun around him. "I will leave at once for Tersine if you think that would be best?" Icen suggested. His voice was strained. The chaos around him mirrored the chaos within.

"I don't think you going for the princess makes the most sense," Maarten corrected. "Only you wield magic in our country. Not even your father. Your Jeony blood from your mother allows you to protect the castle and our country from Entropy's influence. If you leave, there is no way of knowing what havoc Regan could wreak."

"Father has the army when I'm gone," Icen argued, righting the furniture in the room with renewed vigor as shock turned into fury. The fae helped him right the heavier furniture.

"Yes, but you know he has never been a good war leader. That is why he delegated the army to your care." Maarten leaned against the frame, fighting to remain upright. "Your magic strengthens the army in a way your father never could. The army, or what is left of it, will answer to you as named war regent. Treason and treachery and somehow pledging allegiance to Entropy have allowed Regan the power he has usurped, and you need to take it back."

Icen rubbed his face, scratching at the thick scales. "My father must go in my place," he sighed, putting his head in his hands.

"We both know he won't leave you here alone."

Icen knew that his father didn't trust him to not take over the kingdom. "Has Regan influenced me so much?" he whispered. His eyes begged the trembling Maarten to contradict his worries, but Maarten's direct stare was evidence of the truth.

"Your father loves you," Maarten said.

"Do you think I have changed enough?"

Again, Maarten shook his head in silence, turning away. The fae responded to Icen's chaotic mood, slamming the furniture into their positions. While Icen's pride raged within him, pulling him toward offense and retribution, a small, subdued part in his soul battled back. He had to admit that only two months ago, if he had been given the chance, he would have taken over Tersine, and Regan would have been his second in command. His best friend refused to give up on that goal, and Icen mourned. They had competing priorities, and Regan was willing to betray Icen to reach his goal.

"Trust is a long-term gain and a short-term loss." Maarten exhaled sharply. One hand clutched the doorknob, the other was held braced against the frame.

"I'm trying."

"I know. Give me a day or two to recover, and I will go for the princess," Maarten promised. Icen could see the pallor in his commander's face and wondered if a few days would be enough for the grizzled old soldier to make the trip again.

"Do you think you can keep her safe?" Icen's words were laced with barbs, but Maarten did not rise to the bait.

"As much as you can, Prince," Maarten said. "As your fae does not cross the border, and you refuse to show your face, I will bring soldiers I trust. Between them and me, and likely the princess herself, she will make it here where you can protect her." Maarten squinted as he scrutinized Icen. In that moment, Icen realized that Maarten didn't trust Icen with the princess either.

"I will remain in Xahamen," Icen said.

Side by side, Nic and Icen sat astride two black horses, watching wordlessly as Maarten and the men he had chosen to escort the princess of Tersine to Xahamen grew smaller and smaller in the distance.

"Shall we see if we can scare Regan away from your princess?" Nic asked, pointing with his lips to the way Icen's hand wrung the reins in a death grip. Due to his cursed state, Icen's wounds had healed rapidly—more rapidly than the aging Maarten's— and he needed to burn out his anxiety.

"Yes, let's," Icen said once Maarten was far out of sight. They turned east to follow the borderline. Zigzagging their way back to the capital as scouts and hunters allowed Icen to feel as though he were doing something. They passed over the same few miles repeatedly, with Icen hoping to clear the thoroughfare of bandits, rebels, or Regan for Axen to come unharmed.

"Is it true? Does Regan have fae like yours?" Nic asked, drawing alongside Icen once they neared the castle.

"I don't know, Nic." This admission brought heat to Icen's neck. He thought he knew Regan, but now that his supposed best friend had allied himself with Entropy, Icen could only guess what the future held. "It sure seems like it."

The wind around the horses picked up a little, easing the way, even as his concern increased. Icen's fae had been unique to him, his mother, and Nari from what he knew. The mischievous wind-like essence had always been his constant companion. And with Tersine being devoid of magic, only he had remained as a fae wielder outside of Jeony. Having someone else with access to powers such as these ruffled Icen.

"I'm glad you have finally seen the Regan he kept hidden from you," Nic said. "Even though I'm sure it hurt."

Icen set his lips in a straight line. He wasn't sure he was ready to admit that Regan had manipulated his past choices, but Nic was right. Regan had always put his own desire ahead of everything else. This led Icen to more concern. While he himself hadn't always used his fae in the best manner, Icen felt responsible for the consequences of his actions, whether directly perpetrated by his hand or by the fae. As Prince and Jeonian, he was a guardian of the fae. Both his role and destiny decreed him a protector of the world's magic. So far, he had failed in keeping either safe. And Icen wondered how much of the world he didn't yet understand.

Chapter 8-Axen:

The sun sparkled through the clear blue sky, shining on Axen and Kole as they stood outside her travel carriage. He had tied their horses to a nearby tree and would return with them to the capital and their father once Axen was on her way. King Stet would follow them to the Xahamenian capital soon, with the intent to arrive close to the time they did.

"We knew this day would come," Axen whispered to Kole, nudging him with her shoulder. Days before, Axen had finished signing her name to the treaty.

Kole gave her a grim-faced nod. Marriage to another royal line had always been a part of Axen's future. Yet Axen could not deny that the indefinite length of separation never really felt real until now.

"When you are king," Axen continued, but Kole didn't let her finish. He dropped to his knees and wept openly into his hands. Kole's tears were a long-held Tersinian tradition observed before separation that showed Axen great gratitude and respect. The heart-wrenching sobs tore through Axen as she threw her arms around her beloved older brother and lifelong friend.

"It feels like we are losing you to death," he cried. There was so much pain, loss, and grief already from the war, and their uncertain future seemed to be full of violence and separation.

"I won't die. And neither will you." Axen looked up at the three moons hanging heavy in the sky, searching for comfort. "Will I still see the moons in Xahamen?" she asked, her cheek resting on her brother's dark hair.

"Yes. I will look at them every night as they rise. We can watch them together," Kole affirmed. His tears blew away with the morning dew as his countenance hardened. Axen had publicly accepted Icen's marriage proposal, and her father had signed the treaty. Then Maarten had arrived stealthily, explaining where his escort would meet her. They were nearing the meeting place, but Kole was not to join them further.

"We must leave now if we are to meet Maarten at the right time. And also, if we are late, we won't beat your father to the capital," Nari said, mounting the steps into the carriage. The three family members were deep in the Tersinian jungle, several hours of travel away from the castle and everything Axen had ever known.

When Axen moved toward the stairs, Kole made a noise. A brisk little wind whipped the ends of Axen's hair and tunic in a tumbling dance, another new sensation heightening her sense of awe. She turned to see the rising sun glint off the jewel-encrusted hilt of Stet's enchanted sword, which Kole held.

"What?" She looked from her brother to her mother.

"If anyone deserves it, it is you," Nari said. Kole handed the great sword to Axen. Lost in the delight of receiving such a prestigious gift, Axen withdrew the blade in a single, swift motion. The well-worn handle fit perfectly in her hand. A gleam showed that the otherworldly metal of the blade was polished to perfection. The steel mirror reflected Axen's astonished face.

"The blade forged from metal that fell from the silver moon?" she breathed. "As the oldest and heir to the throne, this should belong to you, Kole," she began, but Kole raised his hands to the sky, refusing to take it.

"We decided. And it never was mine."

"But can't only bloodline heirs wield enchanted blades?" she asked. The world spun around her. "You will be king."

"You are about to become queen. And more importantly, a queen who has sacrificed all for her country and the world." He shrugged. "I'm sure the enchantment will hold. It will protect you from any dangers you face." His tears were entirely gone now. "Perhaps one day you will return the favor. Enchanted blades have been exchanged between rulers before. Even if it has been a long time since magic existed here in Tersine, I would happily wield the enchanted blade of Xahamen."

"I am sure when I ask the prince, he will honor that request. He and I can share this one," Axen bit her lip and bowed. Tucking the sword back into the sheath, Axen smiled a shaky smile. "Thank you, Kole. Your sacrifice means so much to me."

She took one last, heartbroken look at the sword of her father's royal line. It was one of five given to the leaders of each of the Five Lands at the founding of the world. Two countries wielded the silver moon's magic. Tersine was one of them. Xahamen's enchanted sword wielded the blue moon's magic. *If Tersine and Xahamen exchanged blades, how would that affect the swords' powers? Or the world's?*

"It doesn't hurt to forge better bonds with our fellow countries," Nari voiced in her somber tone. "In fact, it might help. Being gifted an enchanted blade is said to be a symbol of true benevolence. If Icen can give up his inheritance, it could bring about momentous good for the world."

"It would be nice if we actually knew what would happen," Kole quipped, patting Axen on the arm. "But right now, we take all the chances we are given."

The undercurrent in his voice sent a chill through the princess, even as a welling pride bolstered her spirit. It was an honor carrying the sword strapped at her waist to the royalty of Xahamen. She hoped they would return that gift with as much grace as her father and brother had. Ducking into the carriage, Axen did not stop waving until Kole and everything she held dear were out of sight.

"Why must we ride in the carriage?" Axen complained as the jolting and jostling had her licking her aching teeth and rubbing her bruised tailbone. They had met up with Maarten's company yesterday and had set off with no delay. The second day on the road was fraying her patience. "A saddle is much softer. I wish we could go by horseback. We would be there by now."

"It's safer this way," Nari chided gently. "We will attract less attention the more anonymous we are—and with all our guards, we are already quite conspicuous."

The wisdom in her mother's words kept Axen from saying more, and sleeping in a stationary carriage was much more comfortable than the foliage-littered earth. Outside the window, the deep, tangled jungle of Tersine thinned, leaving gaps between the trees. It unsettled Axen to see so much around her as the open spaces gave way to expansive fields of low shrubbery and tall grass, and then to what appeared to be a barren wasteland of the most powdery-looking soil Axen had ever seen.

"Have we made it to the borderlands then?" Axen asked. She noted that the ground increased in elevation, and the stately, vine-draped trees of home had transformed into oddly short and sturdy, scratchy-barked trees. Not even a single patch of grass broke up the needle-like leaf debris between them.

"Yes," Nari said. She stared out the window, distracted. Her hair momentarily bounced around her as though suspended in water, then it fell. Axen wondered but wasn't sure what to ask.

"Mom, tell me about Xahamen," Axen requested, wringing her hands together as she looked out the carriage window at the passing scenery.

"Xahamen is full of frozen water and mystery. Unbonded fae, a formless energy that allows humans to exercise Cohesion's magic, used to run rampant throughout the Five Lands. These airy creatures of power were attracted to Jozefina's royal line," Nari said.

"But didn't you wield fae?"

This question intrigued Nari out of her fog. "Yes."

"Then you left it all for Jozefina when you came to Tersine to marry, Dad, right?"

Nari nodded, neck muscles flexing. "Yes." Her tight voice betrayed that she was still grieving the loss of her friend. "I wish she was still alive."

"Me too." It would have kept their family from all the years of war.

"I don't know how much good it did, me taking some Xahamenian fae," Nari admitted. "But willing them back to Jozefina was the right thing to do. If I hadn't, they would have faded away like all the other hostless fae when I came to Tersine."

"Do you miss being able to use them?"

"Yes. I do. Not only because they were useful, they were, but because they also fit with my soul."

Axen's eyebrows drew close together. "I don't get it."

Nari laughed. "That makes sense. When you have never felt them before, never experienced magic at all before, fae would be a foreign concept. Fae aren't servants, not like we have in maidservants or manservants. They are like currents in the ocean." She swayed her hands like the waves. "They move and act in a certain way based on the person they are bonded to. This power is instructed and directed by their host's desires, but they are restricted in their actions because they have no agency."

"So they aren't beings?"

Nari shook her head, placing a hand on her daughter's knee. "No, but they do function as an extension of a being—emphasizing the biggest traits of he or she who wields them." Her eyes narrowed and flicked to the scenery outside.

"Call out to the head guard to stop." Nari broke the gray hush. "The world is too quiet."

Along with the change in country, the company grew more alert. Axen's hand rested on her father's sword, and she stayed vigilant.

"Shall we exit?" Nari asked once the carriage came to a standstill, peeking out beneath the blue velvet curtains that covered the carriage windows. She spoke expeditiously, strapping her quiver across her back and placing her bow gently across her lap. Her mother's caution drew Axen's attention. The constant noise of animals, insects, and dripping dew from the jungle had faded away. An occasional wind whistled through the trees. Axen listened to the crunch of the needle-like leaves under the wheels of the carriage and the hooves of the horses. The crushing soundlessness of the land unnerved her.

"I think I can sense magic here that leans toward Entropy," Nari explained. "It is the magic that desires justice and equality. While it is faint, the magic reaches here, unlike back home."

"Entropy is the magic that causes chaos?" Axen asked, feeling that she understood a little better the reason her mother had betrothed her to Icen. She couldn't imagine if the whole world felt like this; the ambivalence sickened her stomach.

Nari bobbed her head back and forth, weighing her thoughts in her hands. "Entropy seeks to stabilize everything, but without the equilibrium of Harmony, yes, it is the magic of chaos."

"Can it hurt us?"

Nari took Axen's elbow in her hand, pulling her close. "Only enchanted objects, people, and fae can hurt us." Nari stroked Axen's hair. "Entropy, and its opposite Harmony, serve Cohesion—the rules that govern how our world works. Entropy is the tendency for destruction and chaos. It is a potency of energy, not an entity. Unlike the fae, it can exert its desires on the world—it is what causes dead trees to topple, rain to fall, rocks to crumble, and people to hate."

Looking over her shoulder, Axen sensed something dark and brooding watching them.

Nari must have felt it too because she murmured to Axen, "The fae here in the woods are whispering a warning. We need to be prepared. Harmony feels weak here. Whatever it is that is channeling Entropy is strong. Stay alert, Axen. If something were to happen to you. . ."

Men gulped food with sword hilts in hand as the breaktime crawled toward completion.

"We'll stay in here," Nari encouraged Axen.

The captain of the Tersinian guard and Maarten stood over their men. Every set of eyes roved as far as they could see.

Nari and Axen reclined into the carriage bench. A warning shout and the sound of clanging swords sent them on the defensive. Several Xahamen soldiers in uniform trespassed into the edge of the clearing and into Axen's line of sight.

The men blossomed into a horde of contrasting cleanliness—some bedraggled and some crisply dressed soldiers—they surrounded Axen's small company.

"Be ready, my girl," Nari warned as they pulled back the curtains, taking stock of their options before taking position in the window with her bow at the ready. "If it is magical, it is best we make our stand before we get too far into Xahamen."

The outermost members of the guard stumbled into battle positions. Their shoulders clanked as they pressed together, forming a shield wall. While there were not enough of Axen's men to encircle the company, the way their wedge danced back and forth kept Axen and Nari as far from the action as possible.

The valiant men lost ground, overwhelmed by the hordes of advancing enemies. The first wedge of defense failed, and soon the second squadron was engaged as well.

Two more Tersinian soldiers stepped between the altercation and Axen, locking shoulders with Maarten and the captain of the Tersinian royal guard.

"We must keep you safe," Nari said, never taking her eyes off the fray. "If these men truly are from Entropy, your life is at stake. If you are lost, it may be too much time before we can strengthen Harmony again. Tersine will fall."

Sucking in a fortifying breath, Axen strategically climbed out the window at the back to protect that weak position. She saw no opponents from her angle.

"How many do you count, Mom?" Axen asked from her new position. The sounds were haunting.

"I can't tell. They keep coming." Nari replied in conjunction with her steadily twanging bow. "Maarten, Axen is out back. Cover her. And Axen, if the next line gets broken, I need you to flee into the woods. Get to the capital and get help—don't get captured, and don't die."

"I count forty," the Tersinian captain of the guard's voice reached Axen. The ringing clang of metal on metal grew louder with each strike.

"On my mark, flee, Axen. Promise me."

Grunting a reply, Axen raised her sword as the second ring of defense broke.

"Now, Axen. Go."

Fleeing was the last thing the princess wanted to do, but she had promised. Ringing metallic chaos and pained screams chased her fleet steps. The underbrush here was plain and sturdy, bringing to her mind the comparison with the dense bush of her home. She knew where to flee there, and she knew how to hide. Tears filled her vision, and it unnerved her that she didn't need to worry about where her next step would go in this barren wilderness. No one followed her, leaving her both safe for the moment and unguarded.

Not far away from the conflict, an unanticipated sound caught her attention, halting her exodus. She shifted on her toes, hefting her sword at the ready. Axen pivoted in a circle, trying to discern what exactly she had perceived and to prevent herself from having a blind spot. As she scanned the area, she quickly noticed the male figure approaching her.

He emerged from between the trees, forming as if from the foliage. His broad, dark-skinned, muscular body aimed directly for her. She cowered in stupefaction as his mud-and-slime-coated muscles rippled with the focused movement of hefting his blade. Snarled hair swirled with flies and fell in mats over the man's face, obscuring his features. Fear emanated from the faintly glowing sword, reaching shivering tendrils through Axen's body.

"Who are you?" she asked, brandishing her sword with a solid stance, wondering if she had wandered into a trap. A strange, warm peace unceremoniously stole her feelings of fear, and a certainty filled its place.

Everything about this attack screamed ambush. *He is here for me.*

"What do you want from me?" Her eyes flicked backward, hoping to see Maarten, her mother, or another member of the guard coming to her assistance. When no one materialized, she turned her full attention to the individual; the sword in his hand gave her pause. "Your sword is evil," she concluded. An undeniable knowledge curled in her mind like an overly warm bite of soup.

He said nothing, looked his blade up and down, and grinned. The light glinted off his pointy eyeteeth.

A dancing breeze twisted by her ear and seemed to whisper, Entropy. The blanket of calm battled within her against the sword's influence, holding her firm in her footing. Its embrace combatted the emotions the sword and the man were trying to overcome her with. Cocooned in the stillness of the reaching goodness, Axen anticipated violence as he approached her.

He halted, and his stench wafted over her, causing her stomach to churn with queasiness. The cool weight of her father's sword in her hands bolstered the princess, and she held it up. She dodged as the man swung the broadside of the sword down against her. The moment the metal of his blade struck hers, the swords beamed brighter. A circle of light formed. It was too bright to look at. Axen felt as though invisible people were surrounding her in the warm embrace of a morning on the beach, supporting her arms. With this help, the evil sword was parried and slid harmlessly away.

Fae, she realized. Fae are surrounding me. The light disappeared in an instant when the blades no longer touched. Why had he tried to strike her?

Both Axen and the man turned to look at his sword, which dangled threateningly from his hand. Even now, she could feel the horror the blade leaked, and yet it was as if the apprehension she felt was being filtered through a cushion of the softest, warmest blanket.

Shaking off his surprise, the man smiled softly, slipping his sword, glinting red and gray, into the scabbard at his waist. "Axen, it is I," the stranger spoke Xahamenian in a voice that was deep and sonorous. His eyes, barely visible behind his cloud of flies and hair, were flat and black as midnight. The princess placed a hand to her chest. She understood many of the Xahamenian words as he continued. "I had to see you before you came to my castle." She pieced together his words as he spoke. "Will you come with me? Or will you continue with Maarten, your mother, and your own guard?"

Tugging her gaze away from the sword, whose emanating dread had caught her attention once again, Axen forced herself to look at the man directly—as their eyes met, his pupils flashed a blood red.

"I, who?" she asked, swallowing hard.

He smiled again. He swaggered a little as his smile grew more feral. "Am I not a beast?"

"Yes, perhaps you are a beast," Axen replied slowly, using her broken Xahamenian. Scrunching her face, Axen began trying to pick apart the feelings that came over her.

Logic told her that he was the beast prince. He had come for her. But the calm feeling seemed aloof at this thought, not quite wanting to believe that this creature before her was the beast prince, the changed person Maarten had promoted, or the youth her mother had described. She wanted to flee, but the prince was too close, and he wielded a weapon she didn't understand: magic.

"Thank you for the generous offer," Axen extended in Tersinian with a grimace, her nose again catching the man's rotten stench. "But I would rather continue on with tradition. I will stay with my guard and your offered men and then meet you at the castle as expected."

A vicious growl flew from the stranger. "Are you saying no?" He almost sounded confused, but the rage his words contained struck at Axen, trying to break through the calm coating of fae that clothed her. Her tranquility held. The beast backed down. "I will let you be. I am a person of honor." With these words, the prince bowed deeply.

Axen recognized the threat in the man's tone, causing her to shiver even through her blanket of serenity. His presence chilled her to the bone, and fear blossomed in her mind again at the thought of marrying him. Stiffening her spine with great difficulty, she nodded an acceptance of the threat. "We will meet again soon, my prince."

The man, Icen, pivoted, striding back into the woods. It was almost as though he didn't hear her last words or understand them. All at once, as the beast prince disappeared, the fae ceased to be her companion, and Axen stuffed her sword back into its sheath, wondering what to do next.

Chapter 9-Axen:

Axen leaned on her knees as she tried to catch her breath. She had sprinted through the sparse wood as fleet on her feet as an eel through the ocean. The fact that she didn't need to process where her next step was going was terrifying and exhilarating. She had never run so swiftly. Breaking into the clearing, she noted that the carriage hadn't moved, but the men were no longer engaged in combat. The uniforms littering the forest floor were only Xahamenian colors, and Axen's shoulders relaxed fractionally as she wheezed from exertion. She needed her mother and clarity.

"Not one of our men died," Maarten called to her as she searched for her mother. "We need to leave right away." He returned to giving the soldiers under his command directions. She was seeking safety and clarity from the threat of men popping out of the woods at random.

"Axen!" Nari cried, beckoning her daughter to join her in the carriage. "I don't know what happened. One moment, we were fighting for our lives, and the next, nothing!"

"Mom, a man in the woods said he was Icen," Axen puffed out the moment her adrenaline let her breathe again.

"What?"

"He wanted me to go with him. I think these were his men." The second the words exited her mouth, Axen realized something else. "Or maybe they were rebels? Is Icen truly the head of the rebels?"

Nari's words quelled as Axen mounted the stairs to the carriage. She waited for her daughter to sit before she responded. "It does seem strange to me that he came to you in the wilderness, especially since we will see him soon. But he wasn't here with these men. Perhaps the rebels were after him?"

"Do you think we can ask Maarten?" The carriage creaked into motion, knocking Axen off balance.

Nari peered out the window. "I don't see him, but maybe we can once we get to the capital? Why do you think he was Icen?"

"He said so."

Nari tapped her chin with her finger. "Maybe. I am sure he has been anxious to see you, and with the rebels, I imagine he felt the need to escort you."

Axen bit her lip. "Maybe. He also had a sword."

"Sword?" Nari encouraged.

"Yeah. It felt . . . I don't know, evil, maybe?"

Nari pivoted to face Axen. "Evil? Why would Icen have an evil sword?"

Shrugging helplessly, Axen waited for her mom to mull over this development. The horses pulled them along briskly, and outside the carriage, a man-made path cut out of sheer cliffs in a rainbow of colors towered over them. At times, the walls were red-and-white sandstone; other times, they were carved from lavender or dusty beige stone.

"Perhaps you were mistaken about the source of the evil?"

Axen spread her hands helplessly in front of her body.

"Maybe, like your father's sword, it is a family sword endowed with fae. Perhaps a new sensation made you uneasy?"

Drumming her fingers on the window's edge, Axen thought about her mother's words. "Everything is so different here, Mom. I don't know what I know anymore," Axen said.

"It is, but you can listen to your heart." Nari reminded her, reaching out to take Axen's hand. "It will keep changing as we get closer to the capital. The cold contrasts greatly with the warmth of Tersine, and the feeling of magic will grow stronger. As we rise into the mountains, the air will grow thinner. But don't fear, daughter. The Xahamenians have hearts as warm as our people."

Allowing her confused mind to wander, Axen spotted towering white mountains far to the east and jagged red-hued peaks to the west. The landscape wasn't entirely devoid of shrubbery. Axen noted an occasional scraggly plant in this transitory wasteland that looked as though it had withered and died where it stood, and then some good traveler had stopped to water it, reviving it on that single drink. Despite the wide variety of rock colors, everything from the plants to the stones looked sun-bleached and faded compared to the vibrant greens, reds, oranges, and blues of Tersine's jungled hills.

With each passing minute, the trees of Xahamen shrank and withered to bare, powdery earth as the lowlands grew to highlands and the distance swarmed her with buzzing homesickness.

"Do you think I will get fae since you had some?" Axen asked to break the melancholy cinching tight around her throat. Her thoughts turned to the blanket-like fae she had experienced in the woods with Icen as she watched the velvety curtains flutter uncharacteristically.

Leaning onto her hand, Nari sighed. "I don't know. I hope so."

"How will I know if I do?"

"I don't know, Axen. Before I came here, I never knew life without them. For the past twenty years, I haven't experienced their touch. If I feel some again, I will let you know."

Looking forward, Axen saw taller and taller mountains coming to meet her. It was as though they were traveling into the sky itself. The men rode through the second night without even asking Nari or Axen what they preferred to do. Their fear of attack was strong, and the head of the guard made what Axen believed was the best decision. They bounced and rolled instead of sleeping all night.

As the morning thankfully approached, Nari shook Axen awake. "I want you to see the city when it comes into view for the first time. There is nothing like it," she said.

Axen blinked back her exhaustion and mirrored her mother's excitement when the city sprang, like a rainbow during the rain, from the rocky crags that jutted up out of the mountain. The battlement wall reached skyward with alarming elevation gain. An ecstatic feeling passed through her when the calming blanket of fae from the forest enveloped her once again as the surrounding scenery shifted from nature to manmade wall. She beamed as the buoying caress soothed away any thoughts of terror.

When the company reached the inner pearly white walls at the outskirts of the city, Axen—despite having lived her whole life in the capital of Tersine—was taken aback by the enormity of the city walls and the castle itself rising above. The lofty walls loomed over everything, their crystal-blue stone façades built into the very peaks and cliffs of the tallest mountain.

"Axen, look back," Nari encouraged, pointing Axen's view in the direction of Tersine. In awe, Axen clearly saw the world fall away to the jungle forest of her homeland and even caught a glittering peek of the ocean beyond. Another shock of realization passed through her. The only thing that had kept me from seeing Xahamen's mountains from Tersine was the thick jungle foliage and my disinterest. The two capitals, though far apart, were closer than she had ever realized.

Sprawling, high-topped glasshouses glittered blue-tinged rainbows as leaf-filled sentinels between fallow winter fields. Men and a low stone wall guarded these. Large chunks of razor-sharp, blue-rainbow glass filled deep gullies. The whole world was a shimmering raindrop, breaking every color into blue or prismatic rainbows.

The armaments and castle were cut from the same crystal-glass, creating an illusion that the castle soared into the sky. Reaching walls absorbed and reflected prisms in a brilliant blue hue. A single iridescent tower at the center disappeared somewhere in the heavens.

Fear and awe battled as Axen investigated how seamlessly the castle's grandeur, sitting at the top of sheer, glittering white cliffs, melted into the mountain peaks below. The lines of the architecture drew her eyes up and up until she looked straight into the cloud-filled sky. The castle filled the whole of the horizon.

"This entire city is made from a mineral called enchanted ice. This ice is similar to frozen water, which is why it sparkles and appears translucent," Nari explained. "Though it can be just as opaque as stone when cut just right."

Axen felt like she had stepped into a dream world, but whenever she caught sight of the men garbed in the royal blue, silver, and red livery and her own forest-green and gold-trimmed outfitted men outside the carriage. This view violently yanked her back into reality.

Arriving within the carriage yard of the castle, the entourage slowly pulled to a stop at the feet of King Caissidde. A few guards swarmed out of the main gate of the castle. Soldiers wore the typical blue, silver, and red tunics and carried dark blue shields emblazoned with a burgundy, fanged lizard. They fanned across the courtyard in pageantry and welcome. Nari's familiar, comforting hand on Axen's shoulder reminded her that, like the three moons gazing down on her from the sky, she wasn't alone, and it pulled her back from the brink of bewilderment.

"Where is Icen?" Axen whispered to her mother as Maarten opened the door of the carriage. The three of them shared a look. Combined with exhaustion, the apology was evident on Maarten's face. After noticing Axen's distraught mien, Nari forced a queenly face of placidity, nodding to Axen to do the same. Axen wanted to ask Maarten about the prince and the forest, but couldn't find the right moment.

"Welcome, Princess Axen and Queen Nari of Tersine. Please enter our home. My sister and I will show you around and to your rooms." Caissidde greeted them as they passed into the courtyard, Nari at his elbow, and Axen at Maarten's.

Pursing her lips in curiosity, Axen noted that as they entered the castle, the nobility remained outside. She could see their brightly colored clothes as they peered curiously through the gates, vying to get the last look at the royal family. Inside, only three guards and one modestly dressed serving woman stood waiting.

"How odd," Axen mouthed to her mother. Maarten must have caught her words, though, because he turned to her in confidence.

"The nobility are not allowed in the castle at this time," he explained in a whisper. "At the request of the prince, only a selected few people are allowed into the castle, including yourself and your parents when your father arrives."

Confused, Axen wanted to ask why, but the dark-haired woman who had stood waiting gripped both Nari's and Axen's elbows as she excused them from Caissidde and Maarten. "I would bet anything these women are exhausted and would love a few hours to rest and freshen up. We will see you both at dinner," she said, turning to speak directly to Axen and Nari. Her lavender eyes matched those of Maarten and Caissidde, but her square white teeth filled a smile. "I am Mette, Icen's aunt and Caissidde's sister. I have been helping with the domestic affairs of the castle since the death of Queen Jozefina."

As her booted feet echoed in the hollow castle, Axen now understood why they had brought no other help with them outside of their personal guard. She felt exposed. There were no close walls, no embracing scent of foliage, and no watching eyes of guards. In her distress, a blanket of calm danced over her skin in a small zephyr.

"Mom," she whispered. "I feel some strongly now. The blanket is dancing comfort over my skin. Is it fae, truly?"

Nari nodded. "I feel them too, my daughter. And they know me. I think they might be some of my old fae." A gratified half-grin crested Nari's full mouth.

Fae. Axen burst with elation at the thought. "Why would fae have me surrounded? Does this mean they are mine?" She thought back to the forest. They hadn't been much offensive help in hand-to-hand combat.

"It's a protection against magic. They could be yours, but it is hard to tell. Many of the fae surrounding us belong to Icen. I can feel his mark on them. Some feel like Jozefina's."

"I am sure he sent fae to protect the princess," Mette remarked from her leading position. "He was determined you made it here in one piece. So many rebels and rogues out at the border these days. He wasn't going to take that risk."

"The prince?"

"Yes," Nari answered, sharing a pleased look with Mette. "I have felt his fae here and there since we crossed the border. I had planned to use any fae I attracted to protect you, but Icen beat me to it."

The hint of the prince's generosity gave Axen some small comfort. But it was at odds with what she knew of him from their meeting in the woods. There must be more to his situation than I understand.

Her eyes wandered after Maarten and Caissidde as they departed until a smooth, water-colored wall in the center of the room caught her interest. A narrow, winding staircase led from it to what appeared to be the castle's tallest tower.

Following Axen's gaze, Mette said, "That is the staircase that leads to the king's personal chambers. Or where your chambers will be after the marriage. As a gift from King Caissidde, these are Icen's current rooms."

A small breeze whistled past Axen's ear, reminding her of a question. "Could a beast conduct something so . . . cozy as this shield of fae?"

"I would wager some belong to you, which is why you feel them so strongly." Nari continued. "But no. Evil is evil and good is good. Perhaps the evil you felt from before was something from Entropy, and not from Icen's sword at all."

"Sword?" Mette asked, slowing her steps. "Icen's sword, really Caissidde's, is enchanted. It is one of the five forged at the founding of the world, and is not evil. It was my father's before it was Caissidde's. I have seen it in use. It is good."

"I saw him wield it, and it felt evil," Axen said.

"You must have felt something else," Mette shrugged. "Or maybe he was wielding it with negative intentions? He is healing now, but my prince has been. . . stubborn."

She must have heard Axen's sharp intake of breath, because she added in haste, "We will have two more guards moved to that floor from your own personal guard. Icen has arranged for the princess's safety." She included the last part for Axen's benefit.

"I appreciate his efforts," Nari murmured with a hidden wink to her daughter.

Despite Mette's kindness, it was a relief to Axen when she and Nari entered the receiving area of their shared chambers. Mette didn't enter the rooms at all.

"I don't think she talks to anyone all day, that poor woman," Nari whispered to Axen as they took a turn around the four separate chambers. With a yawn, Nari said, "I think both of us would like a bath and a nap. With the guards here, I feel fairly secure leaving you alone." Pausing to observe Axen's reaction, she added, "What do you think? Will you be alright if I go into the other room to freshen up?"

Axen nodded. Nari squeezed her daughter's shoulder before she left.

Without her mother's solid presence, the whole world crushed Axen with its newness. Cold drafts whooshed between rooms when the door opened. Axen's eyes took in the foreign castle around her. All the permanent fixtures were made of crystal-blue ice. Her feet sank into the plush carpeted floors as she moved from room to room. Draperies covered every wall. The overwhelm crept up into her throat, choking her. Nothing felt the same as back home.

A warm rush of air swirled around her and carried the smell of flowers to her nose. Her knees knocked together as they weakened. The breeze smelled of Tersine. Homesickness welled up again within her, and that odd, comforting embrace of the fae whipped around her in an instant, holding her up.

Floating in that embrace and leaning on her courage, Axen ducked beneath the free-flowing spray in the bathroom. Steaming water already filled the bath, and a waterfall of deliciously warm water poured from the ceiling over her to rinse the suds off. At home, the bath had to be drawn and warmed, and she had used a hand pitcher of colder water to rinse herself. She leaned into the bittersweet realization that her life would be different with magic in it.

No wonder my mother promised Jozefina to preserve Xahamen's remaining magic. A thudding heartsickness quivered through her pouted lip. *Tersine doesn't know these amenities, and never will without magic.* Her sacrifice only meant an extension to Tersine's existence. Compared to Tersine, Xahamen felt alive.

"Is it magic that causes the water to be hot and fall from the ceiling as though dripping from the roof of caves?" Axen asked Nari as they sat together at the mirror in Axen's room, brushing through Axen's long, curly copper-tinged locks. Even now, a mellow breeze blew through the room, dancing through and drying Axen's hair when in Tersine she would have needed to use a towel.

Nari nodded as she withdrew her hands from Axen's hair in time for the wind to style her curls and braid a circlet around her head, perfectly positioned for her mother to place her tiara. Marveling at this other display of magic, Axen touched her hair cautiously. Nari smiled at her daughter in the mirror. Axen drew her hanging mouth closed.

"The fae seem to favor you." Nari's shoulders relaxed. "I am so glad to see it so."

Even without a nap, Axen felt invigorated and ready to explore more. She, with her mother, Mette, and King Caissidde, went to inspect the sparring grounds. Two guards and Maarten came along for protection. They also toured several enormous glass-encased gardens outside the castle's inner walls. Just like the glasshouses on the edge of the capital city, these glasshouses glittered with an iridescent hue, sparkling as the setting sun hit each facet.

Standing with her feet far apart, Axen took in the beautiful glasshouses. Nari tried to tell Axen something with her eyes, but Axen could not discern what until Maarten joined the shared conversation.

"It is also not the only glass-enclosed garden in the palace," Maarten whispered to Axen, inclining his head and raising his eyebrows as if letting Axen in on a secret he and Nari shared. “You must ask Prince Icen about it.”

Chapter 10-Icen:

The moment Axen crossed the border, Icen felt fae desert him. Excitement filled him. He had seen the caravan approaching since he and Nic had taken to patrolling alongside the main highway between Xahamen and Tersine, and was pleased to know the princess was close.

They followed the company, staying in the shadows and bushes where they could remain out of sight. This served the purpose of hiding Icen's face, protecting his future wife from any threat, seen or unseen. He would do all he could to make sure Regan didn't lay a finger on any of the approaching company. Regan had made himself an enemy of the crown that night when he declared his plans to go against Icen and potentially harm Princess Axen.

While Axen hid within the carriage, Icen drew close now and again, trying to catch a glimpse of her. His heart pounded. Eagerly, he sent more and more fae to guard the princess, disregarding his own safety.

"Would you like to meet her?" Nic asked, chuckling under his breath. He followed Icen in the wide loop around the carriage and mounted soldiers once again. "I don't think she would mind, and you could check and ensure that the fae are doing their job?"

That's all it took to convince Icen to try. Except he had been a coward, and the visit was brief. Princess Axen's well-formed curves tantalized his memory. Her curly hair had framed her face in an angelic halo. The pursed set of her mauve lips showed her concern. She was every bit a beautiful princess, and it only served to remind him that he was a beast.

Despite that, Icen had been loath to leave the company behind.

"Our job is not done," Nic coaxed, leading Icen's horse deeper into the forest and toward the border. The ground fell away as they traveled, opening the borderlands up before their eyes.

"What is that?" Icen asked, pointing to a cloud of dust that expanded rapidly, consuming the road from view. As they neared, the dust kept rising. Even Icen's cursed, excellent vision couldn't pierce the thickening cloud.

"Do you think we should check it out?" Nic asked Icen, fidgeting with the reins and looking over his shoulder more than once.

"I didn't see Stet with the main party," Icen said, biting his lip. "Maybe Regan didn't have Axen as a target after all."

They ran their horses until Icen felt layer after layer of his fae peel away. This close to Tersine, he was nearly stripped of power. Panic welled in him. The last time he had gone deep into Tersine and become faeless, he had nearly died. If he hadn't been cursed to be a beast, he likely would have.

His concern for himself disappeared as he saw the small horse-mounted group of Tersinians pinned down by his own Xahamenian soldiers.

"Arms down!" Icen cried from where he hid. A few Xahamenians looked his way, smirked, but continued their barrage. The cacophony of sword on shield and song of bowstrings vibrating covered any other directives Icen hollered.

"Is it the king?" he wheezed through a tight throat.

"There," Nic called, pointing.

In the middle of the fray, atop a black ball of kicking fury, sat Stet, the king of Tersine and Axen's father. The silver of his sword glinted in the midafternoon sun as it rose and fell on the foes that threatened his person. Men that Icen didn't recognize.

"We need to get Stet out of there," Icen said to Nic, who had already prepared himself for battle. Drawing his hood closer over his face, Icen roared and charged.

Swords and arrows came fast and furious from both sides. The prince and his guardsman shed no blood as they thrusted and parried their way to the Tersinian king. Icen's enchanted sword deflected a life-ending blow from a berserking Stet before the prince spoke from deep within his hood.

"Stet, it's me, Icen. My man Nic and I are here to get you to the castle." Icen tipped his hood back. His black curls and startling blue eyes with the red sunflower trait around one pupil declared his personage.

"I'm glad I didn't kill you," the exhausted king heaved between breaths. The opposition fell heavily on them, and both men had continued to attack and defend throughout their interchange.

"Wedge, men!" Stet called. The thin drummer at his side nodded and rapped a staccato. Icen and Nic closed ranks with the Tersinians, rallying around the Tersinian banner. They bore their shields, protecting themselves and Stet as the well-trained soldiers cut their way through the less-disciplined opponents.

Once on the other side of the melee, the group rode hard away under the rapid fire of arrows. Icen, withdrawing his assassin stars from a pouch at his waist, dropped to the ground, flicking them into the arms, necks, and any tender available skin of the ragtag assailants. Their glinting gave them away just before striking their target dead.

"Go," Icen commanded when the Tersinian party slowed to assist him. "Get to the castle."

Stet nodded and immediately prodded his war stallion into a gallop. The valiant creature kicked and screamed with battle rage. His men followed suit as they shot their way north. Nic remained.

The enemy advanced slowly, wary of the deadly barrage of stars.

"Go, Nic," Icen said. "See to it that Stet makes it to the capital alive."

Nic hesitated, leaning toward the prince and his duty, but Icen's full attention was on the pursuing soldiers who had taken advantage of the prince's pause to begin firing arrows again.

One aimed to strike Nic in the neck, but Icen threw his body in the way. The arrow bounced off Icen's jugular, spinning harmlessly to the ground, and Icen saw Nic's jaw fall open. He turned, mounted, and fled.

The enemies neared by the second, and Icen's arms flew faster than humanly possible, catching and returning arrows to where they came from once his stars ran out.

Men reared hard left and right, fleeing in disarray or falling to their deaths. Once the last of the dust had fallen, Icen stood, boiling from the exertion.

Searching around him, he found the nearest bank of snow, and he threw himself down. It sizzled around him, bringing him back from the brink of boiling to a lizard's death—just another thing he had to deal with being a lizard. His thoughts whirled to Axen, hoping she would reach the capital. Both Maarten and Axen had the skills to keep her safe, even with Regan on the loose and previously loyal men turning on the Tersinian royal family.

Icen knew he needed to make haste.

Chapter 11-Axen:

Axen ran through a series of hand-to-hand combat moves in the empty castle courtyard. Her mind wandered to Maarten's explanation of Icen's actions in the forest. The soldier and advisor had believed Icen had been testing the strength of the fae he had sent to protect her. Something about that explanation didn't sit right. She trusted Maarten, but even Nari seemed skeptical of the explanation. The heavy gates creaked open, drawing her attention, and she dropped her weapons as her father came galloping through, flanked by three guards.

"Dad!" she cried, rushing to her father as he slid from his horse and handed the reins to the nearest guard. He wrapped Axen in a hug. The doors leading to the castle soon teemed with activity from the few guards and people allowed in the castle. Stet took in Caissidde, Mette, and Nari before his gaze turned into a scowl.

"Caissidde," he greeted coolly. "Is your son not here?"

Axen perked up in anticipation. She was eager to receive a formal introduction to Icen and confront him, hoping he had a reason for his violence toward her. A heavy silence followed his question, but Mette smiled.

"He is within the castle, my lord. Please enter," she invited.

Stet's eyebrows dropped heavily over his eyes when Nic clattered into the courtyard a moment later. Axen wondered at his suspicion.

"We need to speak in private, Cai," Stet said somberly. He released his wife from a hug and turned to enter the castle.

This pronouncement evaporated all of Axen's hope that her father would insist that she get introduced to Icen right away. Something else was on his mind.

She followed closely until Nari spoke around the closing door, "We will get you in a minute, my daughter."

Axen hovered in the grand entry, hoping against hope that being left out was an oversight. She could hear the booming cadence of her father's angry voice, rising and then falling quiet. Other voices answered in their turn. She was unsure how it would be taken if she walked in, so she turned to Maarten.

"I think we should wait," he said, leading Axen up the stairs to the small castle library. He stood stiffly at the library door, hand on his sword. Axen took a chair near a window and sat. Her sword clanged against the ice furniture.

"I will go ask your father's guard if they have any news," Maarten said at last. Axen's gratitude played in discord to her dancing anxiety.

“I will go as well,” she suggested, but Maarten shook his head.

“I have a bad feeling about this, and I want you to stay here and be as safe as possible,” he said with a bow.

Wishing she were more confident in what her role and privilege were here, Axen sat and tapped her fingers on the frozen crystalline stones that made up the chair. She could hear the furniture ring beneath her fingernails.

A small tinkling across the flooring caught her attention. Jumping to her feet, her hand sought her sword. Her sudden movements alarmed her guards, setting them on alert. As Axen approached the bookshelves, she saw a flicker of a shadow. Moving toward it, she was hit in the face with a whiff of . . . garbage?

Axen looked to the guards, whose faces contorted with the smell. Turning to the right, in the window reflection stood the beast prince of the forest. He gave a wicked smile and winked, but when she turned from the reflection to confront him, nothing was there. Her guard peered at her, but she gave them no heed as she fled. Determination to confront her parents filled her. She found them standing with their heads together outside the council room.

“Mom? Dad?” Axen announced her presence. “What is going on?”

It was as if they had been waiting for her. They turned, extended greetings with strained smiles. "We have had some significant changes in plans. An army passed into Tersine today, angling for the capital. I wish we had more time to explore and visit," Nari exclaimed, taking one of Axen's elbows.

"But we need to prepare for the wedding," Stet said distantly. Stet took his daughter's other side, leading her back toward the stairs and their chambers on the second floor.

Axen's jaw dropped in surprise. "What?"

Nari took Axen's arm in hers as Stet took his leave to strategize with Caissidde. "There was an attack at the Tersinian border when your father passed through this morning, heading deeper into the country. We must move the wedding up."

"To when?" Axen asked, flabbergasted.

"Today."

A cold thrill shot through Axen. "But I haven't been properly introduced!" Tears of loss sprang to her eyes, and she began trembling. She wanted to speak more, but something held her tongue.

"We are sure your safety is his utmost care, but surely you understand that we can't leave Kole to fight alone. He needs your father."

The comforting feeling of calm cocooned her shoulders, but it was her own emotions rather than an outward threat that battled against the constant peace it tried to provide.

"Mom?"

Throwing her arms around Axen, Nari's calming presence joined the invisible blanket in soothing Axen's fear and confusion.

"He saved your father," Nari said. "He spoke with us."

Fleetingly, Axen could feel the current of fae around her body merge with her mother's, but the situation felt more pressing than that discovery.

"Caissidde?" Axen asked, her stomach tightening.

"Icen."

Axen couldn't hide her confusion and hurt. "Without me?"

Nari spoke quickly, as they could hear steps approaching. "It was so brief. He couldn't stay. But we all agreed, if you do as well, my dear, that our biggest weapon against an invading army guided by Entropy is your marriage to Icen. Axen, he's hideous, but his concern for you was so real. So distinct." Her voice dropped. "Your father was charmed instantly. And I am comforted by the fact that he appears to be the same boy I knew years ago."

"You didn't invite me?" Axen tried to control the tremor in her voice.

"There is so much afoot, Axen. Icen agreed to marry you today. If you want us at your wedding for certain, and you do not want to stay here for an indefinite amount of time until we can return—" Nari's eyes looked directly into Axen's own. "It has to be today. Kole is a fine warrior, but inexperienced in war. If the men he is up against are enchanted or guided by magic in some way, Stet doesn't want Kole or any unnecessary men to die, or the country to fall."

Axen spread pleading hands in front of her chest. "I understand, Mother. I do. I thought I would have more time to make friends and settle in. I thought I would get to know Icen a little first."

The expected knock came at the door. With a silencing shake of the head, Nari turned and opened the door to a slightly breathless Mette.

"I am sorry, my ladies," Mette said. "We don't have much time. Please come with me." As the women walked, Mette spoke rapidly. "Don't worry, Axen. We have everything you will need to be beautiful for your wedding, even on such short notice. As I am sure you discovered when you arrived, we don't need maids or ladies-in-waiting since the magic helps with all of that. And you seem to have attracted some very loyal fae already." Mette attempted to soothe the panic rising in Axen's belly with her words. "I am sure you will quickly feel at home. Prince Icen is so determined that you feel comfortable."

Axen noticed that Mette's eyes held a faraway, sad look that she quickly covered with a wide smile, even as her breath came in quick gasps. Mette's eyes were the traditional Xahamenian soft purple and brimming with compassion.

"Icen made sure everything was ready for you," she urged. Mette nodded at Nari to continue.

"Yes, Mette reminded me that it is customary in Xahamen to spend your honeymoon period alone with Icen. The honeymoon period is typically up to two months; however, it can be as short as four to six weeks if you were to conceive an heir." Nari's voice was unaffected despite the climb. The even cadence of her words contrasted with Axen's flushed face.

Not only was she being left here with strangers, but she would be stuck alone, like a prisoner. She was about to be trapped with a man she didn't understand, who was plagued by a curse, and able to wield magic. Her breath quickened.

Catching Axen's eye, Mette said, "However, regardless of an heir, the honeymoon period concludes two months from this day. There is no pressure to conceive an heir. Though I am sure the Lord Prince would make an excellent father." Mette had said the term 'Lord Prince' in an affectionate tone that caught Axen's attention even as she once again felt embarrassed by Mette's candid discussion of intimate things.

There was so much happening all at once, but she was growing certain of Mette's kindness and affection for Icen, and somehow that made it possible for Axen to finish mounting the stairs despite her own, terrifying experience with him in the woods. When they neared the door of Axen's new suite, what had looked to be dark wood was actually a stunning dark blue, glittery door made from enchanted ice.

Upon entering, Axen noted that the entry room, spread into the sitting room with chairs for sitting, was carved into a layer of white ice.

"On the first floor of the suite, there is this entryway here, and then this sitting room. Come."

They passed through this room and followed Mette up the solitary flight of stairs within the suite to the second floor.

"Everything you see here, the decorations, the furnishings, are all sentimental and have been in the family for generations." Mette paused in an alcove that overlooked the castle entryway, drawbridge, and carriage yard. She opened a door to her left that revealed a study full of heavy tomes set into ice-and-stone shelves.

"There are three rooms on this floor. This study and two more in a straight line."

Beyond the study, they entered a spacious room with transparent walls and a glass ceiling that gave a clear view of the sky.

"This is the second room on this floor. It is used by the King and the Queen, or in our case, it will be used by the Prince Regent and his Princess. You and Lord Prince Icen," she clarified, again saying Icen's name and title affectionately. Past the four-poster bed, another jeweled door led out.

"The last room on this floor is this one." Mette danced around as she pushed the last door open with a flourish. "This room is yours and yours alone."

The chamber was far simpler than any of the other rooms they had passed through, but to Axen, it was a breath of fresh air. The decor and furnishings were reminiscent of Tersine. Axen felt another gust of peace that reignited the calm from the fae. There was a small bookcase filled with books, Axen's wedding trunk, and a single-person bed covered in a gorgeously embroidered bedspread depicting the ocean and the castle of Tersine.

"Icen helped me redecorate this room. He wanted it to be as comfortable and welcoming for you as possible," Mette confided as Axen ran her hand across the bedclothes.

"The king, or his co-ruler, our prince regent, is not allowed within this room without express permission.

Neither is anyone else. Upon your occupation, you will have absolute control over who enters. This is a magic effect from long ago and is based on the Cohesion property of magic that the five kingdoms are founded upon."

"Cohesion is the binding force that allows the magic to serve both good and evil," Nari reminded Axen.

Mette nodded and continued. "Every other room within the entirety of the palace can be entered by the King or Prince Regent, and the Queen or the King's consort. Much like your room, the king and queen's wedding chamber," she opened her arms as though presenting the room around them, "is also protected by Cohesion. It is to protect the monarchs."

With a wink, Mette added, "The prince may try to hide from you, Axen, but rest assured, at some point, he will be unable to keep anything from you. The castle will be entirely yours. You have this one room in which you will be protected from all you fear or dislike, or if you simply need a break."

Returning together to the wedding chamber, the women gazed out over what may have been the whole world. Mountains and valleys and jungles stretched as far as the eye could see. The view showcased extensive gardens within glasshouses, the now-snow-covered orchards, and the ocean far off to the north and south.

"Home," Axen said, pointing out the southern ocean to her mother. Uncertainty over her choice swelled within her. A concerned longing passed over Nari's face as her eyes met Axen's.

"This room is the highest place in all the Five Lands," Nari reminisced distantly. "I was here once before, at the birth of Icen. I remember her fae fussing the moment Icen was born. From that moment on, her fae always tended to be diligently caring. You can feel some of them now." The breeze that darted between them smoothed their skirts down and dragged a pair of chairs close in anticipation.

Axen blinked at the reminder that her mother and Queen Jozefina had been friends. It felt odd to be standing here, betrothed to a man she had barely met, arranged to marry him by the very love her mother now spoke of in reverential tones.

Mette paused in lip-biting giddiness, waiting for Axen and her mother to take in the grandeur. Axen saw her mother melt into memory, the past coming between the two.

"I will escort your mother back down, and I will return to assist you where I can," she said with a nod. "I am sure you won't need much from me. Jozefina's fae, left as an inheritance for Icen, are eager to assist."

Axen was left alone with no hope of being officially introduced to Icen before the wedding. She gazed after her mother and Mette, wondering if she should follow and tell her mother that she would not go through with this. Not this way, not right now while feeling utterly vulnerable, forgotten, and alone.

Two months. If she got married today, she would be trapped in these rooms for two months with a man she had glancing interactions with twice now and had once appeared to want to kill her.

Can I consent to this?

Chapter 12-Axen:

As soon as her mother and Mette were gone, Axen tiptoed toward the exit of the king and queen's wedding chamber. Making to leave, she grabbed the handle, planning to flee the room.

Her breath caught when a sudden gale picked up, whipping her around. Hoping it was just her clumsiness or something benign, she went to turn again but was spun by the wind one more time and forced to look deeper into the suite.

Axen searched the empty room for the enemy. Her wide-eyed expression reflected back to her from the floor-to-ceiling windows. The room itself revealed nothing before the wind gusted again. Baffled and beginning to panic, she looked around her. There was no one—only what she believed must have been the magic.

"Can I not leave? What if I don't want to get married?" she roared at the glass windows around her.

The panes vibrated from the force of the trembling zephyr that spun around Axen. Its shivering updrafts appeared to be as confused as she was.

"Let me be!"

The wind ceased entirely at her words, and Axen felt completely alone for the first time since she had stepped over the Xahamenian border.

"Do not shout." Maarten's voice came from somewhere below. Axen's muscles turned soft in relief.

There must be a protocol in place to keep him from entering the suite, or he would not shout so.

"If you want something of the wind, you have to ask." His voice, though raised, was respectful, "Icen has already permitted his fae to do whatever you ask of them."

"Maarten?" she called, cautiously moving from the wedding chamber into the study just beyond. Her head swiveled as she moved toward Maarten.

"Yes, and Icen is here too. He was just leaving when he said he heard screaming."

Axen stood frozen, half crouched on the step as her heart hammered in her ears.

"Will he let me see him?" Sneaking down the stairs, she soon caught sight of the two men standing side by side in the entryway on the first floor.

Maarten faced the sitting room, and the man, who must be Icen, looked down the spiraling staircase to the main floor of the castle.

"Xahamenian custom forbids me from seeing you on our wedding day before we wed," Icen rumbled.

Sucking in a deep, clear breath, Axen twisted her hands. From her vantage point at the top of the stairs, she would have never guessed there was anything wrong with her betrothed. There were no flies and no lizard features she would have supposed. Her shoe made the tiniest hiss on the enchanted ice as she went to step forward.

"Please don't come any closer."

Axen met Maarten's proud eyes. He was pleased by Icen's response and would not be an ally for introductions.

"But," she murmured, wobbling a little. She took in his strong, broad back, clothed in a dark coat. He was nearly a head taller than Maarten. Long, tightly curled black hair reached past the top of his collar. The well-tailored suit fit him snugly in all the right places. She tried to ignore how it emphasized his strong arms and legs. Axen blushed.

"I must go now, Axen," Icen said, causing her to startle. While his voice sounded old and slithery to the princess, his hesitant words carried a note of calm to her chaotic heart. "You are too tempting."

Opening her mouth to speak, Axen couldn't decide what needed to come out, but her wordlessness didn't matter as Icen vanished into the stairwell. Maarten stood in the entryway to the suite alone.

"If you need anything, let me know," Maarten said. His serious eyes caught hers with their reassurance. "I am here if you need me."

Axen nodded, grateful to have a friend, wondering at how much her life had changed in such a brief period. She had gone from being one of a warm, large family to a solitary prisoner in an ice-cold castle in the frigid north.

And now, I go to marry him. Thinking of the Icen she had just spoken to tickled her with pleasure.

How could she feel pleased that she was going to marry the beast prince? A wave of heat rose in her face at how shallow she was being. How was she standing here, thinking about his physique, and not worrying about the reluctance she had toward their wedding?

My parents trust him. Maarten thinks he is changing. Maybe he still has hard days and hard moments. But . . . She would give him the opportunity to prove himself worthy of her devotion.

Time was short. The wind insistently coaxed her from her thoughts back to reality, dancing along her brow. It tugged her back into her own personal bedroom and guided her to the vanity stool there. She sat. Resistance made no sense. The wind was going to complete their task with or without Axen's consent.

Within seconds of sitting, the mischievous magic washed her hair and dried it, taking it from fly-away to elegantly curled and set with a tiara she had never seen before. Reaching up, she pulled it down to admire the set and the delicate twists of metal that held the stones in place. Round gems of a brilliant blue and vibrant red-glittered sprays of light. Each gem was set into the platinum tiara in a way that reminded her of the three moons.

"Wow," she breathed, running her fingers across the faceted face of the stones. Each mimicked either the blue or the red moon. At its center rested a brilliant rainbow-colored diamond. After placing it back on her head, she admired the ethereal woman who stared back from the mirror.

A wave of gratitude crashed over the princess. She had gone from being afraid of marriage and confused as to why it had to happen so soon, to accepting her situation. She had seen Icen, at last, without a threatening sword. While not much, it had been enough.

Now to be married. Axen stepped from her personal room onto the lush, silvery carpet of the wedding chamber. Awe of the heavens-filled view overflowed her heart as she took in the capital of Xahamen and beyond. The cliffs, the neat rows of houses along the streets, the glasshouses, and the people of this land were to be hers.

She wondered how many of the Five Lands she could see in the twilight panorama. Her breath blocked her view, fogging up the glass in little circular puffs. She traced her finger through the moisture. Fog was not something you could breathe in Tersine.

Axen wandered around the wedding chamber as she smoothed her rumpled wedding gown and wondered what was taking Mette so long to return.

There was no art here, no exorbitant stones or metals. Two doors led out—one to the study, the other to her personal room. The walls were windows, and a fire roared in the hearth. She made her way into the study on her left. Shoving the heavy door open with two hands left Axen massaging her sore shoulder after it swung back and caught her.

Something in the book-lined study beyond had departed in a whisper, and Axen knew it without a doubt. Was it the phantom prince of the library? She tried to laugh it off. It was too big to be vermin.

Steeling herself to confront whatever it was, she tried to exit again. She tiptoed through the study and looked into the stairwell beyond. A form lingered, wafting the faintest hint of a terrible smell.

"Icen?" she asked, clasping her hands at her swordless waist. A wedding dress wasn't much for defense.

The figure paused, then disappeared.

Axen raised her chin in defiance and stepped backward, searching the shadows until the close confines of her personal suite cloaked her. The odd, unexplained experience had rattled her, and in the confines of the tiny bedroom, she strapped a dagger to her thigh.

What a strange wedding accessory, she thought grimly as the heavy layers of her dress draped over the weapon. Please hurry, Mette. Hopefully, what Icen's aunt had said was true, and no creature could enter here.

Chapter 13-Axen:

Axen struggled to listen as Mette chattered the whole way down the winding staircase.

"I thought I saw something while I was waiting," she said, interrupting.

"I'm sure it was nothing," Mette said, not even sparing a blink before continuing her personal monologue. She gave Axen's arm a consolatory pat.

Axen wouldn't let it go.

Had it been Icen returning unannounced? Was it a man at all? Perhaps it was the form of the wind, and it only felt ominous to her because she didn't understand all the magic that gusted around her. These thoughts plagued her, but she did not speak of them to Mette.

On the main floor of the castle, she caught sight of her father, and tears fell unrestrained down her cheeks. For the first time, she questioned whether she could stay in Xahamen when her family returned to Tersine to live life without her. The heavy weight of reality crushed her, but also a steadying, tingling remnant of past love shored up her doubts.

"I think everything will turn out okay." Stet reached for his daughter with both hands and drew her close. He motioned for Mette to give them space with a subtle nod.

Pursing his lips caused the hairs of his moustache to stick straight out as he looped his heavy arm over Axen's shoulder. "Are you ready?"

"You have raised me to be a woman of honor. I will do all I can for our people."

"Yes, but are you ready to marry Prince Icen?"

Axen scratched her face, giving the question deliberate thought. "I don't know if I will ever be ready, but I am willing."

The king nodded and patted her arm. He led Axen toward the chapel doors as he continued to speak. "Icen will benefit from your strength and courage," he murmured, looking toward the heavy, translucent doors of the chapel. Shadows undulated through its thick ice while the candlelight turned into twinkling orbs. "But remember, there is goodness in him too." He stumbled over his words as emotion overtook him, tears cascading down his cheeks to be lost in his beard.

"I'll try to remember," she replied, wanting to believe that Icen was as good as others tried to convince her he was, and yet the presence from earlier invaded her thoughts. *Why hadn't he announced himself?*

"Everyone is waiting," Stet said before Axen had another chance to speak. "Do you need more time to decide? If we leave today, we may not be here for the wedding. But we can honor your choice."

Biting her lip, Axen took an uncertain step forward. She wasn't perfectly certain, but action always premeditated a clearer path.

An unnatural quiet fell between father and daughter as they squared themselves to the task. Before them spread two massive doors. The princess's gaze fell on the intricately carved images in the midnight-colored doors. She squinted to see the images better. On one side stood a beautiful man. The other door held a hideous and fanged part-lizard, part-man. It featured a creature of power and nightmare.

"Dad," Axen breathed, transfixed.

Stet looked at her, then nodded. "He chose the fanged lizard as his addition to the family crest when he was just a nene, a child. It is a strange twist of fate that he turned into a beast to rival the ferocity of this one."

Marveling, Axen stepped from her father's embrace to trail a finger down the carving. "He was beautiful once," she murmured. But the Icen she knew had become a monster, in form and in character. A lifetime of memories played through her mind—rumors of the beast prince before he declared war; the fear of almost losing her father to his hatred; her mother's reassurance that he wasn't a monster. Her courage nearly failed her. As though sensing Axen's fear, Stet looped his arm through hers, bolstering her upright.

"If you do choose to leave now, we will bear any repercussions," he whispered into her ear, giving her one last chance to change her mind. "You do not have to do this. Not for me. Not for the country. Not even for a slim chance to save the world's magic. But whatever you decide, you must face up to it stalwartly. Do not turn back."

With a deep breath, Axen took another hesitant step forward. Stet released her to open the heavy doors with both hands, wide enough to let them through. As she passed by him, his hand went to her shoulder blade, holding her up. He allowed her the space she needed to process this next development, keeping her hidden in the shadows of the alcove.

"Is something wrong?" Lady Mette asked, quiet and insistent as she slipped beside Axen. Stet growled, and Mette retreated.

"I will not turn back now, Father," Axen said, using the formal words to create both a closeness and a respectful distance. "My marriage serves a greater purpose. I cannot let our people down. Perhaps, we won't let the world down either."

"If I were to command you to leave?" He pressed her, and Axen knew it was only to encourage her to set her mind firmly on her decision.

She tightened her lips in determination.

Their eyes locked once more, and his history of strength while making hard choices surged into her. She would proudly face her wedding as her father's daughter and a Tersinian.

"Come, Father, I have a husband to wed," she said, throwing her shoulders back. Every muscle in her body trembled, concealed behind the heavy, draping fabric of her dress. Her twisted mouth hid behind the veil. She could feel her father's heartbreak and pride in the quickening of his breath and the tightening of his hand on hers. Another wave of warmth rushed over her, ruffling the veil and the edges of her hair with their eagerness. Courage straightened her spine. The fae had returned to her in her time of need.

She looked deeper into the room at the large man standing, waiting for her at the altar. Her mother believed Icen to be good and believed that he would treat Axen well. While their history was different, her father confirmed that he felt the same. Her parents had never betrayed her trust.

As they walked the short corridor, Axen heard Stet suck in a deep, shuddering breath. The princess knew the king was taking in every detail. Her father's hand held her fingers tightly, holding onto her for these final seconds that she would be his. He would no longer be her protector. She would have a husband, and as her father passed her hands to Icen's, she shuddered.

Icen's dark hair hid most of his face in shadow. The flies were nowhere to be seen. The thickness of her veil obscured the details of his face, but she could tell that his skin had an odd, shiny texture in places. When he saw her eyes rest on his face, he turned, tossing his hair in front to obscure his features entirely, except for his chin.

Perhaps she would see his face better when she removed the veil. She let her eyes roam down the rest of his body. Everything was covered, as she had seen earlier from the back. His neck hid behind a high, ruffled collar laced to the top. A broad chest and shoulders were covered in a shirt and lapels. Even his legs, chiseled beneath his trousers, were mostly a mystery. Gloves concealed his oddly shaped hands that sprouted extra-long fingers. A surge of indignant irritation overtook her. She wanted to look into the face of the man she was marrying, but she could not.

The ceremony was neither lengthy nor elaborate. Axen heard her name and Icen's spoken within the simple ceremony, given in Xahamenian first, then Tersinian. She caught a few words here and there from her political training, but the reality that she would need to put in a valiant effort to learning the language of her new husband, home, and people settled on her. Formally, Icen presented her a ring of state, and she presented him one in return.

Then, in an oddly intimate gesture, Icen also produced a small, diamond-studded gold band.

Axen glanced at her mother, who had covered her mouth with her hand. Tears flowed freely from Nari's eyes. There was something special about the ring.

A gravelly and low voice—the voice of her husband—spoke. He was shadowed too deeply to discern anything but the light reflecting off his eyes and a chin marred by something such as patches of what may have been scales. Without a clear view, she couldn't decide for sure. To her surprise, a tame, musky smell of a man—of her man—reached her. She was pleased to know that he didn't reek all the time.

"I promise to keep you safe. I promise to learn to love you. I promise my soul to you." The words were fleeting, but they clearly came from Icen. "I vow to keep you and your family safe using anything within my power. I vow to respect and honor you." The vow that came from Icen's shadowed face, given in clear Tersinian and normally only done in marriages of love, was unexpected but poignant.

"I vow to honor you, your country, and this sacred marriage ceremony," Axen whispered in return.

"Do you, Prince Regent Icen, agree to be bound to this woman in holy matrimony, through sickness, health, war, and peace?"

"I do," Icen rumbled.

"Do you, Princess Axen, agree to be bound to this man in holy matrimony, through sickness, health, war, and peace?"

"I do," Axen said, and it startled her for a second when Icen squeezed her hands gently. When she stepped forward to have him lift her veil and perhaps kiss her, he abruptly turned and fled. Axen tried to hold on to his hands, but the strange fingers slipped easily from her grasp.

Why did he flee? But she didn't have time to think about it as Nari was at Axen's side within seconds, taking her daughter's elbow and leading her away.

"Caissidde said there will be two private wedding feasts," she said. "One will be in your and Icen's quarters. Icen has not been in the public eye since his change, and he refuses to attend a feast, which means it would be odd if you did."

Stet moved to join them. "King Caissidde has arranged for another small banquet for us and a few nobles outside the castle. However, as soon as we can, we will discreetly take our leave. It will likely be some time tonight."

Tears rose in Axen's eyes. "So soon?" she asked, hearing her voice wavering and hating the sound. It made her feel small.

"Secretly, Axen. You know how important that is."

Axen nodded, leaning into first her mother's embrace, then her father's, knowing that she couldn't trust her own voice.

"I will write as soon as we arrive home," Nari said. The tender tone nearly broke Axen's resolve to stay.

Axen felt as though her funeral procession was on its way as her mother, father, Lady Mette, Maarten, and a second guard moved with her several floors up the winding tower stair. At the top, Maarten opened the door. Axen's fumbling fingers removed her veil as she looked around for her husband. When he was nowhere to be seen, she turned to her parents for one last hug, summoning her courage. She stepped into the entryway, spying an elegantly set, small stone table.

"Take a seat, Axen, and see if he will join you," Nari said, waving her fingers goodbye.

The door swung shut behind her mother with a thunk. Its noise reverberated through the hollow room. She took a seat and straightened her back before she spoke.

"Am I to eat alone?" she asked. It took all her willpower to steady her trembling voice.

"I am here," a voice said, seeming to come from the ethereal matter between planes of existence. Axen recognized the deep, slithery voice as Icen's.

"But you don't show yourself."

The prince didn't answer until she moved to stand. "Please, don't make me show myself. Not tonight."

"It is our wedding night. I can't imagine a better time for me to see you," she replied, looking at her plate that had served itself. "Yet I will show you trust and respect. If you think it is best, I will not ask you to show yourself tonight."

With great restraint, Axen bowed her head and spoke aloud. "Please have courage, and please let our trust and friendship grow."

Taking a bite, she forced herself to eat in front of the unknown audience until she felt his presence go.

Chapter 14-Icen:

She is beautiful, determined, and I . . . I can't convince myself to present my hideous, beast-like self to ruin her evening. He couldn't fathom why the angelic creature had deigned to marry him—a man who broke mirrors, made babies cry, and was a coward at heart.

An atmospheric shift caught his attention. The fae floating around his body trembled, and a deep sense of foreboding filled him. Regan appeared next to Icen. *This betrayer shouldn't be here at all.*

"She's pretty," Regan said, his voice low. "Shall we go in and get to know her better?"

Icen tried to stifle the adrenaline surging through his body. It wouldn't help him in the upcoming fight. "How did you get in?"

"Were you trying to keep me out?" Regan's voice turned steely. His hands went to his hips. "I thought we were friends."

The temptation Icen had felt to approach Axen tonight, despite telling her he wasn't ready, dissipated instantly. "I don't think you understand what it means to be friends." The prince sifted through the options he had: attack or stall. With Regan's enchanted sword, their power dynamics were equal and didn't favor hand-to-hand combat.

"I tried to approach your woman, but something prevented me. What did you do?" Regan leaned against the wall. His eyes were dark in the shadowed hallway.

"I don't know what you mean," Icen tried to lie again, but Regan's sibilated warning forced him to pivot his method. "When she entered the country, fae left me. I assume she is of the bloodline. Her mother accessed her old fae as well." These words, at least, were true.

Hearts beat in the silence. "Her fae are strong," Regan said at last.

"I don't know. I haven't had much time to spend with her."

"You bowed out tonight?" The way Regan rolled these words off his tongue cut Icen to the quick. "So, are you going to introduce me?"

"She is my wife." Indignation colored Icen's response, but he sucked it back down. He needed to keep a level head. "You know very well that we are in our honeymoon period right now, and it would be quite indecent anyway to bring you into our bedchamber on any night, much less our wedding night."

"I don't care about niceties like that," Regan snarled. "I want to meet her."

For once in his life, Icen forcefully denied Regan something he wanted.

"No."

"No?" Regan's hand went to his sword, but this time Icen was quicker.

His enchanted blade didn't make a sound as it struck deeply into Regan's waist. Blood gushed from the wound immediately. The smell of gore swelled to fill the corridor, and Icen gagged. Their eyes met as Regan staggered backward, his weaponless hand going to his gut.

"You?" The disbelief and hurt in Regan's tone towed Icen's guilt to the surface.

"I'm sorry—"

"Not as sorry as you will be," Regan sneered. Icen advanced toward Regan with the intent to help, but Regan drew his sword—it sang with its following movements. "Don't touch me."

Regan leaned against the wall and disappeared through it. It was a secret entrance, and when Icen touched it, the wall solidified into ice. Icen could no longer deny that Regan also could access magic.

Coating the wall with fae to keep Regan from entering again, Icen raced from the room. He found Maarten sleeping.

"Are Stet and Nari gone?" he asked in a low voice, moving around Maarten's room to guard each wall with fae. Somehow, Regan's magic had overcome the castle's inbuilt defenses, allowing Regan to create a secret entrance. Icen was determined to keep him out.

"Yes, they left almost immediately after the wedding dinner."

"Regan is likely after them." Icen gulped in a breath and focused his mind to attract any fae that wandered unused in the castle. With just a thought, he nudged them to unite themselves with the distant, retreating Tersinian queen. "Hopefully, Nari can pick up her fae and fight with agility," he muttered. Then to Maarten he said, "I need extra guards at our door. I need to reinforce the castle walls. Regan broke in, even though I had closed all our old secret entrances this afternoon."

Maarten was fully awake now.

"I'm going to get Nic. I need to start with my father's bedroom, but I need Axen guarded in case she comes out of her room."

Wordlessly and speedily, Maarten dressed and disappeared one way as Icen went the other. Soon Nic joined the prince, and they melted through fae-guarded portals, proceeding to Caissidde's quarters at a fast pace.

"You are supposed to be on lockdown with the princess. Why have you abandoned her on your wedding night?" a bleary-eyed Caissidde reprimanded Icen.

"Regan got into my chambers, Father. He must have hidden, magical entrances into the castle that allow him to come and go at will," Icen explained, dragging his father to his feet. "The princess is my priority, but I have to protect you too."

Caissidde placed a hand on his chest, his mouth opening and closing without sound. "What?" His wide eyes looked between Icen and Nic.

"Regan wants to take Tersine for himself. And while I think his love for you will keep him from killing you, I am afraid of what he will do to me, or Axen, or Stet, or Nari." Icen ran his hands along the ice-made walls, shivering from the cold until he satisfied himself that no secret entrances led into the room. "I have done what I can to protect us, and I don't know what Regan will do if he can't further his plans through one of us, so I am here to ensure that Regan can't murder you in your sleep if his feelings change."

All the information was too much for Caissidde to take in so soon after waking, but Icen couldn't wait. He needed to protect his and Caissidde's elite soldiers—their bodyguards—and, if he could summon enough fae, the entire castle. The dark hours seemed to fly by as Icen worked tirelessly to seal every wall from breaches.

"I need you to alert the elite forces. Right now, they will be our only defense," Icen said, directing Nic once he felt his magic could do no more to keep Regan out.

"And you need to go back into confinement," Nic reminded gently. "You have a wife to greet."

Icen paused mid-step, taking in the tousled locks and the womanly form tucked beneath a blanket on the window seat of the king and queen's chamber. Her cheek rested on her hand. Little puffs of fog gathered on the window near her face as she breathed. He wanted to wake her, maybe even stroke a gentle thumb across that furrowed brow to calm her mind, but he didn't. He couldn't. It wasn't his place—not until he could courageously face her companionship.

He lifted a hand, directing the fae to carry her to bed. Moving to the frame, he leaned against the wall to make sure the tingling fae there still protected her chamber. She is safe, he sighed, turning to the expansive bed in the king and queen's chamber. Exhaustion from working magic and running on adrenaline overwhelmed him. He tossed himself onto the bedspread, not even taking the time to remove his boots. The last thought he had before he drifted off encouraged him. *Axen was a warrior princess who could handle herself if all his efforts failed.*

Chapter 15-Axen:

The next morning, Axen lay face down on the bed in her new, immaculate bedroom. Gold-and-silver-stitched draperies fluttered from the canopy in the eager wind. Sitting up, she felt twinges of pain from where the decorations on her handmade white dress and the beads from the bedspread had pressed into her flesh. She looked down over the sleep-rumpled front of the dress. Her hard work and her many hours of hope looked as wrinkled and disheveled as she felt. She had waited late into the night for Icen to attend her. The three moons had been long in the sky at her last recollection, and she had curled up on the window seat to watch their glow illuminate the world below. She was surprised to find herself in her own bed.

Yawning, she went to the armoire. The doors swung open as she approached, revealing the veil she had forgotten. It fluttered gently in the breeze among other clothing items. Some articles she recognized. Others she did not.

She withdrew her comfortable, familiar clothes. The wind rushed around her, yanking the items away from her. Cowering, Axen covered her head and her face, but a movement in the mirror caught her attention. When the storm died, she neared it. A woman with copper-and-red-tinged dark hair, perfectly styled in free-falling, loose curls that reached her waist, gazed back. The woman wore a silver dress of a light, form-fitting fabric.

Axen raised her hand to touch her own hair. The woman in the mirror replicated the action. She gasped as the first peek of the morning sunlight reflected through the stained-glass windows and off the diamond ring. The room shimmered with a cascade of rainbows. Axen was filled with awe.

"That's me," she whispered, reaching out to touch the mirror in disbelief. *What was Xahamen doing to her that she hardly recognized herself?* Wiping her fingers across her face, she realized that she wore makeup, something she had never done. Now that she was aware of it, she didn't like the way it felt on her skin.

Another innocent movement caught her eye, drawing her attention to the bathroom door. It swung open slightly. Stepping back through into the bedroom, Axen looked around in wonder. The door to the wedding chamber had cracked open a bit as well, and Axen willingly allowed the wind to lead her through the study and down the stairs, wondering where they would end up. In the sitting room, a table was laid with a mixture of breakfast items. One of the straight-backed chairs scooped her up, tucking her into her spot. She sighed at the windowless cage around her. An ache of curious loneliness tugged at her heart.

Her plate served itself with a light whistling breeze. Noisily, her stomach tried to convince her to eat. She waited, hoping. Just as she was ready to give up and eat, a persona, a whisper of a shadow, loomed in the doorway.

"Lord Prince Icen?" she asked, turning. "If it is you, please speak to me."

No one was visible in the doorway, which created more confusion on Axen's part. There was silence in the room.

"Would you please speak to me if you are Prince Icen?"

An odd, frightening feeling came over her. She focused on what she could hear as she waited for the shadow's response. Between the fae magic that surrounded her and the shivering of the wind, Axen knew the apparition wasn't friendly. Their unease brought to recollection the memory of the hideous presence yesterday in the library. Nerves clawed at her stomach. Hints of an awful stench reached her nose.

When the wind nudged her elbow to the steak knife beside her plate, Axen could simultaneously feel a whispering from her fae guard. There were two presences outside the door. One was Icen, and the other was dangerous.

"Lord Prince," she called out in a quiet voice as she secreted the knife into her hand. She sensed more than saw the presences stir in response to her voice. “Can you show yourself to me?” Her voice quivered, a betrayal.

There was silence, and then a growled “No.” The door slammed shut, making Axen jump. Whoever was out there was gone.

A gentle breeze pranced along the hem of her skirt, swirling up her body in a landspout. Her blanket of fae seemed to weave themselves in and out with the playful wind, nudging Axen’s feet into a lively dance. The fae felt alive.

“What are you?” she asked, trailing her fingers through the invisible streams of air. The warmth around her fluttered in excitement.

“Can you speak?”

There was no audible response, but she was embraced in a crushing hug and then released. An anticipatory stillness filled the air.

“Will you be my friend?” she asked, reaching her hands out in front of her. In her mind, she tried to envision the creatures or energies that surrounded her. She swayed with the warm ebb and flow, as the wind—the fae—twirled her in a circle. Opening her eyes, she noticed a golden sparkle at the edge of her vision. But when the daydream faded, it led her gaze to something that looked like a glasshouse on the roof of the castle directly below them. There, on the roof of the castle, somewhere below her, was a glasshouse full of green against the shimmering ice-white hewn stone.

"What is that place?" she wondered aloud, confused by the presence of the glasshouse and why the prodding fae magic would reveal it to her. There was no other spark to direct her questioning. The calm still encircled her, but the room was a hollow shell. "Where have you gone?" she asked pitifully.

The rest of the day passed in loneliness. Axen paced the wedding chamber, watching the sun pass across the sky. It crossed her mind several times to speak with the guards at the door, but she wasn't sure if that would be violating the honeymoon period or not.

As she wandered, the wind bumped into her, almost like a dog begging for attention. They would hand her little things, like a shoe or a pillow. Their actions made her ponder the nature of the fae.

"Can you do my bidding?" she asked when they had blown in another meal for her. "Like if I wanted gandules instead of stew?"

She rejoiced, pumping her fists, when the wind obliged her. Trying out her newly discovered friend, she asked for her sword, some paper, and finally, for something to do.

The devoted, pressing wind fae met the blanket of fae around her in a ripple. Axen distinctly recognized her mother's touch on this new magic, along with what Axen assumed were Jozefina's fae and even the hinted essence of another persona she didn't recognize, slipping a leatherbound book, written in Xahamenian, into her hand. They insisted she open it, bumping her hands and tugging at the cover. She gave in and spread the silky pages across her lap.

"I cannot read it," she admitted after some of the wind had riffled through several pages and landed on a page with words underlined. "I need to increase my Xahamen reading skills." At her admission, the wind snatched the book out of her hand in a tantrum. Axen yelped.

The wind retreated, and her own blanket of fae bristled against her skin as if in displeasure. The two different groups of fae appeared to be at a standoff.

"Don't be cross, please." Axen rubbed her arms to comfort her blanket. "I'm sorry I can't read the book, but if you bring it back, I will do my best to translate it." Thinking, she added, "And if you have any ideas on how I can translate it, such as a book of basic words, I would appreciate that, too."

The wind humored her, and her fae warmed her with a gentle glow. On the window seat beside her, the breeze deposited the original book along with a small stack of books written in Tersinian. Axen couldn't suppress a chuckle as she came to the realization that the fae probably couldn't read.

"Thank you for these," she said, looking through the books. Nothing in them would help her translate Xahamenian, but the children's stories looked interesting. If nothing else, it would soothe her boredom.

***

When she turned the last page, she held the stack of books up. "These can go now. I will see what I can do to continue translating your book." These words seemed to satisfy the wind.

Axen, though still unsettled by the wind's previous demanding behavior, was happy to be able to control it somehow. The magic did little to assuage her loneliness. She had been a princess constantly surrounded by life and laughter before coming to this land of ice and cold.

The wind deposited more books beside her. She opened the first, and a small scrap piece of paper fluttered out. Turning it over, her eyes read the neat, cramped letter penned there:

"I am trying to heal my heart. I don't think she deserves the broken me. I wish I could tell her that I am the man she deserves, but I am a coward. Will she reject me? Will I hurt her?"

The last line unnerved Axen. If this book had come from the study, as she thought it must, who could have penned these lines except Icen? She looked around her.

Two of the three occasions she had contact with Icen had not been friendly. Did he really want to kill her? Was his desire to harm her something he couldn't control? She shuddered, but the warm, soothing touch of her own fae calmed her. The cacophonic breeze even directed her to the study where another book lay open.

Her eyes spied to another note resting on its open pages.

"Now that her family is safe behind their border, I can rest in peace."

The handwriting was the same, and the message comforting. Axen crushed the note to her chest, reaching toward the book for more.

Chapter 16-Icen:

Icen sat at his desk, head in his hands. He needed to approach Axen. Every night this week, he tried, cowed, and returned to this blasted desk, defeated. All he had been brave enough to do was leave her gifts in an attempt to help her know he was there and that he cared.

He sighed, lifting an illustrated book before his face. This book, a child's Xahamenian language learning book, had come from the fae's idea. As he had looked through his books, they had pulled volumes in Tersinian and the matching book in Xahamenian from the shelves, making a stack. It hadn't taken too long for Icen to put their plan together.

When he had heard her practicing her Xahamenian from the first book he had left her, he gave her more. His personal library had dual-language options that he felt would help. And when he could find the time, he scribbled pronunciation guides to add to the growing piles of notes he had left for her.

The notes. Trembling, he picked up his pen. He wasn't entirely sure which notes she had read, but he knew the fae had shown her the small scraps that he had hidden within his books, away from Regan's prying eyes. He had written them in Tersinian to please his mother at first, but eventually, to ensure they were kept secret. Breathing in deeply, he wrote a note with Axen in mind. Part of him hoped she could find it.

I am intimidated by her. Her fortitude, her will, and her persistence. Perhaps with time, she will be able to accept a beast like me.

Chapter 17-Axen:

That evening, the silent companion joined Axen. It hovered outside her bedroom door.

When the being appeared, the wind had been frantic with excitement, tugging at her to rise. Her blanket of calm had pulsed with eagerness. Hope filled her chest with light until no greeting, invitation, or any other acknowledgment was extended. Her optimism dimmed, and she returned to the rotating pile of books that had become her most faithful companion.

One of the pages held a phrase that she had painstakingly translated.

"The faeren come from the water of the magic fountain. Faeren exist everywhere and are the father of all magic."

These words made sense to Axen, especially as she learned better how the wind worked. She became confident in utilizing the fae that glided across her body for basic things and the fae that she recognized as Nari's and Jozefina's. The fae wanted to please her, even if they did sometimes seem to have a mind of their own. The longer she used them, the more she realized that they did not.

The original book that the wind had brought her was full of the history of the magic of the Five Lands. Her vocabulary expanded, but there were still too many words she didn't understand to read it easily, and she came up with many questions.

"I wonder if Kole would be able to wield fae if he came here?" she pondered aloud, leaning on her hand as a mix of her own, Nari's, Jozefina's, and the unidentified wind danced at her feet, playing with the hem of her trousers.

Axen was pleased to learn so much from the book, even if many passages were indecipherable. She learned of people who had made progress in healing the land's magic—people she had never heard of, such as Jedrek, Aedinn, Palamoon, Aria, but also her own mother and Icen's mother. Each person's contribution had been small but important. The book even expressed that the magic would continue to heal through future sacrifices made by leaders of the Five Lands. Axen hoped, at some point, that her and Icen's names would be listed as those who had contributed to the healing of their world.

In the study, she found another gift from Icen: a handful of throwing stars. This added to the list of bow, arrows, and target, as well as books he had been leaving for her. The new weapon provided her a diversion, and she added that skill to her swordsmanship and archery practice.

When she tired, she read.

Her understanding of magic grew, but her frustration with Icen foiled her excitement. And when the silence grew too heavy, she succumbed to the loneliness and sought out companionship in the only place she could, hoping that by doing so she didn't violate some unknown clause of the honeymoon period.

"Good afternoon, Maarten," Axen said, cracking the front door open a smidge. Happiness filled her at the view. The frame and the wall obscured the dark, old head.

"Good morning, Lady Princess," he replied, looking at her. A frown weighed his face down. "I have Nic with me today."

Maarten was very choosy about who guarded the prince and the princess, making Nic an elite soldier. Like Axen, Nic was young, which was surprising since he appeared to be well-skilled and a guard that Maarten trusted implicitly.

"Any news?" she asked.

Maarten remained silent. She could tell he was chewing over her sudden appearance and weighing whether it was appropriate to say much else.

"My dog had puppies," Nic offered, with a smile.

"And of the war?"

This question took the men longer to answer, but Maarten spoke. "Yes, it has broken out. Tersinians fight at their border, keeping the rebels successfully away from their people. A huge blessing. There are rumors of skirmishes breaking out at the opposite border near Jeony." He rubbed his wrinkled face with the palm of his hand. "Palameru and Dazmorn, the other two of the Five Lands, are too far away, and Caissidde is afraid to spread himself too thin looking for fights over there. If you are curious, and if you look carefully to the south at the barren lands, you may see where your father and brother are. The castle itself is currently secure, but the second wall has fallen to the Entropy-led renegades. More people are fleeing to the inner city."

Axen sighed. "Does that mean Icen and I can be released from our confinement?"

"The king says not yet," Nic said to Axen's downcast face. "With the marginal success we are seeing at keeping the rebels at bay, he wants to give you as much time to achieve Cohesion as possible. If we start messing with your time together, we don't know how it will affect the outcomes."

"You can continue with your efforts. It helps more than you know," Maarten added, though Axen was sure that Maarten must know Icen well enough to know something unusual was going on with their honeymoon period. "Typically even the guards do not speak to the couple during the honeymoon period." His tone was short, but respectful. A light flashed in his face. "Did you know that tonight is the darkness of the moons?"

Axen bristled with indignation at the topic change before seizing the thread of Maarten's idea. "I did not even think about that. I did notice that they were close to the horizon," she responded. The corner of her mouth threatened a half-smile. *Maarten must think that Icen won't hide from me if the world is dark.*

"Perhaps you should return to the lord prince?" Maarten asked when their chitchat grew long. Stifling a groan of dislike, Axen nodded to his wisdom, closed the door, and returned to her self-imposed routine.

As the day wore on, she looked around corners and into shadows, hoping to glimpse Icen. Knowing that a war was raging outside, and that she wasn't actively doing anything to help, didn't sit well with her.

When the night drew close, the three moons set beyond the horizon. Expectancy charged Axen's actions, and instead of retiring to her room or the wedding chamber, she went to the white sitting room. The room was just big enough to allow for her weaponry practice.

She shook her head, dragged the stone table against the far wall, and jogged back up the stairs to grab the target and lug the giant thing down so she would have more room and, hopefully, more shadowed areas for Icen to hide in, if he so chose. *Am I trying to ensnare my husband?*

Setting her quiver and bow along one wall, Axen pulled out her pouch of assassin stars and tossed them at the target, dancing between each throw as if she were dodging an enemy's attack.

Once out of throwing stars, she moved to the target to retrieve them. Drawing them from the leather, she noticed that there were three at the near center of the target. Pulling them out with suspicion, she looked back over her shoulder. While she had finally been able to lodge the stars into the target, throwing them wasn't the same as throwing or blowing a dart—both skills which Axen excelled at—she had never yet consistently come close to hitting the center of the target with the small projectiles. Counting the stars again, she confirmed what she had expected. The three well-placed stars were not among the ones she had started with.

Allowing herself to sense his presence, she located Icen outside the door but did not approach him. "Thank you, Icen," she called, fanning the stars carefully in her hand.

He did not reply, and Axen sensed his departure. She considered chasing after him, but instead decided on a quick and confident, "I will wait for you in the wedding chamber after the sun has set." She turned back to her practicing, her face flaming. While her words had been forward and uncomfortable, she had every right to speak them. Icen was choosing his own isolation, but Axen was sure she deserved at least a little company from the man who had asked to be her husband.

The unknown wind, coupled with Jozefina's, shared in her excitement. As she dressed for bed, she wrestled with them every step of the way.

Once arrayed, she grew drowsy sitting on the great, plush chair before the hearth in the wedding chamber. The fire dimmed to embers. The wind drew the curtains over the expansive windows, limiting the coolness coming from them. Above her, the stars twinkled down, growing brighter.

Her eyelids grew heavy, and in defeat, she moved to the bed, tucking her bare feet beneath the pillows and lying backward, looking up at the sky. She hadn't realized she had fallen asleep until her weight shifted toward the end of the bed. Jumping with a yelp, she reached for the dagger at her waist, forgetting it wasn't there until her fingers turned up empty. Pivoting, she rolled to a crouch on the floor. She saw Icen's surprised face in the shadows. His features looked monstrous in the darkness.

Or maybe it was half-monstrous? Axen's sleeping brain raced to take in all the details she could. She saw his shadowed visage backlit by the dying fire of the hearth and top-lit from the pale starlight. Before she could move, Icen was by the study door leading away from her, hiding in the shadows again.

"I didn't mean to frighten you," he spoke in his tired, deep voice. The words were a little elongated, as though it was difficult for him to form natural speech patterns. It also didn't sound rehearsed, like all the words she had heard in the forest or at their wedding.

She didn't say anything in reply as she slowly rose to her feet, relaxing her guard. They both stood, staring at each other. Axen's heart stopped racing, and her desire for human interaction made her bold.

"Icen," she stated, stepping toward him to try to get another look at the man who was her husband.

A rumbling growl filled the space between them, but the words were indiscernible. Bravely, she took another step toward him. His body faced the door.

Biting her lip, Axen took a recovering sidestep to sit on the feather-filled mattress. She watched to see how Icen would react before trying out her Xahamenian. "Thank you for the books," she said simply, getting comfortable cross-legged on the bedspread. With delight, she noticed that he angled his body toward her slightly. Though still shy, he no longer felt threatened.

"It was a wonderful gift."

Icen coughed. It was almost a laugh, almost a scoff. He didn't believe her.

“You look . . . a beast from here,” she said slowly, continuing to try out his language. “But I . . . not sure . . . what you truly are.”

“I am a monster,” he said, his hissing voice low and sad, but clearly in Tersinian.

Axen didn’t argue. She made a dismissive noise and smiled in his direction.

Icen grumbled and turned abruptly toward her, continuing in her native tongue. “I am, my lady. Everyone fears me or wants to kill me, and I can’t say they are wrong.” His body loomed over her as he bent toward her. “I have hurt people and destroyed families and my own country. I worry about leaving these rooms when even those who are loyal to me have been unable to stand up to this...” he gestured to his face and body in one fluid movement. “I am fighting against losing my country, and to preserve yours.” He swung around and pushed through the door. Having anticipated that as his next action, she sprang after him and snatched at the back of his loose coat.

“Please don’t leave me,” she blurted out in a sob. Her resolution and constitution broke in the face of companionship. His hand darted out and grabbed her wrist, firmly and gently, but her eyes traced the form of his claws and the odd texture of his arm. Patches of scales trailed along the skin of his hands. She recoiled.

Icen turned, lips tightened into a line. The pale light lit the patchwork of scales that interrupted swathes of beautifully smooth skin. Heartbreak was evident in his eyes. Once he had extricated Axen's hands from his coat, he turned and left. The door swung heavily shut behind him.

Axen stared at her bare wrist. She hadn't recoiled from him in revulsion, though she was sure that was how it appeared to Icen. Her response had been from her own desperate action: reaching out in her bedchamber to grab onto a man whom she barely knew. She felt relief the moment he touched her. The odd texture of the scales did not register much, if at all, in the darkness of the night. Her heart began to break. She had begged a man for companionship, and he didn't want her. In her shame, tears fell.

Chapter 18-Axen:

Axen anxiously waited while the sun rose to see if Icen would reappear. Once dressed and bathed, she forced herself into the routine she had been living by, trying not to look over her shoulder at every shadow.

Standing on the stairwell looking into the study, she threw her arms out in defeat and sighed loudly. She pushed open the door to be accosted by the rancid smell she had smelled several times before. Behind the desk, face hidden behind matted hair, sat Daytime Icen. His appearance, dirt and gore smeared, differed from the night before. The beast prince had somehow transformed into a worse monster.

Axen bounced on the balls of her feet in surprise, her hand on the sword she had strapped to her waist, as she had just used the sitting room to run through hand-to-hand sword combat routines. Gagging, she snapped out a quick, "Sorry, you surprised me." She backed out of the room into the alcove to catch her breath. The heavy door swung shut between them.

Icen's chesty chuckle could be heard through the door. "You weren't expecting me after the way you accosted me last night?"

Twin flames burned Axen's cheeks, but she cracked the heavy door open again, wedging her booted feet between the door and the frame. Tears streamed from her eyes at the rancid, decaying odor. She couldn't persuade herself to inch even one foot farther into the king and queen's wedding chamber, and she remained ensconced behind the smell-blocking door.

A tickle of a thought touched the edge of her mind. Icen didn't smell this bad—or really bad at all—last night. The straightening of his smiling, filthy face distracted her. His skin was free from scales. Does this have to do with the curse? In the place of the scales were scars, puckering and marring what would have been charming features. And yet, the scars were not what intimidated the stalwart princess. It was the darkness in his eyes, though mostly hidden behind his disheveled hair, that frightened her.

"Don't look at me as though you fear me," Icen growled.

Axen's hand immediately went to her sword. She scanned Icen's body language. He looked as if he were ready to pounce, but she saw no weapon. The defenseless masquerade couldn't fool her, however, as she knew that the assassin stars were deadly and his aim was lethal. Concern over her lack of armor made her consider going back for a leather vest. Her gaze darted past him toward the wedding chamber, calculating if she could somehow make it past him to safety. Taking a fortifying breath, she knew she only had one way to retreat. That was the way she had come from. She would shelter in the sitting room.

"You can't enter your bedroom, if that's what you are hoping," the fetid version of Icen said, slowly standing. The odor was somehow worse than ever before. His top lip curled up in a snarl. One hand rested on his sword, and his eyes narrowed.

Primal instinct seized Axen. Her mind raced through her options as one arm crossed her body to protect her heart from any invisible attack. If Icen approached her and tried to take her, she would fight him.

He was much larger and stronger than she was. Even with her advanced hand-to-hand sparring experience, much of a battle against someone twice her size would be left to chance.

She ran through the multitudinous ways to dismantle an attack from a heftier opponent, preparing, but she caught herself and stopped. Why was she thinking about ways to protect herself from her husband? Shouldn't he be the one protecting her from himself? It seemed illogical to perform such undignified maneuvers against Icen. Her fae cuddled up around her arms, tugging her away from the study and down the stairs. She licked her lips with the comfort they provided. If she couldn't avoid a direct attack, her fae were as strong as the prince's—they had demonstrated their strength back in the forest. Only if necessary, she promised.

Icen stalked toward her. The look in his eyes—furious, brooding, and fierce—convinced her that an attack was imminent. Adrenaline flooded her.

Backing down the stairs, the door swung heavily shut, cutting off her view of the angry Icen. She darted into the sitting room and threw her entire weight into sliding the stone table in front of the door behind her. If worse came to worst and he was somehow able to force his way through, she would use the entrance where she knew guards were stationed to escape. She was scared, but she was determined to speak with Icen first, if possible.

She also wanted to see the honeymoon period out to honor tradition.

Icen laughed maniacally beyond the door.

You can stand against him, she reminded the terrified part of her before using her sword to chop several wooden pieces from the shelves in the entry room. The doorknob rattled, and Axen scrambled to carve pieces to wedge under the door and under the table legs.

Straining with all her might, she resisted the prince's force as he put his body weight against the door. She feared the table would budge, and she would have to truly fight. Her eyes darted around to find her bow and quiver, which were still lying against the wall.

Axen crumbled to her knees as Icen ceased his pressure. The temporary reprieve allowed Axen to fortify her barricade. With that done, she willed her trembling legs to calm. She knelt on the stuffed chair with an arrow nocked and waited in terror. Not one word of comfort passed from Icen's lips to quell her fears, and Axen forced herself to remain.

Moments passed in silence. Axen wondered if Icen had gone until he spoke.

"Are you afraid of me?" he asked, his voice clear in Xahamenian.

Axen realized that, unlike last night, Icen only spoke his own language. Her mind tumbled over this information in confusion. What was different? What had happened? Last night, he had seemed so fearful and cautious, and today he seemed to thrill in being a predator. What had she unleashed by her touch?

The precariousness of Axen's situation fell on her like a heavy weight, nearly crushing her. Her blanket of fae repelled some of the terror despite Axen's resistance.

Holding steady, Axen's teeth rattled as Icen rammed the door with a roar. His force bucked through the furniture, jolting Axen along with it.

Sucking in a breath, she held her position, arms and bow at the ready, adrenaline eschewing her exhaustion at holding an arrow taut. Two more shock waves passed through her and her blockade, and it held. She sighed.

The following hush rang through the room.

Axen strained her ears. Was he gone or biding his time? Thinking quickly, she sent the fae to readjust several of the wedges that had come loose. Unsure of what to do next, Axen realized that her options were not ideal. If Icen didn't leave her alone and continued to stand between her and her bedroom, she would be trapped here in the welcome parlor, where there was no comfort. Will I have to flee to Maarten for help? She wanted to maintain some appearance of normality and endure the honeymoon period, giving the magic some time to work—that is, if Icen ever came to her. Could I hold out? If she could somehow trick Icen into letting her back into her bedroom, she didn't know if she would ever leave there again. Can I truly believe Mette that he can't enter my particular bedroom if I don't want him to?

There were too many decisions, and Axen didn't feel like she had sufficient information to make a good one. She waited. Icen didn't make another attempt to break through her fortifications. Gathering courage, she set her bow down and moved to the front door, hoping Maarten was back on duty.

Instant relief flooded her body. Her eyes met Maarten's. "I need some help," she said simply, looking between him and his companion. Together, Axen and Maarten entered the room, and the loyal soldier's eyes flew wide. Sharing a look with Axen, Maarten propped the door open.

"Get another guard who is off duty. And be quick," Maarten ordered. He perched carefully on the top of the staircase, gesturing for Axen to join him outside the suite.

"I don't know what to do." Axen squeezed a frightened whisper out. "I surprised him yesterday when I . . . grabbed him." She choked on the words. "And then today, he snapped. He didn't actually do anything to hurt me, but he scared me. I don't know if I acted appropriately, but Maarten, I was afraid."

"His looks are rather terrifying," Maarten agreed. His eyes detached from her face, gazing into the middle distance beyond her shoulder as though he were picturing Icen's disfigured looks.

A contradictory thought crossed Axen's mind. It wasn't Icen's beastly physical features that scared her, but his threatening manner. She didn't bother trying to explain that out loud. There were pressing matters she needed to attend to.

"I'm not sure what to do. I am afraid to make things worse for the world by refusing to go back in."

"Did he raise a weapon to you?"

She shook her head, heat rising in her neck.

Maarten nodded, eyebrows lowered. "Your fear is understandable. Many with a hardened constitution have cowed when confronted with such a monstrosity."

Axen managed a weak smile. "He was blocking me from my room, but now I am afraid that if I go back in, I will be trapped. What if he doesn't want me out? What if I am stuck in my room and he decides . . ."

Discouraged, she looked at Maarten, who peered over her shoulder at her barricade in concern. He did not speak. Not wanting to rush him, Axen waited, though her gaze kept darting down the stairway to see if they had enough time to address all her concerns. When he spoke, Axen felt her stomach sink into her shoes.

"He would never harm you." He shook his graying head. "I can't blame you for wondering, seeing as he hasn't really taken the time to convince or demonstrate to you otherwise. I think you are right that the best thing to do is to have you stay in unless there is an actual threat to you. His behavior surprises me, but he has deceived me before. In the past, he left his dirty work to his commander, Regan. Even at his angriest, I have never seen him become violent. I am concerned that he frightened you, but I also think that he deserves a chance to explain."

Axen didn't readily agree, but she didn't interrupt.

"About your room—I know for sure that he cannot enter if you do not will it." His conviction carried in the strength of his words. "I have been at the mercy of the Cohesion magic myself. If you don't want him to enter, he cannot. Even if you are unsure about him entering, the magic will keep him out. And anyone else as well, including me."

Fidgeting with the end of her sleeve, Axen knew where his argument was headed.

"I think I will be able to get you into your room. One of us will get through to him."

As Axen opened her mouth to protest, Maarten raised his hand to stop her. They both noticed the men coming up the stairway.

"I will speak with the king, and he will decide what is best." He rubbed his stubbled chin. "I promise that no matter what, I won't leave you in there forever. It might take a day or two, but I think Icen will calm down and will explain to you his point of view. He would never hurt you. If you notice, he didn't use his fae to knock down your barrier. He definitely could have."

Axen didn't know if that was supposed to encourage her or terrify her more. She resolved to learn better how to master her own fae, which fluttered around her now in trepidation. If she needed to use them to protect herself, she wasn't ready.

The other guards stepped to join them before Axen's fingers twitched as they tore her barricade down. Maarten caught her eye as he deftly and secretly stored her wedges in the seat of the plush chair and eyed the shelf she had destroyed.

"We will send in a carpenter to repair this after the honeymoon period," Maarten said with a bow. "Now, hold tight. Nic and I will escort you to your chamber so you can prepare for dinner."

Axen clung uncertainly to Maarten's arm and to her sword as they went up the stairwell and passed into the study. Tears filled her eyes as Maarten and Nic left her in her bedroom. The door shut with an ominous click.

Chapter 19-Axen:

Axen did not trust the magic enchanting her bedroom to keep her safe, but with it being the best chance she had, she would not leave. To her great relief, she did not see, hear, or smell Icen for the rest of the day. Her caged body triggered a spiral of thoughts. She wondered if she could really trust Maarten not to leave her trapped until the end of the honeymoon period. If only I could get word to my family. But she knew they were too far away and too busily engaged in a battle of their own. They wouldn't suspect anything was amiss, and she hated to worry them more.

She groaned. Even several of her weapons and forms of entertainment were lost to her. Her bow remained, forgotten, in the sitting room, and the only weapon she had left was her father's sword. She wondered if she would ever talk to Icen about exchanging the sword she had been gifted with his enchanted Xahamenian blade.

The wind tittered around her, plucking at the ends of her hair and trying their best to guess her desires. In passing, she thought about asking the wind to retrieve her stuff, but decided against it. Only a human's touch would do, because the magic had its limits in connection.

A noise creaked into her subconscious, whirling thoughts. Coming to her senses, Axen discovered a ribbon of light meandering its way through her cracked bedroom door from the king and queen's chamber. She tiptoed to it. Beyond the solid enchanted ice, the world looked dark, as if night had fallen. And there was something else. She could feel Icen's presence within the wedding chamber. The proximity choked her. Her hands twitched in anticipation of a fight. She wanted to shy away and relock the door, but with the meddling wind that followed his orders, she wasn't sure that would make any sense. Taking her sword in hand, she waited, watching the door. She was ready to swing in an instant. Nothing was certain here in this frozen land with an ice-hearted prince and a magic she didn't fully understand. Minutes combined into hours. Icen made no move to enter her bedchamber.

"Can you enter?" she wondered aloud. The twinge of tiredness growing in her arms had provoked her words. Her patience for a fight was wearing thin. "If you can, then end this for both of us. I don't know what you want, but I will not allow you to touch me."

When there was no reply, Axen moved closer to the door and stared out. Coughing lightly, she tried to catch Icen's attention.

The prince's head whipped toward her, and Axen caught a glint of light off his . . . fangs? She shuddered. Had she missed his fangs earlier in the daylight because she had been too scared of him? Shaking her head, she steeled herself, watching.

"I don't intend to touch you," he spoke Tersinian again, with his distinct, elongated accent as though it were hard to form words.

Axen's blade dipped. There was a noticeable difference in Icen's appearance, language of choice, and attitude. "Then what do you want? Why did you open my door?" she snarled back, lifting the sword once again.

"I didn't open your door. That was the fae. I could not touch your door unless you willed me to." Every word slithered from his mouth with difficulty. "Not even my fae can enter unless it is something you allow."

Why is he so different in the twilight hours of yesterday? Axen wondered again, more confused than ever. She turned her attention to gain a clearer understanding of his features. In the glimmering light of the moons, he left his face unguarded.

Axen couldn't gauge Icen's reaction to seeing her hiding herself within her bedroom, wielding her sword. His hair mostly covered his face, but she could feel her spirit reacting in fear to his broad shoulders and narrow waist, his weaponry of thick arms and sturdy legs. She bit her lip to redirect her anxiety as he took tentative steps toward her. How can I look at his physique while I am afraid of what he can do to me? While part of her admired his body, she feared his clutches.

“Show me you can’t enter,” she demanded.

“I am afraid you will see me.”

“And?” she scoffed.

“I think my appearance will frighten you.”

Axen swayed at his audacity. “Can’t you tell I am already frightened of you? Your looks don't scare me. You do.”

Icen turned fully to face Axen. “Why?” His voice was confused. “Because of how hideous I am?”

“What?” Axen nearly shrieked from pent-up anxiety. “Do we need to speak in Xahamenian? You are hideous because of the darkness in your eyes, not whatever your face looks like. Is that all you are concerned about? How you look? Maybe worry more about being kinder or maybe gentler.”

Silence fell. Axen’s arms trembled in both anticipation and weariness. “Step forward. Show me that you cannot enter this bedroom,” she reiterated. “Show me, or leave me be.”

Axen observed as Icen appeared to struggle between the two options. His hesitation highlighted his confusion.

“I do not want you to see my face,” he tried to reason with her. “Is there a way I can convince you to look away?” He continued talking with the same difficulty, so Axen decided to switch to Xahamenian.

"Um, no?" she forced out, though a small welling of pride filled her at how well she spoke, knowing her long hours of practice had paid off.

"Eh?" He sounded puzzled and also switched to Xahamenian. "I have not been touched by human hands since I turned into a monster. I cannot deny the sensation, though pleasing, overwhelmed me," Icen said, his words coming out almost more difficult in his native language than in hers. "I am sorry that I scared you."

Was Maarten right? Axen marveled at this complete change from this morning. Would Icen fix the misunderstanding?

Axen bit back mounting frustration. The fear he had instilled in her earlier was slowly returning as he stalled. "I want you to show me that you cannot enter this room."

Shock nearly blew her over when the shadow nodded. "If that will make you feel better, I will do that. Even if I fear you will hate me for it. I didn't realize you had a temper."

Axen paused. She had never been pushed so far out of her comfort zone before, and it was doing terrible things to her patience. Her irritation evaporated with a sigh, but she did not lower her sword.

"Please show me that I am safe in here from you."

"From anyone," Icen corrected, continuing in Tersinian.

Irritation flared in Axen, but she stuffed it back down. She would wait.

The prince drifted warily toward where Axen stood. Anticipating a confrontation, she flexed her arm and leg muscles to steady her trembling body. Adrenaline infused her with strength. Out of the corner of her eye, she could see her blade swaying, and she hoped the prince didn't notice. A worrying fear shot through her. Her knees would buckle if her adrenaline failed. She had never been in a true battle for her life except for the time she met Icen in the woods. But she had others around her then for protection, if needed.

"I know I am terrifying you," Icen murmured. He held up his hands to show he was weaponless. "I can see well in the darkness. Your sword quakes with your fear, even as your eyes flash with power and determination." The prince pondered this, finger tapping his chin. "I should probably not tell you that you are beautiful." His voice was sincere. The shadowed head cocked curiously to the side. His palms opened toward Axen in a gesture of peace.

"I will not harm you, and neither will the magic."

"Then why are you here?" Axen gasped in frustration.

"I am here because last night you asked me to come, and I fled," he said, arms crossing in front of his chest. Benevolence chased away the annoyance Axen had felt. A rising inquisitiveness seized her. Axen watched Icen gingerly reach one hand toward the opening the door left behind.

With a blinding flash and a roar of pain, he crossed the threshold. Icen flew backward over the length of the king and queen's chamber. He smacked the wall with an odd, crunching sound, then slid to the floor in a crumpled heap.

Surging forward with compassion, Axen dropped her blade and rushed from the room to kneel beside Icen, whose breath came in short, panting gasps. Helping him to sit up, vulnerability made her as flighty as a deer, and as Icen cringed awake, she sprang to her feet in retreat. Icen's clawed hand snatched her wrist. The tenderness of his touch and quick release as she yanked her arm away caught her attention. But now wasn't the time to think it through. She fled to her room, the fae lending wings to her feet.

Stretching her neck to see him better over the bed, she watched as Icen staggered to his feet using the wall. He shook his shaggy head, and even though he was in pain, he stayed. A breeze fussed around him, tugging at his clothes and smoothing them down once he was upright.

"Are you okay?" she asked, reaching a reluctant hand in his direction.

"I will be," he panted. His Tersinian sounded slightly easier on the tongue. "Does this help you feel safe?"

Axen nodded, ashamed and confused. How had the man from this morning been so different from the one of the night? "I don't know what came over me. I needed to see this. I needed to know. You frightened me this morning, and I . . ."

Icen shifted his weight from the doorframe and moved toward Axen, stopping a few feet in front of her. "I do know what came over you," he whispered.

An exciting thrill danced through Axen's chest. Breathlessly, she noticed a shift in the man-beast. She watched as despair melted from his words, and hope and peace filled them instead.

"You wanted some security in all the chaos that is your new life. I am glad that I could give you that minuscule amount."

Courage and the desire for companionship moved Axen to push a little harder. "I think that is all you want as well, Icen. Please come join me. Let's talk." She sat cross-legged, her knee tucked on the safe side of the doorframe. One delicate hand extended its friendship into the king and queen's chamber, inches outside the protective shield of magic.

"You aren't going to pull me through, are you?" Icen chuckled nervously even as he approached. "I think I would do it again if you asked me to demonstrate, but I would rather not face that pain if that is alright with you." Tentatively, he took her hand, and she went wide-eyed at his touch.

Feeling her pulse race in her temples, Axen smiled to calm herself. "I don't think I could pull you through, and I wouldn't want to. I believe you that the magic will keep me safe. I want to see your face more clearly." A breeze whirled around Axen, holding small stones aloft near her face. She gasped as small lights winked into existence, glowing from the stones' centers.

The breezy fae carried hints that reminded Axen of Nari and Jozefina, but the unknown fae now had a definite mark. It was Icen's.

She continued to be awed by how different her life in Xahamen was compared to the one she had known in Tersine.

Axen blinked several times to solidify in her mind what had happened. "Do you not wish to share your horror with someone who will not cringe?" Axen asked. She did not release her grasp and forced herself to look toward his face. "Do I, the woman who left my country to marry you in hopes of calming a war, not deserve to see your face? The woman who agreed to marry you before knowing you, on the principle of trust? I am your wife. How am I to come to know and honor you, and maybe love you, if you will not let me? If you will not even let me look at you?"

Icen was silent after her outburst. His free hand slowly lowered to his awkwardly crossed legs. He gripped his ankle tightly to keep from tipping over. She couldn't avoid looking at his well-muscled chest and the large, powerful legs that made sitting on the ground arduous.

"Look at me then, woman," he said. His words were harsh and cold, but Axen could sense that it was in defense of himself rather than in anger or hatred toward her.

Axen leaned forward and brushed the curls back from his face. He flinched as her fingers met the scales and flesh of his face. With the shadows chased away by the small floating lights emanating from the stones, she saw a beast and also a man. All the hints and peeks before hadn't done this moment justice.

Her eyes roamed from his broad, flat nose and his skin patched with scales to his cascading hair. His angled eyes with slits for pupils, and no hair where eyebrows should be, drew her gaze next. Even in the eerie glow of the magic lights, they were a piercing ice-blue, one narrowed pupil ringed by red, and filled with so much hope and trust that Axen knew she could have shattered him with a single word or look of rejection.

His fangs stretched to his chin, but his lips were full, soft, and free of any scales. His cheeks, one nearly covered with patchy, shiny scales, the other mostly human, intrigued her. He sat stiffly, bending toward her at the waist. There was so much raw power coiled in front of her that if he had wanted to, he could have had her at his mercy. And yet . . . she melted. His beguiling eyes were devoid of anger or hatred. The depths of the slitted pupils searched her face with longing, hope, and openness. A single tear trickled down her cheek.

Icen lifted a clawed hand, as though to wipe the drop from her face. However, the barrier of magic that protected the room rippled in warning. Icen withdrew his hand. But the offer filled Axen's aching heart. Overwhelmed by her gratitude at his unguarded yearning for acceptance, she placed her face in her hands and sobbed, "Thank you," over and over and over again.

Chapter 20-Axen:

When Axen awoke, her memories from the night before came to the forefront of her mind. Her exhaustion and worry from yesterday had made her drowsy, and the last thing she remembered was Icen asking the wind to move her into her bed. The door leading to the wedding chamber was shut tight now, and she raced to throw it open, hopeful.

Yet standing outside the wedding chamber, shadowed by the artificial light of the study, stood the beastly Icen from yesterday morning. His smell wafted over her, and she gagged.

This creature–beast, man, thing–that stood before her on the far side of the room may have been shorter, stockier, and stinkier than Night Icen, but from this distance, she couldn't really tell.

"Good morning, Icen. You are different this morning."

The transformed Daytime Icen snarled.

Axen reeled back. Her mind searched for her sword. It was stowed farther into her room. She didn't take her eyes off the prince. Doubt filled her mind. Had he manipulated her into thinking she would be safe in this room so that his changed, morning self could have his way with her? She froze. Weapons. She knew that going for her weapons would be a logical choice. The fae would bring them to her . . . she paused. But would they?

She waited, and though Icen's looming presence remained, he didn't move.

Inching her way into the king and queen's chamber did nothing to agitate him into a response. However, she could see the muscles in his arms and hands twitching in anticipation and irritation. Why doesn't he enter the wedding chamber? She wondered. This recent development made her brain spin. Besides his looks, something else had changed from last night. If only she could put her finger on what it was.

"Won't you come speak with me?" she asked suspiciously. She intentionally spoke in Tersinian. "Over here? Like last night?"

A wicked grin broke across Icen's face, wiping wide-eyed confusion from his brow.

Scrunching her face, she noted his fangs were missing. He had no scales; his body shape had changed; and he smelled horribly. It was almost as though he had turned into a baser creature as a human rather than as a lizard.

"Give me a minute," she begged his pardon, turning into her bedroom and shutting the door behind her. "Wind fae," she said aloud, "please give me something so I can stomach Icen's stench."

Sluggishly, the wind swirled around the room, causing Axen's loose hairs to dance and tickle her nose. Nothing obvious happened, but she shrugged. Magic was still so new. She couldn't tell if the fae had done something. Shrugging, she wedged her nose into the crack in the door and sniffed. Bile burned Axen's throat.

"Um, Wind," she began again, wondering if she had asked them something they couldn't do. "I can't handle that smell, but I don't want to hurt his feelings. Can you please give me something?"

This time, the wind swirled around her, and in a moment, she felt a solid glass jar in her hand. She opened it. Within the jar was a salve that was a little sticky and very potent. Holding it up to her nose, Axen sniffed and sneezed. Taking a glob on her finger, she dabbed it under her nose. To her great relief, this time when she poked her nose through the crack in the door, the smell was far less overpowering, and she managed to open the door all the way.

"How are you feeling today?" she asked Daytime Icen in Tersinian.

An awkward distance and pause stretched between them. Her fingers tingled as she remembered the texture of scales on his cheeks, the expectant hope in his eyes, and the tender touch of his hand. The gentleness of last night contrasted with the overbearing, antsy man before her.

Even with the compassion she felt last night, she wasn't certain she was ready to relinquish the safety of her bedroom to this version of Icen.

"Won't you come to me?" he asked, beckoning her forward. His open-mouthed uncertainty made him far less menacing, but her suspicion grew. Something was off.

"I am sorry I fell asleep last night before we spoke much. I'm not afraid of you," Her words trailed off as the door to the study slammed shut with Icen behind it. Is he throwing a tantrum? They were separated once again.

"What is happening?" she asked herself. Nothing about the Beast Prince made sense. Her expectations for this morning's meeting had been a lot more friendly after their amicable parting. What had she done this time?

When Icen didn't open the study door again, Axen advanced. Warily, she let the wind dress her. She insisted on making sure that her dagger was accessible, and her sword was buckled about her waist. Not willing to take any risks, she even hunted a leather vest from the armoire. She shrugged into it as she fought back irritation. The wind fae had been no help with the armor.

The breeze danced around her. She could almost feel their stress.

"My safety is more important than my appearance," she chastised, wondering if her choice of attire had upset them. She contemptuously eyed the breeze fluttering around her sleeves while she tucked several assassin stars into a little pocket of the shirt. Patting each weapon several times to ensure they were still attached to her, she inhaled courage. She was going against a different version of Icen, and she wanted to be prepared for anything.

Cracking her bedroom door open, she made sure the Prince wasn't visible anywhere in the wedding chamber before she stepped into the sunlit space. When nothing happened, Axen inched her way toward the study door. Her safety was her priority, but her first longing was for companionship. Knocking on the study door, she retreated halfway and waited while the beautiful sunrise sparkled around her.

After what felt like an eternity, the study door cracked open, and Icen spoke in Xahamenian. "You see how my form morphs with the daylight. This form of a man comes with different horrors than the form of a lizard." His tone was threatening.

Axen spoke gently in reply, continuing in Tersinian, "I am not worried about your looks, Icen. Your lizard-like appearance last night did not scare me, nor do your looks." She held her hands out before her, offering peace, though she kept her feet planted, prepared to dash to safety if needed.

"In the daylight, I am a different kind of beast. The kind they told stories about in your country. I am ugly in form and in heart. Sometimes I can control the darkness of my soul, but sometimes it controls me," he said, still in Xahamenian. Axen couldn't help but wonder why he didn't switch to Tersinian, though she was pleased at how clearly she understood Daytime Icen's words. She took a step toward him, bewildered. He only spoke in Xahamenian, but she was disturbed by the furious flash in his dark eyes.

"I feel I am in control today," he said. "Please do not be afraid."

Of everything he had said, those words in his language unsettled her the most. The calm blanket around her seemed to hum in rejection of the sentiment, singing a discordant note that those words were untrue. Even the wind danced around her in agitation, as if the winds themselves were afraid. While Axen didn't understand these warnings, she went on alert. Suspicion supplanted her compassion. Icen's hands clenched when he noticed her behavioral shift.

"Can we talk, Icen? Like we were going to last night?" she asked in her language, her hands unconsciously going to the sword at her hip and the stars at her waist.

Another look of confusion crossed Icen's face. He didn't immediately respond. Axen couldn't help but wonder then if Daytime Icen couldn't understand her Tersinian. More hairs prickled on her neck.

"Come in here," Icen coaxed in Xahamenian, spreading his hands, palms up, in front of him, replicating her sign of peace. His smile looked anything but welcoming. Another inkling of suspicion ticked Axen's awareness. "We can eat in the study." His foreign words sounded like the hiss of the dangerous riptides of the ocean. His ignorance of her language caught her attention. When Axen didn't reply, Icen turned and gestured for Axen to approach.

Axen sat down in the window seat and smiled. When she spoke this time, she spoke in Xahamenian. "Why not here? It has such a lovely view."

This seemed to make Icen scramble for a response. "The sun, it burns my skin."

Axen could feel the lie in his words.

"Wind," she said in Tersinian, curious why he didn't ask the fae to do the same thing himself, "give me something to protect his skin from the sun."

Rage and confusion battled across Icen's face before he stifled both and grinned. Axen's stomach dropped into her boots with an unnamed anxiety as a large, black coat with a matching wide-brimmed hat dropped into her arms. There was no doubt in Axen's mind now that Icen hadn't understood what she had said all morning when she spoke Tersinian.

Cautiously, she approached him, extending the coat and hat for him to take. The moment he touched the extended coat, he yanked, striking like a snake, jerking Axen toward him. A searing pain ripped through Axen's coating of fae. She flew, hitting the opposite wall. The magic slammed the wedding chamber shut, cutting off her view of Icen, who had also been thrown farther into the study.

"Icen!" she called, scrambling for the doorway, worried and confused about what had happened. The light, the throwing—it was so reminiscent of what had happened to Icen last night when he had reached across the threshold into her bedroom.

Worried about the prince's safety, she opened the study door, hefting it wide to see if he was okay. A deep feeling of warning caused by a strange vibration of the fae around her halted her foot before she stepped out of the wedding chamber. Where her foot had passed the threshold, she felt as though a net held her boot, dragging her into the study. She noticed the coat and hat she had requested from the wind, carelessly strewn across the floor.

As she tried to draw her foot back beneath her, a blinding light encircled her body, throwing her back across the king and queen's chamber against her bedroom door. When she shook the impact-induced twinkling lights from her eyes and looked back into the study, remnants of dark shadows lingered. Something evil had tried to snatch her away, but the Cohesion magic had held.

Chapter 21-Icen:

Icen was exhausted. Spending all night with Axen had taken a toll on his body, and he couldn't rest. Every moment since his wedding, he had been fighting to keep Regan and his men from entering the castle. When one part of the castle was sealed off, one of the elite guards would come, warning that Icen's magic had been breached. The constant running was draining. Maintaining the castle's safety, all while trying to convince the fae that Axen didn't need them as much as the rest of the castle occupants did, had been a feat. This reality worsened because Icen struggled to divert any protection from his wife.

"You should be with Axen," Mette clucked as Icen took a glass from her outstretched hand. Gulping the energy-providing drink she had mixed for him woke him up a little as the concoction flowed through his veins.

"I should be with her," Icen agreed. "If I felt like I could. But she is the only truly safe person in the castle." He was confident he had sealed his quarters perfectly, and with her bedroom enchanted as it was, even if someone got in, she would have somewhere to hide.

"Do you give me leave to visit her?" Mette asked. "I can only imagine she is lonely without anyone to comfort her."

"I have given Nic and Maarten permission to interact with her, but if you get the time, I think she might appreciate conversing with another woman." Icen was surprised by the huge amount of regret he carried over not being able to spend more time with Axen, and he was grateful that Mette would consider breaking protocol.

"I am doing my best to spend what time with her I can."

"You should probably bathe before you spend more time with her," Mette commented as she hurried from the room. "You make my stomach churn."

Icen grimaced. He did stink, and he worried Axen had noticed his stench. If he could make the time, he would wash the gore, grime, and dirt from his body. Perhaps taking time to groom himself would help Axen feel safer.

"Any news?" he asked Nic, who had come in after Mette. Icen had been about to head back upstairs to rest.

"Like yesterday, it seems that, in the daylight, the castle remains fairly secure. Take a break. I will wake you if anything is needed."

With an exhausted yawn, Icen didn't even bother moving far. He found the closest chair and fell asleep.

Chapter 22-Axen:

Feeling sore from her recent magical repellent flights and fearing whatever evil magic had tried to capture her, Axen hadn't dared leave the shelter of her bedroom again that day. She was certain that what had kept her in the wedding chamber was also responsible for keeping Icen out.

Sprawling across the massive bed, she stared up at the ice ceiling, puzzling over the tender, meek Icen of the night, comparing him against the true monster of the day. A quiet knock came at the door leading to the study. She wouldn't have heard it if one of the wind fae hadn't tugged her bedroom door open and nudged her to listen. To her relief, Maarten stood within the study with Mette at his side.

"We left another man to guard the entryway, but after yesterday, I had to know you were okay," Maarten said, retreating a respectful distance into the study. Mette smiled and waved. The men were on night watch.

"I can't stay long, but Icen said I could say hello." Mette smiled.

Axen accompanied Mette and Maarten down the stairs to the entryway. "Thank you so much for coming. I was thinking about sitting down for dinner." A breeze blew madly around behind them. Axen could smell tantalizing aromas.

She chuckled at the wind's eagerness. "But I think I will spend a few minutes with you. Today has been confusing and lonely."

"I am so sorry to hear it," Mette's heels clicked on the stairs. "Icen has been exhausted lately with all the work he is putting in to keep those of us in the castle safe. The war is growing more heated."

Maarten led the way to the entrance, where the door stood ajar. Two other guards stood outside. "The watchmen said they didn't see you," he confided after sending the other set of guards to the bottom of the tower. "And then I felt some odd magic when I came to my watch tonight. Something didn't feel quite right. Then Mette asked to be escorted here, and I couldn't say no."

Nic had stepped to the top of the stairs to replace one man who had departed. He faced away, but Axen could tell he was listening in. She nodded. "Something is very odd," she said. "Although Icen came and made peace last night, he acted strangely again later in the day."

Nic coughed, and Axen, in embarrassment, rushed to explain. "Last night, Icen, to demonstrate that I was safe from him in my bedroom, showed me how the magic guarding my room worked. He couldn't enter."

A pleased chuckle escaped Mette. "I am glad to hear he has spent a little time with you," she expressed. "I hope he was a gentleman?"

The question in her words led Axen to continue. "Well, yes, and no. During the day, when we chatted, he didn't appear to understand me. And he wouldn't even try to enter the king and queen's wedding chamber."

Mette's lavender eyes took the princess in. They paused at the weapons on Axen's hips. The wrinkles between her thick eyebrows deepened.

"I have never heard of any principle that keeps either the king or queen, or equivalents, out of the wedding chamber. Icen should absolutely be able to enter," Mette said.

"What happened today?" she asked.

Axen sobered, hands smoothing her sleeves. "He tried to drag me into the study, then we were both thrown by magic. After that, he disappeared." Biting her lip, the princess watched as Mette's mouth formed a straight line. The older woman took a moment to mull over Axen's words.

"That sounds really bizarre," she said. "Cohesion's enchantment should let Icen into the king and queen's wedding chamber. Until you moved in, I was under the impression that he was sleeping in that room every night."

"He was in the king and queen's chamber last night," Axen affirmed. "I don't know why he vanished today. When we were together, he told me that the sunlight from the windows would burn his skin, tricked me into approaching him, and then the lights and pain happened, and we both flew apart."

"I don't know how you talk about bedroom activities so candidly," Nic swallowed. "But the prince is known for hiding from responsibility."

Maarten chastised him with a look. "He doesn't usually go outside without a hood, so I am not sure about the light comment. But I'll remind him he can take care of covering the windows on his own." Axen was grateful for the disapproving tone in his voice.

"And about the responsibility, he is working on fixing that," Maarten defended. As a master of his emotions, he moderated his voice, but the loyalty of the statement was undeniable.

The grizzled soldier tapped his chin. "I will tell him when I see him that he needs to behave himself. There is no reason he should be scaring you." Inclining his head, he looked through his lashes at Axen. "Are you afraid? Will my talking to him about it make you feel better?"

Mette and Axen shared a long, concerned look.

Axen could see a suspicion bloom in her new aunt's eyes as she said, "That would probably help. But there's more. He wasn't in the same mood this morning as he was last night. He wouldn't speak Tersinian to me. He smells horribly. I had to use this to even stand across the room from him." She held the little vial out for Maarten to inspect. Even the hardened soldier's nose wrinkled as he smelled the potent brown and shiny ointment in the jar. He sneezed.

As Axen's anxiety rose, the blanket of comforting fae settled on her shoulders. The soft, believing look in Mette's eyes calmed her nerves. She wasn't alone. Both Mette and Maarten believed her.

Mette and Maarten murmured to each other.

"Do something, Maarten," Mette whispered, chastising him out of the corner of her eye.

"I will leave a note for Icen on his desk to have him come to speak to me," Maarten said. Their support felt validating to the princess. "We will get this mess straightened out soon, my Lady Princess."

"If he interacts with her, the entire problem could be solved in one night," Nic articulated, his voice coated with embarrassment. Axen's blood cooled.

"What does he mean?" she asked, flustered. "I . . . I don't understand?"

The expression Maarten directed toward Nic could have frozen ice.

"Nothing at all, my dear. Some think that if you were to bear his child, the magic would heal," Mette soothed, reaching for Axen's arm to pat it.

"That's what happened to my parents," Axen forced out. "When each of us was born, the magic healed a little. I just thought that. . ."

"Oh, pshaw. Your parents' love for each other and for you was the main reason the magic shifted. Focus on getting to know Prince Icen first. The rest will come." Mette took the conversation in hand, giving a pointed look to Maarten.

With a bow and a click of his heels, Maarten raised his voice and changed the subject. "The castle is under direct attack from rebels at the gate. Icen has been doing everything he can to keep us inside safe." He gave Nic a sidelong glare. "King Caissidde moved many loyal troops into the castle walls. We need help. Right now, the castle will hold, but something permanent needs to be done. The king has determined to see if your family can lend any aid."

Axen nodded. "Am I ablc to leave these rooms?" If Icen were not under the same rules of confinement that she was, she should be able to move about freely too. "Maybe I can do something to help?"

"No," Mette spoke up. "These are the safest rooms by far. We need you to stay here so Icen can focus on the castle as a whole. If you leave, I am sure he will feel compelled to direct his attention to your safety."

"Okay," she reluctantly agreed, trying to shake the disappointment of being treated like a prisoner.

"We will stay in contact over the next few days. We will give you and Icen as much time together as possible, hopefully to activate the magic we hoped would come from your marriage," Maarten said. "You have time, but something needs to happen soon."

Axen nodded. Her concern was redirected to the safety of the warring people. That, and possibly the magic of the world, was more important than her personal dilemma.

"Except something is off with Icen," she reminded. "He's almost two different people."

"Yes. I will do what I can, but I suggest you ask him outright if necessary about it," Maarten said. "Once that problem is settled, I am sure you both will be in a position to help with the war and begin healing the magic. If not, we'll arrange something else."

"Yeah. Maybe she can love that self-centered jerk enough to give him an heir," Nic's voice was carried away as a sudden gust of motherly wind swirled around Axen, lifting her into the air. She almost laughed at their defense of Icen.

Mette curtseyed and stepped out of the room with a few parting words. "Maarten will check in on you tomorrow evening. The guard rotation is down to six men, the most trusted ones. If you need anything, do not be shy. If this problem with Icen isn't resolved soon to your satisfaction, we will come get you. There will have to be another way to stop the rebellion that doesn't put you at risk."

The combined wind whisked Axen up the stairs to the wedding chamber.

Icen waited for her. She scanned him for threats, and found that as opposed to Daytime Icen, he sat quietly on a window seat in the wedding chamber, staring out at the sunset. Her feet whispered into the plush carpet. Relief relaxed her shoulders to see he wasn't hiding in the shadows.

The sunset glittered off his black lizard scales. With her hand on her sword, Axen waited, unsure why the wind had brought her here. Somewhere in the back of her mind, she was concerned about her safety. It was silenced quickly since the Icen before her was the lizard, and she was content that meant she didn't have to fight for her life, at least not yet. She still didn't understand how his transformation from Night Icen to Daytime Icen worked, and until she did, she would need to remain alert.

Icen turned his glowing, ice-blue eyes in her direction, not even attempting to hide his face. His coiled hair still obscured part of his features, and the dimness of the room altered Axen's vision, making his lizard traits more gruesome and frightening. Despite this, the waning sunlight twinkled off his scales and created a halo of rainbows around him. He offered a small wave in greeting.

"Wind," she declared. Icen twitched as though he had been struck. The wind flapped the ends of their clothes. "I need more light, and I need something to put waste in." A bucket appeared at her feet, and the artificial lights lit up the room after the curtains drew themselves shut.

Satisfied, she turned to Icen, hand resting on the hilt of the sword. "I am sorry, Icen. I am going to ask you to do something. I am sure it will not be pleasant for you." She sucked in a breath. "I would like to cut your hair."

Icen's shock was loud in the silence. The slits of his eyes and nostrils narrowed as he spoke. "Why?"

Laughing nervously, Axen slipped her dagger out. "I had a pretty terrifying and confusing day. I hope this change will keep that from happening again."

Icen balked at her request, his face contorting in what appeared to be confusion.

What a strange look he has. Axen puzzled over what was different until she realized that his expression didn't form exactly the way a human's would. He looks more like a scared animal than a human.

Despite his obvious distaste for her request, she didn't rescind it. She hoped this change would help her get answers.

"And this will make you feel safer?" he asked. Axen nodded with vigor.

Her back stiffened as his gaze traced the contours of her face. She extended the dagger on the flats of both her palms. “Yes. I need to clearly see your eyes and read your expressions. I need to know why sometimes you seem so menacing, and other times you seem so . . .”

Icen stepped to her, gently slipped the dagger from between her fingers, and cut the hair in front of his face in one fluid motion. His scaled hand held the dagger by the blade, and it didn’t cut him. “I’m sorry I reacted the way I did. I will try harder.” Hair drifted on the wind around her, floating slowly away from existence.

A new realization chilled the blood in Axen’s veins. Icen could have used his agility and stealth to hurt her. The understanding that he had not thawed her reservations.

“You . . .” She had no idea about the abilities he possessed in his altered state. Her breast heaved from the sudden rush of adrenaline, but Icen paid her no heed. He continued to crop his curls with a diligence that assuaged Axen’s fears. This wasn’t a man out for her blood.

A warm gratitude and trust spread through her, alongside something else—interest. While she hadn’t expected Icen to put up a fight, his immediate response to providing her with comfort and safety was thrilling. His self-restraint in not using his animal ability also spoke volumes to his character.

The wind intruded then, another sure sign that everything was okay. They never interacted with Daytime Icen but appeared very concerned with Night Icen's appearance. His hair was evened out and curled to a shine. Not a hair was out of place when the wind was done. She could almost imagine a hand extending from the mothering breeze to pat the top of his head.

Without any effort exerted on her part, Axen sensed the weight of the dagger as the wind lashed it against her leg. She was free of anxiety for the first time since meeting Icen in the woods.

Axen's gaze lingered on her husband. His short hair entirely changed his look. The large, bouncing, voluminous mane was chopped so short that the tight curls hardly moved. His face, marred partially by lizard-like scales, was noticeably human and very handsome.

Butterflies emerged from the curious cocoon of Axen's stomach. Icen's defined jaw and cheekbones were a strange and dramatic contrast to the narrowed eyes and fangs. While the hair of his eyebrows was hard to decipher, beneath the dominating light, she could see ridges where they should be.

Almost against her will, Axen approached Icen, one hand lifting. "Your . . ." she picked a small scale off the breast of his shirt. Long sleeves with ruffled ends brushed the backs of his square hands, where his gloved fingers were out of sight. Broad shoulders and powerful biceps filled the dark-blue coat's sleeves. It hid the likely patches of scales on his arms from view.

Embarrassment filled Axen as she noticed Icen watching. Her stomach growled loudly, and he growled gently back. A fanged, charming grin split his face, and she had to turn away. Warmth grew in her heart.

Chapter 23-Axen

"You must not have eaten yet," he said before bowing. "I sent dinner away, but I will call it back." The wind picked up speed, tugging at Icen's coat tails to make him stay. They were Axen's allies, but Icen persisted in his retreat.

"No," Axen blurted, and stilled Icen's feet. "I mean—" she scrambled for less demanding words. "Wait, my lord. Please join me." She gestured to the table.

The openness of his expression turned dark in an instant. "Must you force me to bear this?" he hissed, leaning toward her from his place near the door. "Must I be forced to do something that I have not done in months?" Despite his cool tone, Icen's face was free of any signs of anger. She could sense an eagerness behind his façade.

Axen snorted back a laugh. "Must you do what? Eat? Do you not eat?" Axen was content. Maybe her relationship with Icen had turned a corner. Hope filled her.

Icen's eyes went wide at her laughter. One odd eyebrow arched. Axen chuckled and took her seat at the table that had appeared between them. Icen's mouth turned up in bemusement. "I eat."

"Eat with me," she invited.

The wind skipped around her in excitement, and soon there was a second plate and a much larger chair on Icen's side of the table.

"I thought you were on my side," he muttered as his wind fae swirled away. He took his seat reluctantly, and Axen had to remind herself to lower her shoulders away from her ears. She fiddled with the diamond-studded band Icen had given her at the wedding as she scanned herself for weapons. The sword at her hip was a tripping hazard, but she didn't dare remove it from where she could draw it easily. While he appeared and acted more amiable than Daytime Icen, Axen wasn't willing to take any chances.

As she processed her surroundings, the lights in the room dimmed. Axen directed a laugh down at her tunic and trousers. "I should probably dress for dinner."

A low rumbling chuckle escaped Icen before the wind immediately encircled Axen and clothed her in an elegant evening gown of silky silver charmeuse that twinkled in the low light. Her copper-tinged, dark hair gleamed as it rested loose and free on her shoulders. Her face felt different, and she wondered what the kindly wind had done to make her skin feel so dewy. Breathless, she looked at Icen. He turned away slightly to give her privacy. He appeared to all the world as if he wanted to disappear into the shadows. Once the wind died down, his captivating ice-blue eyes flicked in her direction for a second.

Reaching out, she picked up the long-stemmed glass from her place setting. It was filled with a dark, bubbly liquid. "I can tell you are looking at me." She chuckled again, leaning on her humor to cover up the awkwardness tingling through her consciousness. "Have your eyes always been that color?" She took tiny sips from her glass. The emotional shift within her from fear to comfort, comfort to fear, wore on her. She patted her hip, looking for the sword that was no longer there. She knew she could ask for it, but knew doing so would indicate distrust, and the knife at her place setting would work in a pinch.

"That's my mother's ring," he said, nodding to her hand that gripped the flute. She noticed Icen's hands were clutching the tablecloth, wrinkling it. Her eyes moved to the ring that cast tiny rainbows onto the glass.

"It's beautiful."

"I never thought a Tersinian would wear it. Especially after," his voice trailed off.

Axen almost set her fork down, but her stomach roared its protest. "I can imagine." She bobbed her head at him, eating slowly, hoping he would join her. "Thank you for entrusting me with it. I'm sure that was a challenge."

He did not reply. His gaze rested on the plate in front of him. Bite after bite, Axen suffered as Icen didn't move to eat or relax his tense frame. She didn't know what to say to calm him.

"You have unique eyes," she commented, biting her lip.

"I don't know what color they are now. I don't much look in mirrors," he admitted as Axen moved to try the next Xahamenian appetizer. She traced the path where Icen's gaze skipped across the food and table adornment to meet hers.

"They are a beautiful silvery blue. I would say their color reminds me of the blue moon," she said, taking a bite and falling into meditation as she chewed. Part of her wanted to stare to provoke him into speaking more or perhaps to see which parts of his face were human and which were reptilian. The curiosity warred with her desire to help him feel comfortable and less like he was on display. "Although it looks as if around the . . . pupil, there may be some red."

Icen's tongue flicked across his lips, and Axen noticed, with a little dismay, that his tongue was slightly forked and narrower than a human tongue.

"I got the red from my mother. It was the color of her eyes. The blue has always been my own."

"It's lovely. And I apologize for not waiting for you to eat. As I am sure you guessed, I am starving."

"Custom dictates that you would wait to eat as a guest. I am not a host."

Axen mulled that over. "I guess that's true. However, I feel like it would be polite for me to stop and eat at the same time as you." As soon as the words exited her mouth, the appetizers swirled into a vortex and were replaced with bowls of soup.

Icen's face fell. "Please eat."

A searing knife of pity ripped through Axen at his crestfallen form. She racked her brain for some solution that wouldn't damage their fragile relationship and would still invite him to eat.

If she scared him away, she couldn't ask him the questions stirring in her mind. Axen took up her spoon and sipped her broth, watching Icen through her eyelashes. She noticed his hand inching up the side of the table, messing with the spoon that was nearly the size of a ladle. It dawned on Axen that with claws, Icen would struggle to pick up anything delicate.

"Oh, my goodness. I apologize for my clumsiness." Axen dropped her spoon to the floor. In response, Icen waved in a new spoon, which Axen turned a blind eye to, taking hold of the bowl with both hands. Proceeding to hold it to her lips, she tried to sip the chunky squash soup as quietly as she could.

Icen's mouth dropped open long enough for Axen to shudder at the view of his pointed teeth and forked tongue before he remembered himself, and his mouth snapped shut. The sound of his teeth clicking made Axen flinch. She set her bowl down, now empty, with hands that trembled slightly.

His fangs were a chilling reminder that, if he wanted, he could easily hurt her. Disturbing images of Daytime Icen filled her mind. Her hand fluttered to her sword hip, but she recovered, reminding herself to be brave. She focused on pursuing a relationship, for her comfort and for the sake of the world. A small drop of soup meandered its way down her chin, and she picked up the napkin with her full hand like one of her brothers would and wiped her face clean. She sighed as the wind whisked the soup away and a simple, yet traditional Tersinian dish of meat and vegetables replaced it.

Eating the yautia root was easy enough. Axen took hold of the plump tuber. Before each bite, she peeled back the hairy skin. She chuckled to herself when some fell onto her lap and popped them into her mouth. Icen's mouth narrowed in suspicion.

"I have brothers," Axen excused herself, taking the steak between two fingers and gnawing a piece off . . . which wasn't hard, considering the steak was cooked to perfection. She allowed her eyes to roll back in her head as she let out a groan of joy.

"You have to try some," she said. "It's amazing. It melts in your mouth."

She kept her eyes fixed on the meat to keep it from soiling her clothes until movement from Icen distracted her. He had removed his gloves. The sight of the human-shaped, if scaly and nonpliable, fingers with pointed claws at the end relieved her. She had been expecting the entirety of each finger to be a claw. His fingers awkwardly curled up into his palm.

"Do you prefer dancing or reading?" she asked before taking another bite. She kept her eyes level on Icen's face as she asked before turning her attention determinedly back to the meat.

"I haven't needed to dance in a very long while," he said. These words reminded Axen of the decade-long war he had waged with her people. In her periphery, Axen caught movement as he rested his forearms on the table. His muscles were taut. Both he and she were wound tight, as though waiting for the other to spring first. Axen wondered which of them was the predator.

Chewing, Axen tried to make her attention less threatening while remaining alert for danger. "So, you like to read," she decided. "I like to dance, and I like to read. Though honestly, put me in the jungle or on the sparring ground, and I am probably most comfortable."

His eyes bored into her, unwavering, questioning.

Rising rapidly to her feet, she ignored the pain in her hip as she bumped the table. She held her arms in a close-partner dance form.

"I haven't danced in a long time," she hummed softly to herself before gliding across the room. By the far window, she paused, giving Icen the opportunity to eat.

As she returned, she smiled to herself to see that Icen's plate sat empty. Eaten. She neared the table, spinning to a stop, but before she dropped her arms, Icen rose, bowing deeply from the waist. Icen slipped his gloves back on and shuffled toward her. His proffered hand shook.

"I do like to read, and I would like to invite you to dance." His breathing rate increased as he continued speaking. "I am also more comfortable in the shadows than in the light. While hand-to-hand combat isn't my strength, I enjoy the strategy of warfare."

Axen's hands fluttered around her face, trying to dissipate the heat in her cheeks. She would have turned away in embarrassment if she hadn't remembered Icen had put himself at her mercy too.

Her heart skipped a beat. Another hopeful smile creased his face, and it was her turn to go slack-jawed. As she studied his very charming, very fanged smile, a scale on his face peeled slowly away and fell to the floor.

She placed one of her hands in his outstretched one, and the other inched of its own accord to the new spot of human skin that hadn't been there before. Stroking the now smooth spot with her thumb, she caught her breath.

"It really is skin," she whispered. Her eyebrows drew together in confusion. "Why did the scale fall off?"

Icen's beseeching eyes caught hers, encouraging her to continue. Something is going on. Axen covered her mouth.

The prince nodded her on. "The fact that it fell off is important."

She was flustered by the rush of warmth that sprouted in her heart, forgetting what she had just said. Icen's face filled with pure, unrestrained pleasure.

"You . . . are brilliant," he said as though reminding her she could figure anything out if she set her mind to it.

Axen licked her lips, convincing herself to focus on the puzzle of his words and the importance of the scale sloughing off. She was too flustered. "I will think on it," she said, her subconscious mind thrumming over the mystery. Her blanket of fae hummed along to the tune.

An evident disappointment overtook Icen's lizard-like features at her confusion, but he placed his free hand at her waist. "Music," he said aloud. His breeze immediately complied. An invisible orchestra played a mellow tune. Though Icen's steps were a little stiff, confirming the disuse he had claimed, he floated Axen across the room. She had to look down to ensure the fae hadn't actually lifted her body into the air.

They glided arm-in-arm, trying to glean answers from the other without asking a question. Icen's iridescent blue eyes drew Axen into their depths. Mesmerized, she found she had somehow stepped closer to him and stood barely inches away. There was an animal grace to his movement, and where she should have felt radiating heat from a human body, she noticed nothing but rippling strength in each fluid movement.

How had they gone from a standoff across this very room this morning to standing only a breath's distance away this evening? Why did she feel the stirrings of attraction to this version of Icen despite his horrific actions earlier in the day?

Icen's reined movements demonstrated concern for Axen's opinion. Her trust in him grew.

Are human movements odd for him now that he's part lizard? Her eyes trailed to the new scale-free patch on his face. It was as rich and dark as the rest of the human skin she could see. There was so much going on that she didn't understand, but she knew she would eventually if she persevered.

"Is this how you take on a new skin in the morning? Is that why the scale fell off?" she asked.

Icen's silvery blue eyes looked away as his arms fell to his sides. She perceived his struggle to answer. Her intense scrutiny afforded her the understanding that more than fear kept him from speaking.

Pressing him again, she asked, "Why do you not have scales during the day?"

The way he cocked his head in confusion was human-like. Axen smiled a delicate smile.

"I don't," he said. "I always look like this."

Axen's smile fell away, and she withdrew. "What do you mean? The last two days, when I saw you during the day, you wore human skin and none other." She didn't add that he also smelled more like an animal than he did now, and was far more petrifying.

"This is the only hide I know I wear," he said, rubbing the bare patches of skin on his face. His mouth gaped open and shut. She waited for him to say more, but it was as if he couldn't form more words. "But..." As he continued in his attempt, Axen was concerned by the veins that stood out against the skin on his temples and neck.

"Your daytime self said that you were a different kind of beast during the day, and though it was hard to tell about your face, I know it was scarred and not at all scaled." Axen unconsciously stepped back.

A wave of pain passed across Icen's face, and he hunched over as if he had been struck in the stomach. Axen pulled the chair behind him and urged him to sit. "I am so sorry," she repeated several times until she mustered up the courage to place a hand on his knee. At her touch, his tightness melted away. Cohesion? she wondered. Were tender moments like this when they could achieve Cohesion and heal the magic?

Icen spoke, "I don't wear another skin during the day." His pained expression molted into an embarrassed one. "At least I don't think so."

So, he doesn't know he transforms, then. Another thought seized her. "Oh, I don't know when I'll have another chance. Fae, please bring me my sword."

Chapter 24-Icen:

Icen hooked his arm through Axen's, marveling at how soft and soothing her warm skin was through his sleeve.

"Wow," she said, wide-eyed. He tightened his hold on her before they stepped through the wall that was not a wall. She swayed. "I didn't expect that," she added chipperly, nudging him in the side with her elbow.

The enchanted swords clinked together between them as he tugged her down the secret stairwell. "My armory is this way," he said.

"I'm glad you're here," she responded, leaning more heavily into Icen's support. "I feel dizzy."

He cracked a half-grin. Her positive attitude delighted him, since he knew how gut-twisting walking through a magic portal could be.

"You'll get used to it soon." He patted her tense fist. Her fingers tore into his arm. Weightlessness buoyed his step as another sizeable chunk of scale slid to the floor when she shook her clenching grip free.

She bit her lip in her cute, confused way.

You are brilliant, my princess. You will understand all of this soon. He tugged her attention from the next puff of light as another scale fell. "Come on, I need to grab something." Axen followed along, dazed but willing. "My mother constructed this passageway through magic, back when magic was stronger and more available than it is now. I have added a few things. Until recently, I didn't use this for much other than transit," Icen explained, thinking about how he had hidden this stair from her. He hadn't meant to guard the secret, but it had made coming and going without her notice much more convenient.

If the curse would let him clearly tell her how he could break it. Actually, no. Having to share my greatest regrets and sins would be embarrassing. He wondered why it had to be a secret, even if he was grateful it was. Facing his decisions alone was enough of a challenge.

"And . . . are there many hidden passageways in the castle?" she asked, stiffening her spine.

"It takes a lot of fae to create a passageway. It takes even more fae to create a permanent passageway. Even here, near the fountain of magic, there aren't enough currently." They are increasing. He had sensed them and wielded them. Every night, every moment, every touch he shared with her seemed to heal the more withered of the fae that he had long since given up on.

"The fountain?" she asked.

"Yes. The fountain of magic connecting Xahamen to Jeony is here, within the castle," he hedged, pleased when she didn't press more. "Back to your first question.

No, there aren't many secret passageways. This one isn't secret, but the entrances are only accessible by fae magic."

"Only you can enter, then?"

Icen twisted his lips to the side, pensively chewing on his cheek. The fae swirling around her could open secret doors if only she knew how to use them. "Only those who can manipulate fae can open them. So currently, yes, only me. Though possibly with some training, you could too."

"Will you show me sometime?" Axen smiled. Her shoulders relaxed.

"Of course. It will be interesting to see what traits your fae take on. And having more fae wielders sounds like a benefit."

Except maybe Regan's sword. That was something he didn't understand. Regan had broken in on their wedding night. Icen had revealed so many secret entrances to that usurper that he was sure he must have missed one. Perhaps it had been the sword cutting through the fae that kept the doors shut. A shudder wracked him as the chill of the stairway sank into his bones.

"I have entries to this hall from everywhere in the castle. The only places it doesn't open are into the wedding chamber and your personal bedroom," Icen explained with a shrug. "The ancient enchantments there prevent more doors from being built, especially magic ones. Cohesion's power trumps both Harmony and Entropy, keeping both of those rooms safe for those who occupy them." Icen ran his hand along the wall beside him as they descended. As they passed entrances, the room beyond would flash in and then out of sight. “The doors must remain shut to be hidden. And all of these entrances you see are locked, which means someone couldn’t accidentally stumble through a wall.”

Axen nodded. Her hazel eyes brightened. “Oh, so this is where you have been watching me from.”

“If only,” he teased back. The muscles in his legs grew tense and less usable by the second. “I need to grab something,” he said before stepping away from the princess’s grasp. She cocked her head, watching his every move.

“I use this blanket to warm my body in these dank hallways and stairwells as I am exothermic,” he offered after a silence. “If I don’t, my blood freezes in my veins, and I can’t move.” He neared her again. “There are both benefits and detractions of being like . . . this.”

Settling the blanket over himself, he reached out to take her hand and place it gently back on his forearm. The warmth of her skin invigorated his icy blood.

“Ah, here we are.” They turned into the armory. All sorts of weaponry lined the walls, none of which Icen cared much about.

Axen’s eyes grew huge. Icen slowed their matching pace to let her drink it in.

He led her to an enchanted ice dais. Whimsical wind decorations adorned the front panel. A rose, the beloved Xahamenian flower, painted red, was carved at its center.

"What a beautiful place," she sighed, fingering the maga flower that twisted around the hilt and the scabbard of the Tersinian enchanted sword at her waist. She drew it out, extending it for Icen to take.

"When I take this one out for you, the slot will be ready for the Tersinian blade," he said, reaching out to withdraw the warmly-glowing, blue Xahamenian blade from its protective ice slot in the dais. The fae of the sword buzzed around the couple, electrifying their clothes and hair until they settled in a whirlpool of air around the Tersinian blade. The blue and silver light melded, separated, flashed, and married before their eyes in a dazzling display.

"Please do the honors," Icen encouraged. A faint flash of purple light engulfed the couple as the Tersinian sword slid perfectly into the slot. The prince snatched Axen close as a light and a sirocco blasted the couple together. Their bodies collided, arms whipping around one another to steady themselves against the hurricane. Her warmth distracted him from the surrounding chaos. The comfort tempted him to enjoyment, but he would deny himself that pleasure until he could break the curse.

With arms around his princess, Icen dropped his blade. The Xahamenian sword hummed as it clattered to the floor.

"I haven't felt that much unbonded fae in a long time," Icen breathed, backing away from Axen as soon as he was able. Stooping down, he scooped up the sword and offered it to her. He tried to ignore the sudden ache in his arms.

"I think it would make more sense if you gave it to Kole," she said, waving it away.

"No. You need an enchanted blade on your person," Icen insisted. He watched as her face fought through a myriad of emotions. She set her jaw.

"You're probably right," she agreed. "Thank you."

"Shall we go back?"

Axen's eyes had already wandered down the magical stairway. "You said there are benefits to being part lizard?"

Clutching his special blanket closer around his shoulders, Icen backed into the stairwell. "I am stronger, faster, and more agile than a man." His stomach quivered at the direction her questions were flowing. Thinking quickly to divert her query, he redirected their steps to his hidden haven.

"Have you been out of the castle to help with the rebellion, then?" Axen asked. He noticed that she, too, had moved on from the conversation and moved into the shadows of the descending stairwell.

"Out of the castle? No. I need to remain here to keep the magic shield strong," Icen said. Axen glanced at his face. His fangs glinted with his eager smile, and she returned it as she tugged him farther down the stairs.

"How much do you know about the magic?"

"Not much," the princess admitted. She preceded Icen down the stairwell, running her hands along the walls in a mimic of Icen on their way to the armory. There were fewer entrances here, but there was one farther on in particular he was angling for.

"Let's head farther down. I have something to show you."

When they reached the dead end, Axen huffed. "I did not find the secret entrance I was hoping for."

Icen bobbed a bow. "It's right here," the prince obliged Axen's curiosity with a flick of the wrist. A door appeared.

Axen leaned into Icen. He could feel her shoulder against his arm, and it made the blasted door nearly impossible to open with his cumbersome paws and claws. Shoving the door open, he wiped at his face and took in a steadying breath.

In the room beyond, bookshelves rolled from floor to ceiling. The sconces along the crown molding lit themselves, and Icen watched as they drew Axen's eyes up several floors of books.

"So many!" she exhaled. Icen watched in delight as her form merged with the ocean of colors, words, and information. His eyes went to the ring of rainbows dispersed by his mother's ring, on his wife's hand, in his personal, secret library. Another breath of pleasure filled his lungs. He tried to squelch it.

"We don't have this many books in Tersine," Axen held a stack of books with unmasked reverence. "Dad never really could spare enough scribes to transcribe anything that wasn't necessary. And all were volumes of the art of war, rather than literature."

"Your climate is not so friendly to paper as ours," Icen shrugged, noticing the way her eyes brightened with his interaction. "At least the cold is useful."

The prince trailed his princess past the spines in a rainbow of colors, and he stood at the bottom of each ladder she scaled.

"There are books in Xahamenian, books in Tersinian, books in languages of all the Five Lands, books in languages with written characters I have never seen before," Axen called down to him, reading several spines aloud. "Books of astronomy, books of mathematics, books of religion and geography." Her voice faded as she neared another shelf.

"It's a vast sea of knowledge," he confirmed. Euphoria enticed him to recklessness. He wandered to the far end of the room, impatiently awaiting Axen's notice.

"Don't spend much time in here, eh?" she teased, waving her hand in front of her face as dust puffed up from the ladder and drifted lazily through the room.

"It's the decaying magic," Icen rumbled back, feeling her as much as seeing her draw close. "It's impossible to stay ahead of the degeneration."

Having effectively captured her full attention, Icen pulled back a heavy rose-red drapery to reveal several large windows, taller than the ones in the wedding chamber. They opened onto a brightly lit wall of vegetation.

"Roses?" Axen asked, placing her hands on the glass. The thorned rose stems and jagged leaves pressed themselves against the other side of the window, revealing in some places their white underbellies. Each thorn was tipped with deep red, the forerunner to Xahamen's chosen royal color. "Isn't it too cold for plants?" Her fingers left behind the faintest of smudges as she turned to Icen.

The peaceful feeling exuding from Xahamen's fountain of magic enveloped Icen. He knew by the easing of the wrinkles at the corners of her eyes that Axen was beguiled by it too.

"I thought you might like this the best," he spoke to the window. "My mother tended this before me. Before her, it was neglected for many years. You can still feel her touch on the fae by the wind that is especially caring. Some may be Nari's, too, but my mother's fae is fussy like a mother hen."

"Oh, so the fae that tries to dress me came from our mothers?" she sighed. "The garden is gorgeous." Her breath puffed around her face in a ring as she rested her forehead against the crystalline glass. "It is a special glasshouse. Maarten told me to ask about it the first day I was here."

"This garden is Xahamen's magic well. Power, and sometimes fae, arrive here from the Jeonian fountain. The power energizes the fae before it returns to Jeony to be invigorated again. That is the Cohesion cycle of the magic in each of the Five Lands." A smile danced across his lips. "That fae is the strongest, though right now, there isn't much. In the past, it has also brought in unbonded fae from Jeony."

"And what does your fae feel like?" Axen asked, eyes torn between his face and the verdure.

Icen didn't want to answer this. It felt too intimate. "My mother told me my fae feels like a guard dog."

"Oh, it's the wind that keeps me safe?" Axen clarified.

Icen shied away from her smirk.

"How do we get out there?" Axen's fascination attracted her back to the windows, where she searched along the wall.

The turn of the conversation disconcerted him. "You can't go in there," he barked. No one could see his failure within. "It's forbidden." He wasn't sure why he had spoken those words. There was no rule about who could enter the garden. He reached up and rubbed his forehead.

Her fingers curled into her palms as she took a giant step backward, away from the garden. They balled in front of her chest, frozen, waiting for permission to relax.

"Oh, okay," she managed to say. "Thank you for showing me. Will I be able to come back here?"

"Of course."

Her disappointment at him refusing her entrance to the garden seared Icen's conscience. He opened his mouth to explain his fears of letting her come too close; to tell her that he wasn't ready to share this part of his life with her, wasn't ready to let her that close to himself and his responsibilities. He bit back the words. Axen swiped at the dirt on her bodice. Steeling his resolve, he silently promised that he would soon show her the garden . . . probably.

"Yes. I would very much like it if you would come back." It wasn't everything, but it was a start.

Another scale fell from the back of his hand, disappearing in a puff of light.

Chapter 25-Axen:

With dawn approaching, Axen patted her cheeks to try to keep herself awake. She was certain she wasn't dreaming; life had been idyllic the last few nights she had spent with her new husband.

"Jaque mahte," Icen said triumphantly. His ice-blue eyes surveyed the layout of the game board.

"What a game," she chuckled. Icen's wind-like fae swept away the game pieces with a miniature land spout. Axen had never played Ajed before. It was all about strategy and battle tactics to pin down the head of state into surrendering. They had spent four hours strategizing, advancing, and chatting.

"You did well," Icen said, tapping the empty table. His claws clicked on the enchanted ice.

"I learned quickly." Axen inclined her head. She knew he had gone easy on her the first few times they had played in the early hours of the morning. But at some point, she smirked, he knew I was going to be a challenge. Like how I feel about asking him about the war. She caught him looking at her, and offered a faint smile.

"I wasn't expecting that to be so intense." Icen rubbed his neck with the palms of his hands, the claws scritching across scales. They both stood and stretched out the cramping they experienced from hunching over their pieces.

Once limber, Axen moved to the window. "I told you that war is a way of life in Tersine." Most lately because of you. "That's why I wonder if soon you could teach me to use my fae?"

The sun was below the horizon. Her pink and purple morning hues paraded themselves across the sky.

Icen sighed, tapping his knees with his hands and moving to stand beside her. "As it works right now, your fae provide you a sturdy shield against attack. With us being close to one another, my fae will protect you. But soon, I will teach you how to encourage them to follow your will." He didn't touch her, but his gentle eyes embraced her form in a manner that tickled Axen's warm skin into gooseflesh.

"I am glad of the small moments we have been able to steal," he murmured.

It had only been a few days, but a delightful chill tempted Axen to take his hand. Her fingers twitched against her self-restraint. If she touched him, she knew he would depart, and she wasn't willing to be alone yet, not if she could help it.

A flurry of fae whipped around them, dropping a paper into Icen's palm.

"How goes the battle against the rebels?" she asked, tracing her finger over the roses carved into the window seat. Her gaze was trained on Icen, waiting.

"Tersine's tide is turning," Icen disclosed, showing his teeth in a yawn. "It happened last night sometime. The shift was apparently 'dramatic' and the ties to our union 'unignorable'. All the rebels have been pushed back into Xahamen."

Calm filled Axen's heart. Her sacrifice, her marriage to Icen, was making a difference. Were they falling in love? A delicious glow toasted Axen's nerves from the inside. "I'm so glad."

Beneath the chill outside air, the three moons lit the blue-white landscape. She sighed, turned, and reluctantly meandered deeper into the room, eyeing Icen in her periphery.

Why can't you hug me? Is that too much to ask? It had been weeks since she had received physical affection, and Icen's companionship tantalized her with the possibility. *I'll be okay.* She wrapped her arms tightly around her middle.

The Xahamenian sword glowed from where it leaned against the table. In a fluid motion, she withdrew it from its sheath, spinning it to test the balance. The fae trembled along the razor-sharp edge, interacting with her blanket of fae.

A thought seized her. "Drastic and sustaining, the same night we exchanged blades. How fascinating," she murmured as the air hummed with the rapidly increasing circular motion of the blade. "Or was it our visit to the fountain that healed the magic most?" Her attention focused as she directed the blade through several smooth slashes, satiny parries, and abrupt chops and blocks.

"I would assume both," Icen responded, but Axen only partially heard.

The meditative actions nudged her desire to hug Icen from her mind. She placed the blade back into its scabbard and leaned it against the table. With one last look at it, she scooped up a sparring staff. She brandished it threateningly toward Icen, then winked. The veneer on its wooden shaft shone a playful challenge. While she was confident in restraint-fighting, even with a sword, she would rather not make a mistake and accidentally harm Night Icen. Daytime Icen was a different story.

"You are always looking for a fight." He winked back, already prepared. A staff dangled loosely from his grasp. His eyes followed Axen's movements with intention.

Hair billowed around her as she advanced.

"Your gracefulness with a weapon always astonishes me," he said, bracing the staff in front of his body. "I feel the same way about all the people from Tersine I have ever come against in battle or in practice."

"We fight to stay alive." Axen shrugged again, whipping the staff back and forth. The firm wood pressed against her forearm and quivered from the force of the tightly controlled strike. "Before you, we had marauders from the sea."

"I'm sorry," Icen said, striking as Axen moved forward. His eyebrows drew close as if in repentance. "I know I can't change the past, but I am determined to change the future."

The solid, almost hollow sounds of wood striking wood deafened Axen. She pressed unrelentingly into Icen, toying with him and knocking him off balance and back on again.

"I trust so." Axen laughed as she poked Icen in the chest and toppled him over on the wedding bed. Her thoughts turned to current war, and the one her coming here had ended. She did not draw nearer, though he lay there a long time, staring up at the blinking stars. The sight of him across the bed, carefree and relaxed, filled Axen's heart with happiness. A warmonger no longer.

"If I ever want to find joy, I cannot go back to fighting without a just cause." He extended his hand, and when Axen placed hers in it, he drew her toward him, tugging her down onto the bed.

Axen looked at the prince quizzically from the corner of her eye. He motioned to the sky with his chin.

She eased her body into his side, placing her head against his shoulder. He shifted, and her head tipped back against the bedspread. She lifted her hand in frustration. A reprimand beguiled her tongue—but Icen spoke first.

"I can't touch you like this," he said. It was almost like he had read her mind, but she knew he hadn't.

"Like what?" she pressed, holding herself while swallowing back the sting of rejection.

"When I'm not completely a man."

"Why?" she pushed again.

He gaped, mouth open like a dying fish.

"Let me guess. You can't tell me. It's one thing you aren't able to say?" Over the last several nights, Axen had learned Icen wanted to answer her questions, but sometimes something physically held his tongue hostage.

"Maarten left me a note," she said, changing the subject. Placing her hands behind her head, she kicked her booted feet where they dangled off the edge of the bed, bouncing the feather mattress. "He believes that our advancing relationship is shifting the tide of magic in our favor. 'Small moments of Cohesion,' were his exact words."

"Please wait. I want to tell you." Axen's knees wobbled as Icen took her hand. "I need a little longer."

"I can wait." Her hope quieted her fidgeting.

"Have you looked at me tonight?" he asked in return. His question was probing, leading her toward an answer, toward a hope that somehow his appearance was the key to why he didn't touch her . . . yet.

She had looked at him. Her secret thoughts burned at the forefront of her mind. "Obviously, I have, Icen. But why not do more than that?"

Icen's hand clutched hers a little more tightly. Axen squeezed it in return. A fire inched up her arm. "You deserve better."

"Better?" The lights in the room dimmed to reveal the expansive night sky above their heads.

"I am afraid. Being vulnerable is hard. I . . . fear rejection and failure."

"Doesn't everyone?" A shooting star caught her attention, and she pointed. Her heart thudded in her temples.

"I see it," Icen rumbled. "I wish I could better control the change, but . . ."

"Me too," Axen said as thoughts of Daytime Icen nauseated her. Icen's shift from a kind, lizard-skinned man to a violent, frightening human haunted her dreams.

"I would never hurt you, Axen."

Axen trembled as she heard the sincerity in his voice. She believed that this nighttime version didn't think he would hurt her, but the daytime version . . . Her sword fingers twitched. "How do you know you won't?" she asked.

"I know that if I hurt you, it would . . ." His sentence ended in a gagging sound, a sign that the magic wouldn't let him finish the sentence the way he had wanted. "I . . . I don't want to hurt you. I spend most of my time trying to protect you."

Axen knew this to be true. Icen would never intentionally hurt her, but that still didn't diminish her fear. "Don't you think it would increase my safety if we could stop the war?"

He didn't answer right away, but his fingers kept a solid hold of hers. "Yes."

"So . . ." Axen pressed, rocking over to her side and running her gaze along the curve of Icen's lizard-like nose and prominent lips. She could sense his hesitancy to continue in the way a muscle in his cheek jerked.

He fell silent. To Axen's gratification, he didn't move. Seizing the opportunity, she snuggled closer to his side. Their eyes met. Axen's gaze shied away from the intensity, but felt no fear. "With me . . . . here . . . you are safe. With my magic . . . with our fae . . . the castle is safe, the world is . . . safe." He glanced at her mouth. Her lips curved as her eyes drifted shut.

He jumped to his feet. "I have to go. Something is wrong."

Axen's empty hand dropped to her side. Hadn't he wanted to kiss me? A whirlwind of questions continued to consume her heart. Her fae mirrored her discontent with their frenetic gusting. But the comfort of knowing Icen wanted her safe and to take care of her was a warm blanket in the confusing northern castle and land of ice and snow.

She couldn't enjoy the rising pink, purples, and creams of the sunrise as she waited for him to return.

Chapter 26-Axen:

That evening, after the sun went down but the sky was still pink, Axen settled herself into the wedding chamber to await Icen. A giddy tingle filled her chest as the chamber door opened. The prince wore a short-sleeved, pale blue tunic with a loose collar. Her eyes meandered down to the scale-patched skin on his neck and arms. Today, fewer clumps of black scale disrupted the even, rugged skin.

"The fabric's chafing makes my scales very sore," Icen rubbed his arms to get her attention. His icy-blue eyes, one pupil ringed by a red sunflower, examined her through his heavy black lashes. While there was a twinge of pleasure in the set of his brow, she could tell his shyness came from his concern that she would either be disgusted or displeased. Since Axen felt neither, she took his arm and stifled her own hesitation.

"Your skin feels warmer tonight," she remarked. Besides her brothers, she had never seen a man in such a state of undress, and she kept swallowing and clenching and unclenching her teeth. "I heard people in Jeony wear clothes like this," she said, biting her lip to settle the nerves that filled her core.

"Yes, it is very hot there," Icen replied. "This type of clothing is not common here in Xahamen. It would be too cold for most people to wear these, even in the summer." He gestured to the roaring flames in the fireplace. "Without a well-stoked fire, I would freeze to death, since my cold tolerance is lower than that of a normal human. The comfort is worth the trade-off sometimes."

Unable to resist, Axen stroked her husband's arm. "What did you do today?" she asked, discreetly shaking a shed scale from the palm of her hand as she wandered to the settee. The scale turned silvery-blue and disappeared in a puff of light as it descended.

Another little detail, dangling as a fragment of knowledge, knitted itself in Axen's mind. Soon, I will get a satisfactory answer on his shift between day and night, the scales, and how I can win his affection.

"I slept, checked the castle for secret entrances, and slept more," Icen replied, though he looked at her with suspicion. "How about you? Did you see the daytime version of me again?"

Shaking her head, Axen chuckled a little. "I don't know how to convince you that you have appeared to me in a different form by day than at night."

Icen's newly regrown eyebrows furrowed in consternation. "I don't think I have, but there are lots of things about myself right now that I don't know." He took her words seriously, but there was something he couldn't say. "But no one else has told me I have beside you."

The warm yellow of the sun danced its burning light along the distant skyline, the celestial orb dropping beneath the horizon. As it disappeared, the three moons and the stars lit the world in an ethereal glow. Axen relaxed against the headrest. The fire warmed her, and the glass ceiling framed the thousands of stars. Her contentment grew as the settee tilted under Icen's weight. His thigh brushed hers, and she held her breath.

"Shall we have dinner in the sitting room for a change of pace?" Icen asked, sitting stiffly.

Batting her eyelashes playfully, she placed her hand on the tense curve of his biceps and quirked her eyebrow. "You must eat as well." Last night, he had only managed a few bites before losing his nerve. Axen hoped for more. "I much prefer not eating in front of an audience."

Icen chuckled and stood, leading Axen through the study, down the stairs, and into the sitting room. The room's light dimmed as they entered. Axen covered the smile tickling her mouth with the tips of her fingers.

"I think the fae have ulterior motives," Icen grumbled at the romantic atmosphere before them. Soft string music larked in the background. His strong hands took the chair on either side of her as he pulled it out. Axen swallowed back the giddy bubble of emotion that welled in her chest by smoothing the napkin across her lap with fixed attention.

As they ate, an unanswered question kept circling back into Axen's mind. She didn't want to ask, but her curiosity gnawed at her. "Why did you start the war with Tersine?"

The food on his oversized fork plopped onto his plate. He coughed, wiped the napkin across his face, and spoke. "I thought your mother killed my mother."

"What? Why would you think that?"

Twitching like a cornered animal, he said, "It was my closest friend, Regan." She could hear the anger in his voice. "We were close growing up. He must have fabricated the story. I don't ever remember talking about it with anyone else." Icen's form shrank. "He convinced me that your mother took my mother's fae with her when she left. I never even tried to see if his stories were true." Icen's voice lowered. "I only allowed myself to see that my mother was weak and vulnerable. I thought she succumbed to Entropy."

Axen nodded, tapping her finger against her mouth. She wasn't quite sure what to ask next. Icen forged ahead.

"I allowed him to anger me toward Nari. He also wanted a kingdom of his own. That's why we went after Tersine."

This was new information. Axen hoped it wasn't one of the topics that Icen couldn't talk about. "How did you learn that it was the opposite and my mother actually tried to help yours?"

His eyes bulged with his effort.

Axen prepared to change the subject. Her words halted when Icen spoke.

"I asked my father to confirm the story when this change came upon me. That time I was willing to listen." He rubbed his wrinkled forehead. "If I had listened to him before, I would have been grateful to your mother. Instead, I gave her grief."

Whatever affected this change, it taught him that my mother was innocent. "She wanted to keep your mother alive, but I don't think it was ever her choice." Tears pricked her eyes. She was proud of her mother's actions, and simultaneously sad that the war—and all the accompanying loss—had come from a grief-blinded young man. A rogue in a friend's clothing had capitalized upon that grief.

Icen's jaw worked before he continued, "When I first . . . became like this—" he gestured to his body with one hand—"Regan had been with me. I didn't want him to see me, so I sent him ahead. I needed time to get used to my new appearance."

Axen ate as he spoke. Her eyes danced lightly to his exposed collarbones before she realized what she was doing and forced herself to look at the shimmering rainbows cascading from Jozefina's ring.

"When he saw me transformed for the first time, he panicked and disappeared. I couldn't blame him. And I didn't. That's when I knew he wasn't the friend I had painted him to be."

"You told Regan that you weren't going to help him conquer Tersine."

Icen spoke the next words with great emotional difficulty. His blue gaze met hers, something tight and unresolved in it. "When we, Regan and I, first sent my father to Tersine to meet you, it was to capitalize on the agreement my mother had made with yours that resulted in our betrothal. After the failed kidnapping, we were going to press you to come here and marry me or at least convince you that we were going to wed." He stopped, shoulders slumping.

The silverware in her hand clattered to the table. The constriction in his voice caused her to slide to the end of her seat. His body, poised for flight, unnerved her.

"It was hard to let go of the anger and the desire for revenge I had cultivated for many years." Icen's voice came out hard, but pleading. "We were going to trick you here, and . . . well, use you as a hostage to take over Tersine. I figured it would give Regan what he wanted with less bloodshed."

Axen managed to get herself to her feet. She whispered to the wind to bring her a sword. Icen must have heard, but he did not move. His head bent, and he moved onto his hands and knees in submission.

"I don't believe this," Axen said. If Icen had wanted to trick her into coming, into trusting him, and into her father and brother losing her country by holding her hostage, he was successful.

"We knew that your parents would trust my father. With the promise between our mothers, I knew that if we played our cards right, your mother wouldn't go back on her word, even if she didn't trust me anymore. If my father thought I was improving . . ."

Axen's hands trembled as she raised the sword, searching for an escape route.

Is this a confession? Is he going to tell me this marriage was an elaborate kidnapping? Shallow breaths hissed between her teeth. Every instinct in her screamed run, and yet her feet were as heavy as boulders. She wanted to hear Icen's entire confession first.

"Regan tried to convince me not to go back on our agreement, and I almost fell for it, but Maarten warned me that Regan, his selfishness amplified by Entropy, had greater plans."

Her mind raced, wondering how she could get herself to Maarten. She wasn't without friends in this forsaken place.

"I will die at your hands. I will not harm you," Icen said, leaning forward, neck out. "I don't know if you can do it. When I asked Regan to, his knife slid from my throat without leaving a mark. I don't think I can die yet."

Axen did not strike, and Icen continued.

"Maarten intervened. He tried to separate Regan from me, but Maarten did not know that I had long since let Regan in on all my secrets. And by then, my best friend's revenge had taken on a life of its own. He sold his soul to Entropy and now wields an enchanted sword. He not only wants Tersine, but he wants Xahamen too." His body shook violently with the emotion of his tale. "When I became this monster, Regan believed Xahamen was his. He wasn't entirely wrong. He had already usurped all my power in the army, and I have been too much of a coward to show my face and exert any semblance of control." Several scales fluttered away from his body.

Jozefina's fae tugged at Axen's grip, trying to dislodge the sword, pleading with her for mercy.

"At first, Regan wanted you for his own. He believed that with you as his wife, he could obtain Tersine. Maarten intervened. He told me about Cohesion's secret enchantment of Commitment. That meant that if I could get you to agree to marry me, of your own accord, Regan could do nothing about it." Icen's body trembled. "I sent Maarten to ask you. But then, when Regan couldn't . . . take you, he realized he only needed you dead to appease Entropy.

"And here, you—not knowing what hangs in the balance—blessed my life and our world with your integrity." He choked out the last word, and Axen looked at him more closely, her heart softening and her sword lowering in turn. "You said yes. Because of your love for your country, for your family, for our world. In doing so, you gave us the chance to fall in love and save the world. And me."

"Because I agreed to marry you, I gave us time to save the world, and you to do what?"

"Yes. So I could b—" Icen made a strangled noise deep in his throat that turned Axen's stomach. She moved to stop him as his hands went to his own throat. "The curse," he hissed, dropping heavily forward onto his hands. "It won't let me sss—"

Axen froze, arms outstretched toward him. "Break the curse?" She wrinkled her nose. "What does the curse have to do with our prophecy to heal the magic?" She tapped the tips of her fingers against her belt. "Icen, I need you to look in my eyes as you answer this next question."

A great groan wracked his body, but he turned himself onto his side and looked up. His ice-blue gaze fixed on her, and her body reacted before she could stop it.

"Do you plan to kill me?" She didn't look away, and her breezy blanket of fae held her up, whipping the ends of her hair into knots.

"No."

"Do you plan to hand me over to Regan for his purposes?"

"No."

"Am I in danger?" The warm covering that had been her constant guide and companion told her that his words were true.

"Yes." Icen's eyes flicked to the door before he whispered. "But he doesn't know what I just told you. He can't speak Tersinian."

Chapter 27-Axen:

"I could have sworn I heard his footsteps," Icen said through gritted teeth, pushing Axen behind him. Her calf bumped into one of the straight-backed chairs. The princess stared at the rich texture of hair, cropped short, at the nape of his neck, as a myriad of suspicions trickled through her thoughts. *Answers at last.* When Icen's fae tugged shut the door leading deeper into the suite, she pressed the prince further.

"He wants me dead." She watched Icen for the confirming nod. "To give Entropy more time to wreak havoc. He can't kill you because your curse makes you invincible."

"That's why I have been so worried about keeping you safe," Icen said, waves of scales falling off him in rainbows. "He would hurt me any way he can: the castle, my father, the leadership of this country will fall to Regan, but you are not bound here. Not by magic. Not by me. Your room's Cohesion will keep you safe, but with the magic being slow to heal and Entropy's strength constantly increasing, I think the safest place for you is with your family." He said the words, but his eyes betrayed them. If she stayed, she knew she couldn't remain silent. She had too many questions.

"No, I cannot flee. I came here to try to heal the magic. If I leave, I have failed." Axen remembered her standoff across this room. If she hadn't fled after that, she wasn't about to leave now. "We are married. It would be impossible to achieve the level of Cohesion we need if separated."

Her comment made Icen pause. "Even married, we cannot overcome him yet. He is too powerful at present." He placed heavy hands on Axen's shoulders.

The princess set her jaw. "So are we. We both have fae. Harmony favors me. It favors us. We are supposed to reunite Entropy and Harmony, achieve Cohesion, and keep the magic flowing into Xahamen. It was prophesied."

"The tide turns too slowly," Icen groaned and shook his head. "I can't lose you."

Axen turned away, releasing Icen to his trembling. She peered at the opening that led up the staircase.

"I don't understand . . . why don't we act? Aren't we growing closer? What is stopping us from reaching our first standard of success in healing the magic and rallying around it?"

Axen watched his gaze drop. "What is it?"

"It's me."

"You?" she angled her head in confusion. "What have you done?"

"I try to do what I can from here, without showing my face. I have positioned loyal soldiers strategically. But it's not enough." His voice was free of any defensive note. "I had no idea that Regan had enough men to fight on two battlefronts."

"You knew about them when you sent Maarten to me." Axen scrambled to catch onto one of the many thoughts tumbling through her mind.

"Regan intercepted him. Maarten would not break. He told Regan that he was scouting for my father. Regan didn't know about the Commitment principle. I think Maarten has kept it secret."

"Are you still trying to take control of my country?"

"Tersine? No." Axen's heart tickled to life. "As my wife, Xahamen is your country too."

Axen gasped in delighted surprise. A fleeting smile crossed Icen's face.

"I want to take back the reins of this country. Our country. I want to defeat Regan and protect Tersine," he gulped, clutching at his heart. Icen paused, clearly bearing an internal weight but fighting through it. "I'm the problem. I'm not where I need to be."

Axen stumbled when a flash of light indicated to her that many scales had fallen from Icen's body in a glittering, blazing wave. "We both know what we can do! Icen . . ." Her voice grew to an excited pitch, even as she tried to control it.

"You are beautiful."

Axen took a sharp breath and looked around. "Thank you. I know." One eyebrow cocked playfully as the princess observed Icen's shining, icy-blue and red eyes.

The levity of her words brought a pleased dimple to his cheek.

Was this what she had hoped for? This warm, hopeful look in his eyes?

"You were beautiful once yourself," she said. "I saw your likeness carved in the doors of the chapel. What a gruesome beast you became." He flinched, and Axen raised herself onto her toes. Even with the extra height, she only reached his chin. "The curse—is that what keeps you from allowing me in? Or is there something else that keeps your affection at bay?" She could smell him with their proximity. His odor was musky, almost feral—the scent animal-tinged at the edges. Nothing of his aroma hinted at rotting garbage. The distinct difference made her wonder. "We know that falling in love, or us having children, can heal the magic. What I don't understand is how we can fix this . . . ?"

Her eyes traced his form before lifting to meet his gaze. The wind, Icen's fae, danced along her shoulders and coiled around her neck in solidarity.

"You must be able to give me direction. Is it like children's fairy tales where true love's kiss can break the curse?"

Icen covered his face with his hands. "No. It is not like that." She could feel embarrassment radiating from him, but Axen's eyes widened with understanding as Icen continued, "You are only here to fulfill the promise between our mothers, fulfilling the hope they had in helping heal the world, and because . . . I want you to be here."

The last words stopped Axen in her tracks. "I am not here to heal you from your curse?"

Swallowing hard, Icen squeezed out a "no."

"So I'm only here to heal the magic and jointly fulfill the prophecy with you."

Icen's chest heaved. "Breaking the curse is my responsibility."

"If you can do it, why haven't you done it?"

"That's why I feel so inadequate." Icen went to continue his answer but found that he could not; words refused to form on his tongue. "I guess that is something I cannot talk about."

Axen took all this in stride. Answers were coming slowly, but they were coming. "Do you have to break your curse before you can fulfill your side of the prophecy and help me achieve Cohesion?"

Looking away, Icen replied in Xahamenian, "Yes."

"Well, that settles that. While I am curious about how you'll break your curse, let's focus on healing the magic." *Falling in love, without getting sliced to bits by Daytime Icen.* "Will you visit me in the daylight?" Until she was certain that Icen wouldn't kill her, she feared falling in love with him only to be caught unawares. If only she could convince him that his daylight version and his nighttime version were at odds with each other, and her comfort.

"Not yet," he said in Tersinian. "I have too much work to do. Once the castle is secure, I will be here as much as I can."

Axen heaved a huge sigh. "Does it not occur to you that it shouldn't be 'I?' You should be saying 'we.'"

From the corner of her eye, she watched him intently. He bit his lip and stood, reaching to touch her but stopping before he did. While the raking claws still unnerved her, the warmth of his skin shocked her. His desire for acceptance sang so loudly that, despite her courage, she cowed.

"Remember the prophecy? We must heal the magic, achieve Cohesion," she added.

Icen moved his gaze to her hand. His breathing grew shallow and quick. To her surprise, he took her hand. She could feel his eyes on her face, but she dared not look and chase him off. He twisted his mother's wedding band on her finger.

"Yes. I need to be saying 'we,'" he agreed, bringing his other hand to their conjoined ones as he brushed a kiss across her knuckles.

The tightness in her chest loosened as his kiss lingered. Unable to stop herself from peeking, she noticed how thin and dainty her hands were, dwarfed by his enormous, clawed ones. Her heart soared. They were getting somewhere.

"You are right. This is our only chance. I will not touch you until I can come to you fully man," Icen said, his voice husky. "You deserve at least that much." He rocked forward slightly, distracted.

He turned his attention to the door. She watched his eyes. There was a lot of pain in their depths. There was also something that made a delicious shiver race down her spine—not in fear, in delight.

"I will return. I will keep trying. We will heal the magic, or I will die trying." His last words hung in the air as he departed. "Something is amiss. I need to check it out."

Something in him in that last moment, in his eyes, behind his deformed, marked, fanged, and beastly face, made her unafraid. A profound eagerness drew her to rise to her feet and seek him out.

"Icen," she called, her heart trailing after him. "I can wait for you, but I don't know if the world can."

Chapter 28-Axen:

Axen knew Icen's curse was the last thing standing in the way of their relationship and the magic's healing. If they could break it, if *he* could break it, the war with Regan's rebels would end—their growing love was already making a difference. The magic would heal as she fell in love with her husband, if he loved her in return.

She tried to dismiss her discontent as she armored herself, slipping throwing stars into the pocket of her leather vest. Neither Icen's nor Jozefina's wind fae fought her. They blew in her quiver, piling on top of it several jeweled arrows, and nudged her to belt on the Xahamenian sword.

Having a husband who beguiled her by night and frightened her by day was her biggest problem. His distance from her wasn't giving her a fair chance to win his heart—or him the chance to earn hers.

Finding the secret entrance was more challenging without Icen's assistance, but walking through it didn't disorient her as much this time. Her fae had been eager, tugging and nudging her until she found the wall that was not a wall.

It is my responsibility to heal the magic, too. She would focus on what she could control, and support Icen where she could not. Whatever it took, she wanted to figure out what Icen was up against with his curse. That's why she stood, surrounded by books in the place that had a plenitude of magic and endless knowledge—the library.

She jumped a few times as she heard noises. Some came from within the glasshouse, others from the hidden stairwell.

Which is a threat?

This was the first time she had roamed anywhere in the castle during the daytime outside of her protected suite, and her senses were on fire. Daytime Icen was still a threat, and even if he were asleep like he claimed he would be, Axen feared Regan and his rebels. Moving to the window, looking into the glasshouse, Axen ran her hands along the windows and the surrounding walls to see if she could discover a way in.

Her ears were alert. She wasn't going to be caught lying down. Part of her knew full well that Icen had forbidden her from entering the glasshouse, but her curiosity to enter the jungle and experience the fountain of magic, and maybe encounter a sleeping Icen, drove her subterfuge.

The door creaking open jolted adrenaline through her body. It could only be Daytime Icen. Blood pounded in her ears.

"Oh, Harmony," she pleaded. "Keep me safe." Her fae danced around her, tickling the ends of her hair in warning.

Daytime Icen. Regan. So many foes. The putrid smell reached her nose and permeated the dusty room. Her fae bolstered her, blanketing her in calm and comfort.

The odor fell on her, but a voice hissed from the stairwell beyond.

"How did you get in here?"

Axen's eye twitched. The voice was Night Icen's. She swayed, and her blanket of fae circled her, blowing her upright.

"Answer me, Regan," Night Icen's voice spoke again. "I am giving you a chance to defend yourself. You appear to be stalking my wife. Without a valid explanation, I will run you through."

Stinky. Violent. "Daytime Icen is Regan?" Axen whispered to the fae. They tugged at her clothing and weapons in response. She turned slightly to see what was happening behind her.

Two hulking forms stood in the doorway leading to the library. One shadow took the other by the neck, disappearing into the shaded alcove beyond. Their voices echoed across the library.

"There is no reason I can't enter the library," Regan chuckled, but Icen growled him back into silence. Regan's voice turned cold when he continued. "You had my last man killed."

Axen tensed, tiptoeing her way across the carpeted floor of the library. Nearing the door, she dropped to a crouch and snatched a throwing star from her pocket, wishing she had a dart gun, but also not knowing if it would do any good against Regan.

"You and your men are no longer allowed in the castle."

"I don't think you have a say in that, Icen."

Icen's deep-throated snarl frightened the princess. "I am married now. Men cannot be coming in and out of my chambers at all hours of the day and night without my consent—or hers. Much less a traitor to the crown."

Axen shuddered. She had been vulnerable to attack—to Regan—and hadn't known it. Foolishly, she had attributed his appearance to Icen's curse, making him appear as two different people. She swallowed hard again. The hand on her sword hilt tightened. She could feel the petals of the rose carved there.

"Oh, Prince. Don't pretend you care what happens to the girl. It was your idea to hold her hostage." Regan chuckled. This time, the chuckle had a bite.

"We are not working together, Regan."

"Why did you marry the princess if not to get me Tersine?"

"To heal the magic and to . . ." Icen gurgled, paused, and recuperated. "If only you had tried to understand."

"I understand. That's why I have been trying to kill her."

A silence followed. Axen filled it with her frantic thoughts: She hadn't been wrong. Daytime Icen, actually Regan, was trying to hurt her.

"You are why she thinks I become fully human during the day? How have you been getting in?"

"Fully human? Do you mean this? What I am now? This horrible, deformed, scarred creature I became serving you?" Regan leaned toward Icen, trying to make himself appear bigger. "If she believed me to be you, all the better. People have said we look like brothers."

"You are not my brother. Your body has decayed, and your odor grown rank. Nothing about us is the same anymore."

"You just said your wife believed me to be you," Regan contradicted. "Are we both disgusting? Perhaps she wouldn't know the difference if you died, and I took your place?"

Axen heard the thud of someone's head smacking against the crystalline walls.

"You will not touch her, or I will kill you," Icen threatened. The promise in his voice filled Axen with hope.

Jumping fully to her feet, she rocked forward and took a ginger hold on the doorknob. A fight was at hand.

"I think the girl has caught on to us. I can see your sword's glow beneath the door," Regan barked. "I guess I am outnumbered."

The animal savagery of his tone and the fact that she had lost the element of surprise made Axen's stomach turn. The door between them was only an obstacle and no longer a weapon.

"Do you think she can stand against me as long as you can, Prince?" he sneered. The sound of metal on sheath echoed in the stairwell. "I honestly don't care who dies. It would please me if it were you, but it would serve Entropy best if it were her."

"You know you cannot kill me," Icen dismissed, his calm voice sounding closer to the door. "Our skills and amount of fae are too closely matched. Even if you have that cursed blade."

"But I can kill her."

Axen whipped open the door, throwing the star into the center of Regan's chest. It plinked against his armored sternum and rattled uselessly to the floor. Her eyebrows furrowed. That should have stuck. Something inhuman protected him, too. *Maybe it was fae?* Death stood before her. She needed to focus.

Icen, whom the star had narrowly missed, looked over his shoulder at her with a mild measure of surprise before he moved toward Regan, sword raised.

Before it fell, Regan blocked it, the red of his enchanted blade growing brighter and hotter, slowly melting Icen's sword.

"Oh, Princey Princey, standing up for something now? If you had a spine before, we could have been kings together!"

Axen withdrew several stars at once, lobbing them at the malodorous, possessed demon before her. Once Icen could disengage, she tossed him the glowing Xahamenian sword. Together, they made a united front.

"Leave, Regan," Icen commanded, though he whispered a command of attack to his fae. "And don't come back."

A mix of Icen and Axen's fae swirled around them, *whipping hair, weapon and clothing. The fae from Regan's sword were slowly subdued into nothing.*

Is this what achieving Cohesion looks like? Axen marveled as their fae pressed their weight into Regan, subduing him.

"It looks like you two are learning to work together. How precious!" Regan coughed, sidestepping through the wall. His parting words echoed around them. "I'll find a way to kill her, Icen. And soon your curse won't be able to keep you alive."

Icen thrust his sword into the disappearing wall, but it struck the ice blocks with a ringing clink. He turned toward Axen. "I will keep a constant vigil until I am again assured all secret entrances are sealed. For now, though, I need you to keep to the wedding chamber or your bedroom."

Axen's eyes fell on the melted and twisted blade that Icen had tried to wield against Regan's enchanted one.

"That blade can kill me, and it can kill you." Axen looked up as Icen spoke. His eyes lingered on the spot where Regan had disappeared through. "Entropy's desires are slowly overcoming Regan's. It sounds like Regan wants to be king, but Entropy needs you dead. It pushes him, like a whisper in his ear, to achieve its one purpose." His voice dropped. "It will consume his life and body."

"Is Entropy a being?" Axen asked, forcing back the panic. "That being that we just saw?"

Icen shook his head, eyes shut tight. "Entropy is an energy, a desire. It is the world's propensity to fall into chaos. I think because Regan has aligned itself to its influence so much, that he believes himself to be Entropy. One man, one body could never hold all the essence that makes up Entropy."

Axen nodded, eyes wide. The man she had met in the woods on her first trip into Xahamen, the man in the study, the stench, all that had been Regan. Not Icen. Icen had never tried to kill her.

Tears filled her eyes, and her knees trembled. She didn't resist when Icen bent down, scooped her up, and whisked her up the stairs. He settled her into the wedding bed, tucking the blankets around her.

"What are these?" he asked, gesturing to the stack of books at the bedside that her fae had brought from the library.

"I'm hoping to find another way to hurry the magic along and understand your curse," she whispered. His clawed fingers reached out, snatching several books from the pile.

"These might be helpful to you," he said, placing a hand on her cheek. "I promise I will return soon, my princess. I will not abandon you."

Axen tried to focus her eyes. "You need to make a Tersinian promise," she intoned. Her gratitude brought life back into her weary soul. She stuck out her pointer finger. "Promise me."

"Okay," Icen agreed, peering down at her, newly encouraged. "What do I do?"

Axen traced her finger across the middle of his chest in the shape of an "x." "Now you cross mine."

With his sharp claws, Icen did the same, careful not to tear the cloth of her shirt with the sharp tip. An internal and an external burning commenced in Axen's chest where his finger touched her.

"Is it supposed to burn like this?" He grabbed at his neckline and gasped as he looked down his shirt. The skin above his shirt betrayed the tips of an image glowing a spectacular silver. Each line curved, forming a shape that she couldn't see beneath the cover of his shirt.

"Promise me, Icen, that we will unite our goals," she repeated, feeling the wind pick up around her. Her hand went over her blazing heart.

"I promise," he said before turning and disappearing into the study.

As he left, the burning subsided from Axen's chest. She looked down curiously at where it still tingled and noticed the symbol of a maga flower, shimmering like the silver moon, tattooed where Icen had crossed her heart.

"What new magic is this?" she wondered aloud, cupping her hands over the beloved symbol of the representation of her love for Icen. This manifestation of her love for Icen, a tattoo—a heart-bearing—that betrayed her feelings for him. When no answer came from the silence around her, she turned to her books, reading straight through the night. At some point, her eyes crossed and blurred, despite her best efforts to keep them focused on the page.

She no longer feared the sunrise because she knew she would be safe. Her dreams were filled with ideas from her studies on healing the magic. The end of Entropy's reign was near.

Chapter 29-Axen:

Icen's hand was on her cheek, gently waking her—though maybe he wasn't trying to wake her at all, only to pull the book from beneath her face. Axen muttered something unintelligible to him before she heard an unexpected noise outside the chamber. The door swung open. Its echo ricocheted off the windows. Both Icen and Axen stared wide-eyed at King Caissidde and Maarten, who stood in the doorway. Axen was in her nightgown, and Icen in his short-sleeved, collarless shirt. They were on the bed, Axen lying down as though her head had been on Icen's lap, and Icen sitting with a hand caressing Axen's hair.

She shrank beneath the coverlet, trying to mask the deep crimson flush that seared her cheeks and neck. Icen inched himself to block her from view.

"Pardon our intrusion. I probably could have guessed, but I didn't. I'm sorry," Caissidde babbled. The King, then Maarten, backed out of the room.

Icen muttered a quick command to Jozefina's fae, which swirled an appropriate outfit onto Axen. She patted down her fresh tunic and breeches as she stood.

"I will stall them," he said, helping her to her feet.

A smile found its way through her embarrassment. Icen was on her team. He had returned, and the books detailed clearly how he was supposed to break the curse—it was truly entirely up to him.

"Alright, then." The tremor in Icen's voice convinced Axen that he was equally flustered. He ran his hand through his short-cropped hair, shutting the door behind him.

Alone, Axen fanned her face. She didn't want to know what Caissidde and Maarten thought of what they had seen. Stiffening her spine, she followed.

"I can't believe this. I can't believe this," Caissidde muttered to himself. He was lightly shaking Icen by the shoulders. "You," he said, turning on her with a hopeful, disbelieving smile. "How is this happening? Do you love him? Is that why the rebels are retreating? Why are you still so . . ." King Caissidde turned his confused attention from Axen to Icen. The King's eyes took in Icen's scaly skin. "Oh, never mind," he coughed. "That was not at all what I expected, and Maarten hadn't warned me. I apologize. I would have never thought—anyway. Icen, we need to talk."

With a sweep of his hand, Icen's fae bumped a chair behind each occupant except Maarten, who stood guard by the door. Axen sat. The chair skimmed across the floor to stop next to her husband. The prince offered his clawed hand to her. Touched, she accepted.

"Much progress has happened, but we found a dead man within the castle just a few minutes ago. There is no explanation except that your shields of fae are failing. People are entering the castle secretly, somehow."

Axen bit her lip as she watched Icen's face. She could feel Maarten's eyes on her.

"We know," Icen disclosed, inviting Axen into the conversation. "With Harmony growing stronger and forcing itself equal to Entropy, Entropy will not rest until Axen is destroyed."

"The castle isn't safe for her," Maarten concluded. He continued to evaluate Axen's responses, and she shifted. Her friend's face betrayed none of his feelings about what he had witnessed in the wedding chamber.

"Our suite is safest for now," Icen added. "But the rest of the castle, no. We have been breached, and while I will continue to do what I can to maintain our magical protection. I don't know how long that will last."

"Do we take the princess?" Maarten broke his scrutiny to speak to the king.

"And disrupt this?" Caissidde gestured to Axen and Icen's conjoined hands. "We need more of this. It might fix, well, everything."

Yes, Axen wholeheartedly agreed. *But first, Icen must fight through his own demons.* That is most important—healing the curse. "I will continue to do my part," she averred. "And Icen is trying." She met his twinkling eyes and nodded. He returned the gesture.

"You know?" he murmured.

"Yes." She brought his knuckles to her lips, and their brush calmed the tension in his shoulders. "And I know you cannot tell me, because your silence protects you from interference. It truly has forced you to heal alone."

Maarten stood back. His arms crossed tightly across his chest. There was a worried crease between his brows.

"Do we maybe have . . . hope for an heir?" Caissidde asked.

"It hasn't even been two months yet, Father," Icen bristled. Axen covered her mouth, hiding a grin.

"From what I just saw—?"

"You saw nothing, Father."

"You weren't romancing the lady?" Caissidde waggled his eyebrows.

Icen leaned in front of Axen, shielding her.

"One can be hopeful." The king bristled. "You are doing something about the magic, about the lizard skin, and about the rebels?"

Tense silence fell over the room. Axen looked at Icen. His eyes were already on her. "Yes," Icen said quietly. "Every minute we can hold out, the better our chances."

"So, an heir?"

"I couldn't do that to her, Father. Look at me."

"Perhaps not," Caissidde conceded.

"Love is not necessarily a physical act, my King," Axen interjected, squeezing her husband's fingers. A puff of rainbow light from Icen's direction brought a smile to the edges of her eyes. "And it cannot be forced."

"I am sorry. I spoke out of turn," Caissidde admitted, sizing Axen up as she rested against Icen's shoulder. "Harmony's power has already increased in Xahamen because of your actions. I fear losing him, or you, or more of my people to Entropy. We have lost so much."

Partially because you refused to stand up to your son. Axen snorted like a bull. "You have a lot to forgive yourself for too, my King. Icen could not have acted if you had exercised your own dominion."

The Prince gasped at Axen's obvious statement, and Maarten's mouth quirked in a half-grin.

King Caissidde slapped his legs and roared with surprised laughter. "You are right, little lady. We all have faults and reasons to forgive ourselves."

Every pointed gaze turned on Icen, but Axen continued. "No one can escape this life without harming others." Icen's eyes met hers, and a darkness of shame warred in their depths. She was glad he knew she knew. The books he had given her had been quite clear, and she had no doubt that his curse had come about because of his own actions, for which he needed to atone to the best of his abilities and then forgive himself. His chair clinked against hers. His tense muscles twitched with such force that she was afraid their company would notice. Thinking quickly, she attempted to give him some space to process their situation.

"Icen's scales have been falling off rapidly," she said, gazing at Icen from the corner of her eye for permission to proceed. He sucked in his lips, then nodded.

Caissidde himself looked surprised. "His scales fall off?"

Maarten perked up.

Axen looked at Icen. "Would it be okay," she asked, leaning closer to him, "to show your father?"

Icen's expression teetered between livid and horrified, but he choked out, "Yes."

Axen seized the opportunity, reached up, and placed her hand on Icen's cheek. The effect on his mood was immediate. The lines in his forehead melted away. His jaw tightened beneath her hands, but she hoped that his humility in this moment would make progress toward breaking the curse.

"You don't have to do this," Icen whispered, though his hopeful eyes said otherwise. "You don't have to touch me at all. It will happen when it happens."

"Oh, hush, Icen. You haven't asked me if I wanted to. You keep assuming that I wouldn't want anything to do with you." Axen blushed at her bold, whispered words. They were only intended for Icen's ears.

The prince looked down and swallowed. “You are welcome to if you would like.”

Axen ignored the onlookers and pressed her forehead and nose to his. “We are getting so close to healing the magic,” she whispered, her voice barely audible. When she pulled back enough to see his eyes, her heart trembled within her at the intense devotion glimmering there. “Don’t give up on learning to care for me.”

He did not speak. He did not have to. He promised they would work together, and now, Axen knew without a doubt that they would. The fae picked up speed, blustering their way through the papers on the table, spinning the beige parchment into the air. Icen’s hand went behind her neck. His arm became a shield to her tender skin. She relaxed into him, sighing.

When the fae calmed, and Icen dropped his grip, she sat back. Cool scales stuck to her forehead and nose.

“Watch,” she commanded as she brushed the scales to the ground. They disappeared in rainbow flashes of light, one after the other. “He is truly trying to break the curse,” she said. “Time is most important in healing.”

A thunderstrike of a noise filled the study, followed by a horrible stench. Filthy men crowded the room.

Icen’s arms wrapped around Axen.

“Get her out of here,” he whispered the command.

Her fingers dislodged from his shirt as his fae swept her into the wedding chamber. Amidst chaos and grappling wind, Icen disappeared alongside the intruders.

Axen's tear-filled, wide eyes only saw the horror-filled faces of Maarten and Caissidde. "Icen," she panted. "Where did he go?" Her empty arms ached.

Chapter 30-Icen:

A sedate, insistent breeze tantalized Icen into wakefulness. Several rose buds bobbed and tapped at his arms and legs. He was on his back, looking up at the canopy in his glasshouse, his garden. His muscles were stiff from the cold, and it took a great effort to sit. He wasn't alone. Regan and his men lay in a comatose circle around him. They were stirring.

Icen grasped for his sword. He noticed that the fae had brought him the Xahamenian blade. A thought crossed his mind: *This needs to get to Axen*. He held the Tersinian sword in his hand and the Xahamenian one at his waist. Stiffly moving to his feet, he leaned heavily into the wind that blew around him. *The fae must be abandoning its post shielding the walls of the castle from breaches, or it is stronger now than when I was here last.* He marveled at how much Harmony had grown, even without his curse being broken. His chilled body rebelled, but with the fae's assistance, he was able to heft his sword aloft. The steel radiated a faint silver.

Waiting, Icen watched the men shake their heads and rise to shaky feet. The glowing red sword in his hand swung around so violently that it blurred. This man, before him, bore little resemblance to the friend he remembered.

Channeling Entropy, he howled from the depths of his rage, driving at Icen with a club-like blow. The prince trembled at the look in Regan's eyes. There was no more love, no more patience, and no more of anything that made Regan human. The light their swords emanated at contact caused Regan's men to cry out in pain, but Icen and Regan's fae shielded their eyes from damage.

Icen pushed fae away from his body to bind each of the rebels. He could still feel more of the fountain's fae amassing around him. *Have we achieved more Cohesion? Or am I breaking the curse more to allow for my half to be strengthened?* His excited mind flung the amassing fae toward Regan, toward Axen to protect her, and to his loyal soldiers. If the fae he had utilized to seal off the castle from attack were abandoning their positions, Icen had to ensure those he loved had enough to keep them safe.

Regan attacked fiercely, driven by loss and a manic attempt at control. Icen pulled his attention back to staying alive. Entropy consumed Regan. The pressure it exerted on Regan's mind was unfathomable to Icen. The body of the man he had once trusted with his life flashed between health and skeletal bone and trembling sinew.

Weakened by the cold, Icen was surprised when one of his wild swoops with the Xahamenian sword bit Regan's side. Blood poured from the wound. It should have been an ending blow.

Regan didn't wield Entropy so much as stand within it. It moved through him, feeding the rage, pride, and destruction Regan had cultivated in his heart. That much was clear to Icen. He could feel the energy of chaos pressing on his mind. It sought to consume Icen, as it had Regan, a last-ditch effort to stabilize itself.

"Regan," Icen gasped between gritted teeth. "Fight its influence. Like Jozefina and Ṇari, our friendship can save you."

The flicker of humanity blossoming in Regan's eyes between blows gave Icen hope. His heart breaking, the Prince tipped backward, carried by fae away from the fight. He kept his quavering blade between him and Regan. Icen watched from a safe distance as Regan's sword trembled. The tip lowered inch by inch. Icen's heart soared—Regan was fighting Entropy's influence. His best friend would be restored to him.

With a mighty groan, Regan fell forward. The evil sword clattered to the cobblestones beneath him. Icen extended his fae to catch his friend, moving along with the air current. By accident, his clawed hand raked across Regan's cheek, and as his hands touched Regan's shoulders, a sharp pain tore through his side.

"Oops," Regan said, standing to hold Icen at his mercy. "Now we are closer to being even. You have cut me twice. I get one more chance." Regan's eyes unfocused. He cocked his head to the side as he listened. "Alas, I cannot. I can feel the well strengthening. So another time then."

Regan pointed the tip of his sword toward the glasshouse's ceiling. A stream of red light from the sword cracked and then shattered a hole in the ceiling.

The garden grew cold. Icen's muscles froze along with the air. He groaned, feeling his wind fae bear him up. They fussed around him, making an impenetrable wall. If Regan had desired to end Icen, the fountain's fae had gained so much energy, Icen knew the evil sword couldn't penetrate them and get to him. Entropy and Harmony were nearing equality once again here in Xahamen. If only he had already broken his curse, he would be able to stop Regan rather than freeze to death.

"I must go after your wife now." Regan's bony frame shrugged as he looked around at his fae-subdued men. "If you can convince your lizard legs to carry you, I suggest you stay here in the garden where Cohesion can keep you safe. Otherwise, I will kill you too."

"Don't hurt her," Icen begged, still searching for Regan's humanity, the friend and brother he remembered. A desperate hope that he could convince the friend he loved to stop his reign of terror compelled him to speak. "Don't hurt my child."

Icen's feet felt chained to the floor as his muscles grew colder by the second. The pain in his side ebbed away.

He tried to swing his blade at Regan, but he was too slow. He saw the shock on Regan's face at his lie.

"You are having a baby? That makes this more interesting." Regan chuckled.

With a wicked grin, Regan turned and raced away. Balled on the ground, Icen wished he could break his curse, because if Axen died, his regret would keep him as a lizard forever.

Chapter 31-Axen:

"You must leave now. With Icen gone, and the castle breached, the only place Entropy can't reach you is Tersine," Caissidde and Maarten insisted. They secreted her away on a back passage of stairs that led down at a precarious slope to the castle's catacombs. Nic had joined them and held up the end of the line. Maarten led the way. When Icen disappeared with Regan and his men, Maarten hadn't hesitated in planning their escape. Axen's safety was his immediate priority.

"If Icen dies, you can still heal the magic. If you die, we start again," Maarten insisted after the end of their fruitless search of the tower and the library. Her mental image of standing in front of the windows, searching, throbbed in Axen's heart. Icen's wind fae had left her, leaving only her protective fae blanket.

She shivered. The underbelly of the castle was dark and dank. Water dripped from the arched ceiling onto her head. She still clutched the iron sconce she had almost swung through the secret garden's window when they had searched but not found Icen.

"Do you know anything about the garden?" she asked Maarten. Her words disappeared into the darkness.

"It was Icen's mother's before him. No one other than Jozefina entered the garden except Nari. Only those who wield fae can enter without assistance." He looked sideways at Axen, as though implying something. Axen shook her head. She did not understand.

As she continued her subdued way through the pitch-black corridors beneath the castle with her two guards and her father-in-law as companions, she wrestled with her feelings. It had been two days of wandering in darkness since Icen had disappeared, and they had no direction or answers to Icen's whereabouts.

"I still don't know why we didn't stay," Nic glowered somewhere behind her. "She could have stayed in her room. What if we don't make it to Tersine in time?"

"You could have guaranteed the magic would hold if Icen died?" Caissidde grumbled back. "I, for one, am not willing to lose my son and my daughter." Grief thickened his voice. Axen's hand went to her heart.

"The room's enchantments are older than anything I know," Nic returned. "Just like the enchantments of the swords, they are unbreakable. A broken piece of Entropy or Harmony wouldn't be enough to overcome the wards."

"Yes. It's what keeps ilk like Regan from entering and murdering those who help the world reach a state of synergy. It is Cohesion's end to have all things work together, good and bad, to maintain the delicate balance that allows life to flourish," Maarten's voice thundered a chastising note. "But to have the princess live as a prisoner? Would you sentence our future queen to that fate?"

Nic's silence was telling.

Axen's legs ached from the distance they had walked. Her heart battled against the gnawing sadness that Icen was lost to her just as she started to fall in love with him.

"Take a breath and hold it," Maarten warned before he hauled her straight through a wall. Bracing herself, Axen prepared to slam into the stones, but the facade led to a hidden passage beneath a tumbling waterfall. Nic was beside them in an instant, thrusting a quick bundle into Axen's arms.

"It's a dry cloak," he said.

Axen thought that the wind would take care of that for her. As she opened her mouth, she remembered she actually couldn't feel the wind at all, except a small tickle at the back of her neck.

"Can you give me dry clothes?" she whispered to the rustling coolness. Her clothes transformed from soaking to damp, and Axen realized that without Icen near, as he had told her, his fae wasn't as capable. She didn't know enough about wielding them to galvanize her own fae into action. *I should have pressed him to teach me sooner*. She also knew she couldn't focus on past mistakes.

Maarten rejoined them, two horses' leads in his hand. Nic followed up close behind with his own.

"This is a waystation," Caissidde said. He stood with Axen while the soldiers grabbed provisions. "We are in the Xahamenian wilderness. I have kept these outposts ready in case we need to flee the castle because of the rebellion." He patted Axen's arm. His lips trembled as he continued. "I will return to the castle and keep searching for Icen there. We will straighten this all out as soon as we can."

Axen could see several men now in a small rock hut to her left, and the glaring eyes of one of them made her nervous. Before she could ask about him, Maarten gestured for her to mount and slapped her horse's rump. Its beautiful white flanks contracted and expanded, launching the horse into a breakneck pace. She let the steed fly beneath her. Her bow and arrows at her back and the borrowed sword at her waist. The enchanted Xahamenian blade had gone missing. Without knowing how to use her own fae and without an enchanted sword, she was vulnerable to attack here in the wilderness. *We'll make it to Tersine.* Her hope fell flat.

Maarten and Nic rode on either side of her. Despite the freezing temperatures of the high forest, it wasn't until the horses and riders were slicked with sweat that they stopped. Axen could hardly bend her legs as she toppled unsteadily to the rocky ground.

Ensconced in the tumbling rock landscape was a small cottage. The three riders quickly scrubbed their horses down and entered. Maarten moved to build a fire, and Nic set about making some food from the small cupboard. Axen scratched her cheek to keep herself focused as she peered out the window. She couldn't identify any of the landscape. The sun angled through the trees. Its path ensured they were truly heading south.

A prickly warning crept over her, tempered by the calming blanket she wore. The Princess took the throwing stars from her pocket, concealing them in her hand. As they ate, the sun set.

No one in the group sat still for more than a second or two, and each frequently found peepholes in the walls to peer outside through. The forest became devoid of noise just as Axen's disquiet alerted her to fifteen well-camouflaged soldiers.

"Maarten," she whispered. "I count fifteen."

Maarten nodded and reached for his quiver. Nic did the same. The three of them sat poised with arrows nocked, waiting. A familiar smell assaulted Axen's nose, and she whispered Regan's name to her companions. Both Maarten and Nic nodded nearly imperceptibly.

The man himself materialized before the window. His hair was pulled back, red, angry claw marks stretched across his skin. The wound was recent. Scabs were still forming, and the attached skin flapped.

Axen lowered her weapon, calling out the window to Regan in a sound that wasn't quite a greeting and wasn't quite a warning.

"Hello, Princess," Regan gave a deep, showy bow despite his rough garb. He looked different from the time they met in the forest and outside the library. His skin was sallow, pallid.

Axen nodded at him in reply. While her bow rested on her back, ready to be used, she held a throwing star concealed in her hand. She didn't want to be without protection.

"Don't speak much, do you?"

"Not unless I am specifically addressed to do so," Axen replied in hushed tones. "Especially not when I am outnumbered." The men in the forest drew closer, weapons raised and aimed. "Why am I in your company? Are you taking us captive?"

Regan chuckled. "Yes, we are."

"Where are we?"

"In the middle of my army."

Axen scoffed. "I thought your army was attacking the castle."

"Well, yes," Regan scowled. "And have been forced back from Tersine's border, and here. There are more of us than that. Silly woman."

Axen tried to maintain her composure, squeezing her knees together.

"You have known the Beast Prince."

"Icen, you mean. Your best friend?"

"Of course, whatever you call him. I saw him too, maybe better than you, after the transformation." Regan gestured passionately with his hand. "He was hideous and deformed, with long fangs reaching down to his chest, and claws as long as my arm. Hunched and walked on haunches. And yet, somehow that beast managed to impregnate you." Regan licked his teeth in disgust. "Even now, with more human skin than that day, I don't understand how you could have let him."

Axen couldn't hide her confusion. "Wait, what? How do you know that? Did Icen?"

"The Beast Prince? Yes. He told me after he decorated my face."

"Why won't you say his name? You were friends. He told me you were like brothers." Her eyes flitted between Regan and his guard.

Regan spat. "He was weak, Prince Icen. So is my body. These pathetic human creatures."

Axen gasped, clutching at her chest and turning to Nic and Maarten. They stared at Regan.

"Who do you think you are?"

"Who? No one. What? I am Entropy. You puny humans refuse to make sacrifices to fix the magic, and Harmony is so weak. I decided it was time," Regan sneered.

"He sold his soul to Entropy," Nic muttered. Axen could see her guard shift into a more advantageous position to attack the monster outside.

"To the darkness," Maarten corrected. "The kind that would consume us all if we don't continue to fight back. He's still Regan. His will is swallowed up in chaos."

Axen's mind raced. Icen was alive. Regan, as deranged as he was, had confirmed it. As her being pregnant wasn't possible, she wondered what Icen was playing at. Why would he tell Regan this bizarre lie?

Tears formed in Axen's eyes at the prospect of losing her husband. "Did you kill him?"

"Not dead," one of the men sneered.

"Icen is no longer." Wind fae rushed from Regan's blade, wrapping around the man's face. He crumpled to the ground. The other warriors fidgeted, eyes wide as they shared glances.

Regan had truly become a monster.

"Don't worry, Axen, we aren't going to kill you. Not yet," Regan said, spitting through the open panes at her feet. Regan laughed, and the men with him stared, yet Axen found comfort in the steady weight of Nic's elbow resting against her shoulder. The arrow in his bow extended past her face.

"Why doesn't he attack?" Nic whispered.

Axen listened for Maarten's response—there was none other than a groan of wood as he tightened his hold on his weapon. Her heart surged with hope at the reminder that she had two men there to protect and stand with her. Hope ignited in her belly when the little knot of wind fae behind her neck grew larger, tucking beneath her hood. She hoped they were proof that Icen was still alive. Her breath caught in her throat, and the tears fell unrestrained.

"Don't cry," Regan said. He dipped his fingertips into the blood dripping down his cheek. He flicked a death star into his other hand so fast it vanished from Axen's sight in the space of a blink. She didn't flinch. She didn't speak. Her eyes held her repugnance for Regan.

Regan wanted to be king. Entropy wanted her dead. If Icen wasn't dead . . . A chill of horror weakened her knees. *What was this betrayer playing at?*

"Steady, m'lady," Maarten whispered into her ear. His hand went below her shoulder, supporting her. "He's playing at something. If you die, Entropy will control the world. Do not fall for his tricks."

This whispered courage bolstered her, and she managed to stare at Regan in defiance. She knew now that the creature before her, a man who had given all this agency over to his selfish desires, was losing. *Why hadn't he killed Icen? And why hadn't he killed me already?*

In retaliation, Regan tossed the star, dancing it across Axen's right cheek. It bit through her skin in a dotted pattern and wedged itself solidly into the wall behind her. Refusing to give him any satisfaction, Axen didn't cry out. A surge of comfort from her fae bolstered her, and she held herself upright, staring directly into Regan's arrogant, otherworldly, and furious eyes. Her cheek throbbed, and warm drops of blood dripped down her face.

"You are evil," she stated simply. "But you cannot kill me either."

Regan eyed the small drops of blood on her cheek with a blossoming grin. "I can't? Hmm."

Nic offered her a handkerchief to clean her face. The dots were needle-tip small and stung bitterly, but Axen had much to process. She dabbed the blood away.

"The blood. It shows you can be killed." Maarten intoned breathily into her ear. "He will attack soon."

The fourteen captors drew closer by some unseen command. Her blanket of fae blew hotly around her body, prickling up to shield her from whatever attack was coming. The heart-bearing tattoo at her chest surged with ice as a little wind that held Icen's mark fluttered through the baby hairs framing her face.

Inspiration skittered through her. "Please let Icen know what has happened and where I am." She could feel the breeze's hesitance to leave her as they retreated and returned several times before they disappeared. Axen's eyes followed Regan's hand to his blade.

Icen tried to rise as his fae tugged at his cloak and lifted his arms. He waved them away several times, trying to send them back to Axen, but they were insistent. Consciousness toyed with his senses until, at last, he opened his eyes.

He hadn't been able to move as he watched Regan and his men leave, and despair had held him hostage for too long. "Axen," he wheezed before allowing the fae to lift him to standing and push him toward the hidden door. He plodded through the castle, the fae bringing him both enchanted swords. Their lights were glowing faint blue and silver, bolstering him with a little more strength.

He wondered, as he fell down the castle's front steps, if this was where his stand would end, but the fae pestered him, dragging him upright to meet an approaching Kole and Stet.

"Brother!" Kole hailed him, running to lend a shoulder. "Where's my sister?" he asked. "We broke through, and we are here to help."

"I . . ." Icen coughed. "I think my fae are trying to take me to her."

"In this condition?" Stet reprimanded. "You will do no one any good."

"I must go," Icen insisted, his passion lending strength to his chilled form. "Though your warmth is already doing me good."

Stet joined Kole, and they wrapped Icen in a bear hug, chuckling. "You should have just asked for a hug," Kole teased. Once Icen was only trembling from his wound, he looked to his family.

"I must go, but before I do, Axen left this. It's yours." Icen extended the Xahamenian blade. The moment Kole touched the hilt, the world turned a blinding blue, and Icen's fae whirled around him, picking up speed and strength until it formed a land spout around him, whipping the shrubs and smaller rocks in a violent spinning storm.

"The magic, it's healing!" Kole cried, pumping a fist in the air. Stet saluted his son-in-law before the wind fae carried Icen above the forest, allowing him to beeline his way to his destination.

Several hours passed as the land rushed beneath him. A cottage, flanked by a few more than a dozen elite soldiers, came into view. Icen saw red. Regan had to be here. He pulled his sword from its scabbard and thrust his fae forward to force the other men away. His fight was with Regan.

A tornado of fae engulfed each of the men, keeping them from the battle. Icen looked on in awe. He had never seen his fae so powerful before.

"You," Regan howled, leaping at Icen out of nowhere the moment Icen's soles brushed the ground. The red of Regan's sword shed flashes of light when its steel bit into Icen's silver blade. Hostility burned between Icen and Regan, and their fae whipped at their command, two hurricanes smashing broadside into one another.

"Where is she?" Icen raged. He drove into Regan with violent fury. Their blades sang as they spun, struck, and spun again. Fire, water, wind, and rain pummeled each dueler. Icen was running on borrowed time, adrenaline keeping him upright. The burning from the rose tattoo on his chest alerted him that Axen was near, and pressed him to continue. Outside the garden, their fae, their invincibility, and their enchanted swords were a perfect match. The fight came down to their battle skills.

Despite being unwounded in this fight, Regan's voice came in ragged gasps. "I want the throne. Give it to me." A more resonant tone filled Regan's words with power. "We want the world to fall into chaos."

Icen no longer held remorse for breaking his promise to Regan, because the creature before him was no longer his friend. "You don't deserve any of it. You should be executed."

Both blades sank deep into the flesh of their opponent. One cut at a time, one fallen fae at a time, scales tore into chaos. The swords appeared to take on minds of their own as their enchantments took over. The magic endowed within each blade fought either for the future of the world or to destroy it.

"Icen." He heard his name from Axen's lips. He didn't turn. He didn't look. He couldn't, no matter how desperately he wanted to see that she was safe. Hearing her voice, alive, gave him a much-needed push. With everything he had left, he swung. The sword, fueled by long-endowed magic, added to the strike. It cleaved through flesh, and Regan fell onto his back, clutching his stomach. Icen staggered, his injuries burning with every step. Entropy's blade had peeled Icen's skin and left a gaping wound.

"You are still hurt?" Icen remembered back to the first time he had swung at Regan in the study. It felt like a lifetime ago.

"Your blade's fae tried to burn away my wickedness," Regan snarled, rising to his feet but swaying wildly. "It hasn't succeeded yet."

The burning smell that accompanied Regan's sword, which he had discarded after cutting halfway into the Prince's arm, drew Icen's attention. While Icen's arm glowed red, beneath the flap of scale-marked skin was human flesh, clean and new. The smell, the reek, was from decaying flesh—evil being burned away.

"Icen, I'm here!" Axen's voice pierced Icen's revulsion. He gave one last look to Regan, who stared up at the sky.

"Are you dying?" Icen asked, too wary to draw near his former best friend.

"Yes," Regan said. Icen gritted his teeth against the terrifying truth in his words.

"Icen?" Axen's voice came from behind him. She caught his eye before looking at the fallen man.

"Go to your wife and leave me," Regan hissed. The shell of a man turned to the woods, crawling away.

Icen wondered if he could end the deranged man, but the word "wife" filled his heart with light. He turned to Axen and gathered her into his arms, holding her tightly to his body to feel her warmth and heartbeat.

"Where is he going?" Axen asked when they pulled apart, though her hand still rested on his chest.

"To die alone," Icen said. His lips resisted a frown as his eyes closed.

Chapter 32-Axen:

The four made it back to the castle as if on wings. The fae caressed Axen's face, despite Icen transporting them in gale-force fae winds to the castle's entrance, where men were fighting.

"We will go help your fathers," Maarten hollered as he and Nic peeled away from Axen and Icen, running to a stop after exiting the wind. "You two need to get somewhere safe."

Icen ducked through the alcove window in the wedding suite with Axen in tow.

Safe. The word echoed in Axen's head. *Is anywhere safe except Tersine?* "Why didn't you kill Regan?" Axen asked. She hated that her voice betrayed her fear.

Icen didn't answer right away. His silence helped her understand.

"You don't want to kill anyone anymore, do you?" she murmured. His twisted, broken frown gave her all the answer she needed.

"We need to get to the garden," he insisted when she tried to enter the king and queen's chamber.

"You need to rest," Axen said. She tried to say it brightly and hide her fear. Icen looked wretched.

"The fountain is strengthening," Icen said. His breath came heavily. He leaned on Axen for support. His visible skin was nearly clear of scales. There was a story there, but she would have to wait for it. "The garden needs help. None of my efforts have worked to heal it."

They nearly slid to the bottom of the secret staircase as Icen stumbled, but between Jozefina's fussing fae and Axen, they remained upright. Every muscle in her body screamed as they reached the library.

To enter the garden, Icen had to hold Axen close as he leaped through the glass windows from the library, opening a portal midair. She heard the steady thump of his heartbeat and basked in the new warmth of his body where she clung to him. She braced for an impact that never came.

The next sensation she felt was Icen tumbling over and a warm humidity hugging her in Icen's absence. She looked up to notice the glasshouse was failing to protect the precious plants within. The top opened to the sky. Snow falling through the hole disappeared somewhere high above them.

This isn't right. Axen was certain, despite never having entered before.

The smell of decay and rot of the gray, brown, and black plants embraced her. With little time to spare for exploration, she helped Icen back to his trembling feet.

Looking between Icen and the garden, she realized that both were all but dead.

"Over here," Icen directed, his body leaning heavily in the direction he wanted to go. Axen supported much of his weight as they made their way to the very center of the jungle, where a pair of lonely vines, one maga flower and the other a red rose, twined weakly together. Black-and-gray powder coated their leaves. Two solitary buds hung down heavily as though they didn't have the strength to face the sun anymore.

"What happened, Icen?" Axen asked, wide-eyed.

"This is why I feared letting you in." Icen shook his head in dismay. "The garden is dying. It has been for years. However, I think it is keeping me alive right now, which is why it has decayed so quickly. This might be the end of the Xahamenian magic fountain."

"Can we do anything to save it?"

"I don't know. I thought it would be strong now, but even with the increase of its own fae, it won't be able to achieve enough Cohesion without me," Icen coughed, his feet shuffling forward. "The garden began dying when my mother did, and I tried hard to fight back the decay. I have never been successful. Regan let the winter in, and I don't know what to do. But if we don't do something, this is the end of the fountain."

Icen's face had grown hollow. His arms hung flaccidly at his sides. "When Regan's men attacked us in the study, my fae instantly reacted to protect you. It transported the men and me here." He pointed to a clearing not far away. "The fae knew that here I would defeat all the rebels. However, before I could, Regan stabbed me with his evil sword." He clutched himself around the middle, his breathing quick and shallow.

Axen trembled. The man before her shriveled and aged. "Please, tell me what I can do," she pleaded, guiding his trembling form to the glass-stone bench beneath the sickly twining rose and maga. It was all she could do to help him get comfortable. The wind had stayed with them.

"I don't know. I hoped that by coming here, we would gain wisdom."

Axen could feel Icen's wind fae rustling through her hair as she cut Icen's clothes away from his wound. She gagged. Icen's skin was rotting away. The smell blinded her with memories of Regan, Daytime Icen. She almost backed away in fear.

"His sword did this?" she whispered, meeting his eyes. The bright blue dimmed with pain, but the red flashed.

"Yes."

"That is why Regan wasn't worried about you anymore. He knew you were dying," Axen muttered. "And that is why you told him I was pregnant, to give me more time and keep me alive."

"I hoped that it would buy you time. If he thought you were also invincible—two beings who could attract fae rather than just one—he wouldn't kill you immediately." Looking around her at the dying garden, the plants shriveling beneath the load of keeping Icen alive, it felt like hope was lost. The garden that had sustained the magic of Xahamen on its own for years was a wasteland.

"With us both alive, we still have a chance . . . Icen?" Axen shuddered.

Icen shut his eyes. The warrior's death rattle sounded deep in his chest.

"Is there anything I can do?" she whispered to him.

Icen didn't respond. His beautiful, dark skin beneath the few remaining scales turned gray. The wind fae with a mark Axen didn't recognize nudged her in the back and lifted her arms, as though trying to guide her, but when she left her limbs to their mercy, they didn't direct her anymore.

Pressing her ear to his chest, Axen listened to his heartbeat until the erratic sound stopped. Grief tore through her. Icen's wind fae whirled into an instant hurricane of force and thorns as they whipped the dead rose matter around her, cutting her. Crying out, she caught the wind's attention enough to get them to stop. The pain was there. The damage was done. Her body dripped with blood from the cuts of a thousand rose thorns, and her heart bled with the fear that they had lost this magic fountain forever. The wind lifted her arms toward Icen, begging her to do something to keep him alive.

Tears filled Axen's eyes, blinding her as she placed her hand on Icen's cold temple. Her hands stroked the curve of his jaw and cheek.

"Icen," she murmured, sitting up, hands on either side of his face and her forehead against his. "Oh, please wake up. Please."

No breath tickled her face. The warm skin she had waited so long for was growing cold.

There was an unusual crackling rustle above her, and Axen whirled, realizing with horror that the vines were extending sticky white roots over Icen's form, coating him in a living coffin.

"Oh, no!" she cried as she tried to peel the clinging root hairs away. "Don't take him from me yet. Please."

Ignoring her, they slowly crept across Icen's chest, and though Axen tore her nails and peeled her knuckles on it, the progression did not stop. She clung to Icen's face with trembling fingers, kissing his cheeks and forehead over and over.

"Please wake up. Please wake up. Please wake up," she chanted. "I love you. How will you ever know that I love you if I don't get to tell you?"

The gentle, invisible hands of the fae blowing around her held onto Axen, coaxing her away from her husband. Strange flashes of light danced on the wind at the edge of Axen's vision. The fae held her fast as a thick, blue-hued sap obscured Icen's face from view. A sudden and complete silence stole the breath from between Axen's lips, and her sobs broke off.

The whole world hushed, reminiscent of a heavy snowfall. Despairing, Axen wished to run and hide, to yell and scream, to break this black shroud that clung to her caged heart, but she couldn't drag her gaze away from Icen's face. The grief crippled her, and she fell against him with her head on his motionless, root-encased chest.

Her warrior's ears picked up the sounds of footsteps approaching her. Fear gripped her chest. She snatched up her Tersinian sword and wobbled to her feet. Icen's wind fae held her fast as Axen caught sight of the flashes of light approaching. The sturdiness of the wind surrounded her, as if with a thick coat of armor. She knew then that Icen's wind fae would not let anyone or anything, friend or foe, touch her should she not wish it.

From the growing darkness, the flashes of light formed a circle around Axen. As it tightened, Axen held her breath. The shine was so bright that she squinted her eyes and was still blinded. The orbs of light drew close enough and dimmed by a degree. Within their glow, Axen saw a woman. She was sublimely beautiful and reminded Axen of Icen, with paler skin. The princess sighed and grinned. Billowing hair floated around the deceased queen's face like a crown. Her red-sunflower eyes resembled those of her son.

"Queen Jozefina?" She reached out to take Jozefina's outstretched hands. Axen could see many things. She could see the nebulous forms of the fae—little wisps of light and color dancing in a cloud around the apparition. Lines of power emanated from Jozefina herself, clear and shimmering and blue in a halo of light. Streams of light flowed from Icen and the single rose and maga plant. These streams of red, blue, and silver, twined into a rainbow of light at the top of the garden, uniting with the dome that reformed the garden's protective covering.

They, mother-in-law and daughter, rose into the air, passing through the roof of the glasshouse just before it sealed completely. Axen glanced toward Jozefina, who gestured toward Icen, entombed at the center of the garden. Grief stormed through Axen. Her breath hitched in a little sob.

"Don't cry, dear one," Jozefina whispered, lifting Axen's chin and wiping away the tears on her cheeks. Pointing, Jozefina directed Axen's gaze to follow the blue lines of power that radiated and faded in the distance. The two women rose high above the castle, high above the Five Lands, until they could see the layout of the whole world.

At the zenith of their flight, Axen saw that each of the Five Lands had a strong band of light connecting it to a central point in Jeony. Two of the lands, Dazmorn and Palameru, had two. The small refugee camp of the Star People glowed orange. The color contrasted starkly against the softer colors of Entropy, Harmony, and the fae.

"This fountain was the main line of power from Xahamen to Jeony," Jozefina explained. "It is nearly dead. Only one umbilicus reaches Xahamen now, much like Tersine."

"Because of Icen?" Axen asked, chin quivering. Jozefina's arm went around her shoulder.

Axen saw the single lines leading into Xahamen and Tersine. Magic flowed only one way—for Tersine, it flowed into the country, and from Xahamen it flowed out. Just like she had been told, Tersine was only being kept alive by draining the magic from the Jeonian font. And now it was draining Xahamen too.

With the world sprawling beneath their feet, Axen noticed the variation of strength in color and light. She could tell some lines were stronger than others. All were weakening as the orange magic invaded its place.

"Entropy remains in Tersine, keeping it alive. And despite all you have accomplished, because Icen still hasn't broken his curse, Entropy is nearly lost to Xahamen. If left this way, all the fae will soon leave Xahamen too to alleviate the strain it and Tersine place on the fountain."

Axen covered her eyes. Dark failure threatened her peace. "Xahamen is dying now too," she said.

Jozefina nodded. “It is. Each line of magic severed from the true source brings our world closer to collapse.”

Shivering, Axen noticed a line that didn’t arc where it should. It pulsated, sending a full arc of magic from Jeony in their direction, stopping midair.

“The power coming into Xahamen, the line of magic, why doesn’t it connect to the garden?” she asked, astonished. “Why doesn’t it reach the fountain?”

With a smile, Jozefina twined a thread around her hand. There was a tug at Axen’s chest. Looking down, Axen saw that a line of power emanated from the maga tattoo over her heart. The heart-bearing tattoo glowed so brightly it could be seen through her clothes.

“You, Axen. You are holding the magic here, with your love and promise to Icen to work with him.”

“Is he dead?”

Jozefina shook her head. “Not yet. He is close. Entropy’s sword cut away the last of his curse. But there is one more thing he must do before he is ready to achieve Cohesion with you.”

“What must I do now?” Axen asked. “Isn’t he supposed to break his own curse?”

“He is. But if you are willing, he will need you to buy him a little more time.”

Back in the devastated garden, Axen moved to Icen's enshrined body. As she placed her hands on the roots, strength pulsed into her. The rose and maga held their small buds up toward the snowing sky. One tear fell onto Icen's chest and then another.

"Icen," she whispered, her voice cracking with emotion. "I love you, and I forgive you for not being ready." Taking hold of the rose and maga vines, she urged them toward her heart-bearing, the tattoo that marked her chest. In the instant the buds touched it, light and sound completely disappeared.

There was a temporary melding. Axen could feel Icen's presence connect with her soul. *Icen, please forgive yourself.* She tried to convey her thoughts to him as their souls passed through each other. She hoped he would remember her plea and forgive himself for all the damage his pride, shame, and greed had brought on the world.

His mind responded with a desperate longing and fear. His soul clung to hers for long moments, and Axen gave as much peace, calm, and acceptance as she could before they separated. Her body melted into the cocoon, taking Icen's place.

Axen saw Icen standing, the maga and rose pressed to his chest, before she shut her eyes.

Icen

He stepped back, looking himself up and down, noticing his hands were free of claws. The cocoon luminesced softly before him.

"Axen?" he asked, looking at her trapped face.

"I will guard her, son," Jozefina whispered in an unembodied voice before fading away. "Heal yourself."

Icen nodded, a confused but determined look on his face. He bowed for several long moments, his fingers resting on the head of the cocoon. When his grief was manageable, he called to his fae. The garden sprang to life around him, fighting through the fallen snow.

"This is to be the most beautiful part of my garden," Icen said.

Icen's fae surrounded Axen's tomb, shielding her.

Caissidde, Stet, Kole, and Nari gathered around—and Kole punched Icen straight in the face. "What did you do to my sister?" he howled.

Chapter 33-Icen:

Icen and Caissidde were surprised and grateful when Stet didn't abandon the alliance after Axen's sacrifice. While Kole had been furious, he had been reasonable enough to continue the war in his sister's name.

Wounded of the last, vicious battle lined the halls of the castle. The death throes of chaos penetrated the greediest and most wicked Xahamenians for several months after Axen's sacrifice. When the surrender came, the weather warmed up.

"No more Regan. No more chaos. No more war," Maarten muttered to Icen with a knowing glance. Regan hadn't been seen in months, and Entropy's influence waned.

Caissidde and Stet stood side by side on the battlements, overlooking the war-torn land. Icen surveyed them from behind. The green of spring covered many scars, in hearts and in the soil.

"Entropy and Harmony continue to maintain a delicate balance," Stet murmured. "Yet Regan is nowhere to be found."

Icen rubbed his head. His curls were growing out again, and they sprang backward under the pressure. Icen, Stet, and Caissidde had been having this perplexing conversation for days now while treating the wounded in the castle as best they could and sending the rebels home with signed truces.

"There weren't many leaders besides Regan," Stet said. His eyes roved down the parchment in his hand with the list of exiled rebel commanders. Regan's signature was not among those on the document.

Icen brooded. While his black eye from Kole had long since healed, the pain from losing Axen had not. "Her face is still there, perfectly preserved," he whispered. He had lost Axen the same day Regan had disappeared, and speaking of the one always led to memories of the other.

His father and his father-in-law turned to him. The kings' eyes were clouded. "I wish we could figure out what to do. It's as though your curse transferred to her in an odd twist of fate."

"The garden has healed. And so has the magic, it appears," Stet comforted, patting Icen's stooped shoulder.

"Only because of Axen's solitary sacrifice," Icen admitted. He latched onto Stet's wrist as though it were a lifeline.

A sad smile crossed Stet's lips. "I wish it did not have to be this way. But Nari and I both had fears that something like this was going to be the result of sending our daughter here." Stet gazed out over the greening land once again. His grief lined his face with heaviness. "It was the risk we took, knowing she could be part of healing the world's magic."

Icen went to apologize again. Stet deflected it with a raised hand.

"We are so proud of her. Do not say anything to degrade her offering." The Tersinian king looked up into the blue, cloudless sky. "Axen wouldn't have done aught she didn't choose for herself. We raised a strong daughter who knew her mind, and neither of us regrets that."

Icen did. The ice-dagger of his own rose-shaped heart-bearing tattoo burned at this remembrance. His hand went to the sting at his chest. His clawless fingers cupped over his heart. It throbbed in a way that wasn't his own, a painful reminder of the woman he had lost. *If only I knew how to get Axen back.*

"Go to her. I am sure Nari will be pleased to see you," Stet encouraged, nudging Icen's shoulder with a strained smile. Icen's heart swelled with pride. The Tersinian king was a man of honor and had inspired Icen to be the same. With Stet's help and Caissidde's support, Icen had worked hard to repair what he could of his childish mistakes and forgive himself for what he couldn't fix. Letting Axen sacrifice herself for him was the last thing he struggled with letting go, but he knew that it was important that he did.

Grief was acceptable. Self-blame got him nowhere.

None of the members of the Tersinian royalty held Icen in contempt, at least not for long. After the fist-fight, Kole quickly burned through his anguish by keeping the rebels at bay. They all agreed, as Stet had said, that Axen wasn't one to be manipulated or forced into anything. She had gone to her fate with dignity, and they would all give her the respect her sacrifice demanded without demeaning it with questions or anger.

Icen padded into the garden. Nari was with Axen's living coffin. The garden had let her come and go as she pleased. The queen's eyes stared at the pages of a book. Her own wind fae rustled around her, willing to please her.

Icen's fae hovered here as well. They refused to leave Axen's side. The garden's rich, spicy, vibrant smell filled Icen's chest. The health of the magic here was a heady perfume, bringing Icen a measure of comfort.

"Hello, Icen," Nari greeted. She looked back over her shoulder as she stood. "I sent the guards away. I wanted to spend some time alone with my daughter."

Despite her steady voice, Icen could see the swollen eyelids and glittering tears on Nari's eyelashes. Icen would have apologized, but he knew Nari would have none of it. Apologies were useless when some of those he had hurt most had already moved past blame.

"It is hard to lose people," she murmured. "It feels even harder to be left in between. Neither here nor there.

She is neither dead nor alive, and yet I don't know what to do to bring her back to this side of the divide." She bent to set her book down on the bench and rubbed her bare arms. "Having returned here to Xahamen, I feel some of the fae I left here giving me strength. I wish they would tell me what to do."

Icen took Nari's elbow. Her words scratched a memory at the back of his mind. They turned to look at Axen's peaceful face. The maga and rose vines behind her form had now grown strong and healthy. One giant bud shared between the two plants appeared large and heavy.

"Thank you for forgiving me for tormenting you and your people, and for taking your daughter from you."

"There is nothing to forgive anymore, Icen," Nari said. "I know you would bring her back if you could." She turned and left him alone. The soft, mossy path subdued her footfalls of retreat.

If he could—the words which had before been like ice to his heart touched his soul. If he could, Icen would trade his own life for hers. He would find a way. It made him feel light. When his mother returned to tell him what to do, if bringing Axen back was an option, Icen would do so without a second thought, no matter what it would cost him.

Placing his head where Axen's stomach was hidden away, Icen sighed. "I wish you were here, Axen. I wish you could see me now. When I was broken, you still saw the good in me. I believe that you loved me and that your love is what caused me to heal." A sob broke his confession. "Thank you for keeping our country strong, for saving Xahamen. There is nothing I wouldn't do to repay you, and yet . . ." he trailed off, noticing a bud with gold petals peeking around the sepals leaning down toward him, reaching for his heart-bearing tattoo. Paralyzed, Icen watched as the bud, moving of its own volition, touched his heart. The moment the unblossomed flower bumped him, the sap covering Axen's face fractured.

A howl tore from his tight throat. He wept openly. Horror and heartbreak overcame him. Falling to his knees, he rested his head on Axen's tomb and wrapped his arms around it. He could feel the roots shriveling, drying into a powder that sifted through his fingers. Through his desperate clutching, the gold-petaled bud persistently nudged him, seeking out his heart-bearing tattoo. In his grief, Icen swept it away, sprawling across his wife's withering coffin. The last crumbling pieces drifted gently away—breaking the Prince's heart. Icen's cries of grief echoed throughout the glasshouse.

He could hear tapping on the glass. Maarten had heard him. The Prince didn't have the strength to rise. Not a single mote of dust marred his shirt to remember her by, and the ice-stone bench was empty, devoid of a single sign that Axen had ever been there. Yet still, the heavy bud grew larger, more gold petals revealing themselves. The bobbing head of the flower slipped insistently between his arms, knocking him off balance.

He moaned in agony as the nudging grew to a crushing weight. He struggled to lift the bud, sinking farther to the ground. In his awkward, prostrate position, he couldn't get enough leverage to shove it away. *Help me!* he commanded the fae.

Icen's fae whirled around the bud. A twisting column of dust that peeled open the fragile shell. The beast prince watched, transfixed. He had never seen this color in a rose before. The petals were a brilliant gold with veins of silver.

Unable to move beneath its weight, Icen groaned in dismay. The bud elongated. The wind danced around him in excitement—he could almost hear a lively tune on the breeze. Excitement filled his breast as the bud grew warm. Wrapping his arms around it, Icen could feel the subtle shift from flower bud and petal to a soft, feminine form as Axen morphed from a flower to a human clothed in a silver and iridescent gown.

Her copper-tinted hair spilled over both of them. Icen shifted himself to a seated position as he cradled Axen to his chest. His eyes remained affixed to her face. Her eyelashes fluttered. Her eyes opened. Once a mixture of green, brown, and amber, they now contained flecks of silver and gold. Icen was mesmerized. Their gazes locked. He did not speak first. He dared not breathe.

"Icen," Axen whispered. "I missed you."

Icen lowered his mouth toward Axen's, stopping a breath's distance away, and waited. Axen accepted the kiss, eyes resting shut. Her hands rose to wrap around his neck. Soon, tears wet the kiss as Icen held his wife close for the first time. His hands wiped both their tears away as he kissed her fiercely.

When the couple emerged from the garden, Maarten cried out in disbelief, the old soldier clutching his heart.

"It can't be," he said, bursting into surprised and delighted tears. "Is it truly you, Princess?"

Axen twinkled with her joy, tucked beneath Icen's arm. "Yes, it is I," she said.

Icen's fingers traced her face, disbelieving.

"How?" Maarten asked. "How is this possible?"

"I can explain," Axen replied. "How quickly can you gather everyone?"

Without another word, Maarten dashed away. The couple floated along behind, the fae sharing in their joy. Icen's eyes never left Axen's face. She could see the fear there, the question.

"I know where Regan is," she whispered to him. "Have you caught him yet?"

Shaking his head, Icen looked at her even more intensely.

"I'm not going anywhere, remember?" She laughed. He tightened his grip around her waist. Tingles erupted in her belly at his hopeful look of promise.

"I'm not going to risk it," he rumbled.

Axen's face burned with pleasure and embarrassment. Icen's eyes returned to her mouth. His arm encircled her snugly, warmly, promisingly.

"Mom!" Axen cried when Nari's tearful face appeared before her in the entry room. The princess pried herself from Icen's hold, one finger at a time. Stroking his arm attentively, she stepped into Nari's open arms.

"Axen!" Stet roared, catching both his wife and daughter in his arms and shaking them back and forth in his abundant joy. "What happened?"

"Let's sit," Axen directed, "and I will explain."

Icen snuggled close to Axen. His arm remained protectively around her as she spoke. His actions left Axen breathless and curious. This was not the cautious Icen she had left behind. She wanted to lean into his embrace, but taking a bracing breath, she explained all she had seen when Jozefina had visited her.

"I had to wait until Icen forgave himself before I could leave the prison his curse and Regan's blade had created for him," Axen said, looking to Icen to make sure that it was okay with him that she shared this bit. He nodded his encouragement.

Peaceful fae settled themselves around Axen. "Regan is here, in the castle. He lies weak in the infirmary. He traded his life for the strength to wield the blade of Entropy." Her gaze grew distant as she relayed all she had learned. "Without the interference of the Star People's magic, this would never have been possible. Since Harmony disappeared from Tersine, Entropy took advantage of the void and occupied the empty space. Regan forged a sword that trapped some of Entropy. The sword needs to be found and destroyed, but with Cohesion achieved here in Xahamen, the Star People's magic cannot gain another foothold. Likely, the remaining three lands will struggle until they have also reached Cohesion as well."

Nari nodded along. "Yes. This supports the prophecy that my bloodline, combined with the royal bloodlines of the five kingdoms, can bring Cohesion to the world's magic. Until my people's, the Star People to whom I was born, magic is neutralized by binding it to the magic of the Five Lands, countries without Cohesion and without our bloodline may face the same fate we just averted here."

Axen took her mother's hand. "And Tersine's line of Harmony will not be healed until our bloodline is united within each of the Five Lands." Looking up, Axen finished the tale. "Entropy abandoned Regan's hollow shell of a body the day Icen rescued me from his clutches. He was left to wander and suffer."

"How awful," Nari murmured. "I wish we could somehow save him."

With a sorrowful note in her voice, Axen replied, "He does not wish it, Mom, or we could."

In a secluded corner at the edge of the infirmary, Regan tossed and turned. He was twisted into a monstrous wisp of the man he had been, unrecognizable to anyone except Axen's enlightened mind. Dark, vacant eyes stared up in disbelief as he saw Axen and Icen's fingers intertwined.

"You . . . One of you was supposed to die," he rasped out. "How did this happen?"

Icen opened his mouth to explain. Regan interrupted.

"Leave me to die," he begged. "Do not torture me anymore. I see darkness in the future. There is nothing left for me in this world."

Grief contorted Regan's scarred face into a mask of horror, but neither Icen nor Axen balked. Nari, Stet, and Caissidde had accompanied the couple but hung back. Nari stepped forward and placed her hand on Regan's chest. He tried to push her away. His weakened body shriveled like a leaf in the fall, writhing in agony. He didn't want compassion, but Nari persisted. She rested her hand on his chest fully, and Regan's twisted features relaxed. His eyes closed. His heart beat three times—then stilled.

"I gave him peace," Nari said. "What little I could do, since my fae is still weak."

The company bowed their heads in respect, grateful and grieved. Too many people had been lost, and even one as wicked as Regan still was a great weight.

"Thank you, Mom," Axen spoke for the group.

"Thank you, Axen," Icen murmured, wrapping Axen tightly in his arms. "I'm certain Entropy and Harmony weigh equally now in Xahamen. Thank you for waiting for me. I want you to know, I've healed."

He turned to the group. "I would love to host a real wedding feast in Axen's honor. We can celebrate our freedom, our alliance, the magic healing, and our future."

With her nod of permission, Icen placed a tender kiss on Axen's waiting lips. "I can't wait to achieve Cohesion with you every day."

Acknowledgements:

For all those who believed in me, encouraged me, read awful drafts, and still cheered me on:
Alissa, Courtney Bellingar, Jean, Shaylin, Hope, Madelyn, Amy Trent, Sabrina, C. Rae, Dee, and Melissa. And those who tried. This book has been through some pretty rough stages.

To my editors who pulled me back from the brink of quitting:

April, your kindness and joy and level head has been a gift. From beginning to end, you stick with me!

Ela, your expertise in polishing my manuscript made it shine in a way I never thought possible.

Robyn and Amy. There are no words to thank you two. I hope God fills your life with every tender mercy possible.

And all my ARC readers. You are the real MVPs, who have helped me hope for a future as a writer.

About the Author:

Jazmin Lister is a true Renaissance woman. She has loved literature since a young age, reading literally every book in her elementary school library. She has also read several dictionaries and thesauri from cover to cover, finding new and interesting words. Her passion for literature pushed her to get a BA in English from Southern Utah University. When prodded, she will also acknowledge having received a BS in Pure Mathematics at the same time. She has since obtained a Masters Degree in Mathematics from the University of West Florida, become a Certified Master Gardener, run a market garden and greenhouse, taught herself her heritage language of Spanish, and homeschools her children. She also enjoys teaching orchestra, hiking, rock hounding, metal detecting, reading, playing the piano, and, when she can get there, exploring her beloved Isla del Encanto—Puerto Rico.

Sneak Peak: Depth of the Ocean

Part 1-The Team

I rushed from the College of Science and Engineering's conference room, my presentation board snug beneath my trembling arm, my briefcase in one shaking hand. Tears poured down my face. I tried to hold the torrent of emotion in until I escaped the many condescending eyes, some of which I previously considered friends and colleagues. Frustration ate at my stomach. I had spent months curating the list of people in that room in hopes of finding someone trustworthy and willing to dive with me.

My ideas, though admittedly strange, were based on research and experimentation. All my data was easily readable and understandable on my slideshow with complementary poster board presentations. From fear to disbelief, the range of skepticism and contempt had been huge. I didn't understand why. My years of research produced solid evidence of the likelihood of colonization success, something an ocean-loving, eleven-year-old me had only hoped possible.

Now, at twenty-four years old, after obsessively collecting degrees, including graduating Valedictorian from Duke's Marine Biology program, men and women I had built relationships with, worked with, admired, and even trusted, rejected me completely and decisively. More hard work wasted.

I pulled my sleeve up over my hand in an attempt to comfort myself as I groped for the doorknob to the stairwell. Tears blocked my vision. In this rarely-frequented stairwell, I knew I wouldn't be disturbed. It was one of my favorite sanctuaries. However, this time in my melodrama, the door opened too quickly, and I tripped in my blind getaway; the contents of my briefcase spilled the length of one of the flights of stairs. My tears filled the depths.

If the US military wanted to purchase my patents so badly, why didn't anyone else believe that my inventions would work too?

A hand-drawn picture of a half-shark, half-squid caught my eye. I had drawn this picture as a small child. My parents had framed it. The dim light caught on the wrought silver, flashing through my tears. It was the image of an imaginary creature, a lusca.

Over time, my ocean obsession grew exponentially. My parents would gift me mermaids, talking fish, shells, books, and classes that supported that obsession. And once I grew a little wiser and my desires morphed into colonizing the ocean floor, they helped me build my very first submarine-style boat, taking me to the beach for hours and hours on end while I tinkered and experimented. They built me up, encouraged me, and then they died.

"Curse them all," I spat out, snatching up the picture and stuffing it back into the briefcase. I couldn't take any more emotion at this moment. I wanted my parents to be proud of me, and for the moment, my mind spiraled into a void of despair.

"Miss Sinclaire!" A voice echoed down the stairwell to tap me on the shoulder.

My hand immediately crept to my pocket, scrambling for the handkerchief stored there earlier, almost as though foreshadowing this scenario. Dabbing at my eyes and nose, I turned. A hard look pinched my features. "Would you like something?"

The young, warm, male face behind me startled me. "Do you really have a working model of the Midnight, Deep Sea Zone suit, and the Ultra-Submarine?" The young man bubbled, nearly exploding at the seams as he waited for my reply.

I searched his face for any allusion to ridicule. His wide-set brown eyes were clear and focused. Deeming him sincere, I answered, "Yes, I do, Mr . . . ?"

"—Correa, the name of César A. Correa is at your disposal, Miss Sinclaire." His hand extended in my direction, and I shook it curiously. "Are they really ready to be used? They have been previously pressurized and are now in working order?"

Balking at his obvious enthusiasm, I whispered with wide eyes, “Yes. Both my MDS suit and the U-Sub are fully operational and await a bit of field work.”

Mr. Correa threw his arms around me in a moment of gusto. “A bit of field work? Doesn’t that sound modest for someone who wants to explore the final Earth frontier?” I wasn’t sure how to take the hug, so I patted him awkwardly until he released me. “This is your lucky day, Miss Sinclaire,” he disclosed. “Although none of those buffoons and scaredy cats in the room back there will come with you, I happen to have a couple spare months lying around. They are waiting to be filled with such an endeavor.”

Presentation boards clattered to the floor again. My red leather briefcase landed with a thud as realization knocked. “Am I awake?” I gasped. “Who are you? How do you know any of this?”

Chuckling, Mr. Correa gathered my belongings. “Well, I heard you were having a conference meeting today with a few people from the university. I wasn’t invited, but I did look up all those recent articles in the newspaper. You didn’t say much there, but one of those older men who exited the room was more than happy to share the details I missed.”

“Where do you get off spying on people?” I asked, suspicious, I had heard this kind of tune before, usually to be followed up by bribery or lying. "I know people like you. The government has sent you to steal, or try to buy, my ideas." I gulped back my next question to keep myself from sounding unintelligent and bitter as I took my boards and case back from his extended hands. He was still very close to me, and I could smell his rich, earthy aroma.

I was surprised as I heard him laugh. "You think I'm from the government? That's fair. You probably have had all sorts of people come to your door looking for a get-rich-quick scheme."

I gave him a side eye as he handed me papers, pens, and red lipstick. "Are you not?"

Mr. Correa bowed from the waist. "I am the solitary grandchild to two sets of grandparents who loved me so much and left me an inheritance. If there is anything I have an abundance of, it is time."

I stood agape. Unable to take my eyes off him, I felt like I was seeing him for the first time. His buck teeth were perfectly framed by vampire teeth, and I shook my head, confused at what I was feeling. I was even more confused when disappointment seized me as he looked at his wristwatch and said, "I'm sorry, but I seem to be a bit behind schedule. I am very interested in hearing your proposal. Would you mind discussing this tomorrow over . . . lunch? Here is my card. Call me later to set a time."

With those rather flighty-sounding last words from Mr. Correa, he was gone. And my heart refused to stop racing.

I was left with a phone number and more hope and dread in my heart than I allowed it to retain in years. Was this the person I had been waiting for? Clutching at my belongings with a vigor I had not possessed scant minutes earlier, I carefully reorganized all my materials into neat stacks. Then I hastened home, hugging the curves along the narrow, windy roads of Mayaguez to the vibrant green and steep mountain roads of San German. Soon, the rural coastal plain of Guanica came into view, the Caribbean ocean filling the horizon, and I skidded to a stop in front of the little yellow ocean house with all the flurry of a child bearing good news to their guardian.

My grandmother, my childhood guardian, knew I was excited before she saw me enter. As the front door banged against the entry table, she hollered from the kitchen, “Sit down, you crazy girl, before you faint!”

I galloped into the kitchen before plopping myself on a worn bar stool; a goofy smile plastered to my face. My fingers thrummed out the rhythm of my heart on the countertop as I closed my eyes for a moment and pinched myself, praying I was not dreaming. The pinch hurt, and my joy grew.

When I opened my eyes to the chocolate pie of congratulations in my Abuela’s hands, I immediately burst into tears. I whipped out Mr. Correa's business card and waved it in the air. "He wants to talk over lunch tomorrow," I sobbed. "I can't believe it. I might actually have a dive mate!" Taking the pie from her to set aside, I launched myself over the table to throw my arms around the woman I loved the most.

"I am so proud of you, Aleja, but please stop choking me," Abuela crooned. The silver-haired, spunky old lady had been my guardian since I was nine and had seen me in such hysterics before. "Calm down, mi Alejandrina," she continued. "I have always known this would happen. You are my beautiful nena who acts a little crazy at every moment of success."

I snorted. "Abuela," I said as soon as I could breathe. "I cannot mess up tomorrow. This could finally be it. I have interviewed so many people and been so cautious. I still wish I didn't have to find someone. If only Mari would be willing to come with me . . . or you?" The tension sobered me while my excitement evaporated. My relationships were few and far between. Other than two good friends and Abuela, I didn't trust many people. And of those three people, one feared the ocean, one was infatuated, and the other believed her wiry arms and legs, and bedtime of eight o'clock made her too old to go. And while I was too paranoid to take a whole crew, Abuela wouldn't let me go down without at least one other person.

"Pshaw. If this isn't the one, there will be another," Abuela contradicted. "It took years and years for your parents to acquire enough funding for their Amazon expedition, but in the meantime, they spent so much time exploring and researching here in the Caribbean, they made many other breakthroughs. This is your first rodeo."

I wanted to believe her, but the fear of never achieving my dream still burned like a fresh scrape.

"Let yourself have hope this will work out, Aleja," Abuela admonished.

I'm sure she saw the sudden obtrusive thought that brought my mood down. "What if this is a prank or joke? What if he doesn't really want to come? What if he is only curious and he just wants to meet to satiate his curiosity? What if he is actually a government spy?" The last two people applying for the position had shown way too much interest in my project, and with some digging by my law enforcement friend Rafi were exposed as government agents. "This is way harder than I ever thought it would be."

"While you do have many things working against you, Aleja, you deserve miracles," Abuela replied steadily, ignoring my worry with a pat of her hand on my own. Her black eyes and gentle face remained placid. Swallowing hard, I hugged Abuela tightly once more before disappearing upstairs.

I lay on my bed, rehearsing what I would say when I called Mr. Correa. Once I was satisfied with my script, I moved to my desk and began scratching down how I would present my idea tomorrow over lunch. These thoughts led me over the past fifteen years of my life.

My grief from losing my parents so young was no longer stabbing. I was no longer a gangly, eleven-year-old girl, stumbling my way through the corridors at Yale, or a thirteen-year-old at Duke who didn't look like I belonged in more ways than one. My hair was too dark and wildly curly beside the smooth locks of my already older peers. My features were too Anglo to be considered Puerto Rican and yet too indigenous to be considered beautiful in a typical American way. My Taino and Boricua ancestry was demonstrated in my high cheekbones and upturned and unusually small nose, and full mauve lips. On the mainland, I was considered foreign, and on the island, I was considered unremarkable other than the fact that I was often labeled a gringo due to my mixed heritage. My life was full of contradictions and disappointments amidst hard work, loss, and the unwavering support and love of my Abuela. Despite my fears, I forced myself to call Mr. Correa.

To my horror, his secretary answered on the first ring, and I prepared myself for the inevitable rejection.

"Office of César A. Correa of Correa House Investments, how may I be of assistance?" Her voice was friendly yet formal.

"Ummm," I began with a rousing silence filler. "Hi. This is Alejandrina Sinclaire. Mr. Correa asked me to call."

"Ah, Miss Sinclaire, we have been awaiting your call. Give me a moment, and I'll connect you . . ."

I waited for the space of a bat of an eyelash.

"César Correa here. Miss Sinclaire, I presume?"

Jumping at the sudden change from the secretary's soprano to the deep masculine resonance of his voice, I felt a rush of nerves as I replied, "Yes, this is Alejandrina."

"Now that I see you are eager for this business lunch, I must ask you. Do you prefer seafood or Chinese cuisine? I need to make a reservation."

Never one to be shy, I declared my preference for seafood. Nothing could beat Puerto Rican Chinese food, but a sit-down style restaurant might be better for our work conversation.

"I shall pick you up at around noon tomorrow, if you would kindly provide me with your address." His taking command of the conversation unsettled and excited me a bit.

I promptly dictated my street and house number. "It's the bright yellow house with the flag on the patio," I added for good measure.

"I will see you then," he stated firmly, a definite finality to his tone. "Goodbye, Miss Sinclaire."

"Goodbye," I echoed weakly as the phone clicked and our connection was severed. Feeling suddenly drained, although the purple light still warded off most of the evening shadows, I peeled off my clothes and sank into a bath. When I came out, Abuela served me a piece of pie.

"So . . . ?" she prompted as she took a bite.

"He is going to take me to lunch tomorrow so we can talk more about my proposal." I knew my voice was tinged with disbelief.

Abuela shrugged and laughed. "I knew he would."

"What if he isn't a spy?"

Abuela's smile faltered a minuscule flicker. "Then I guess you head to the bottom of the ocean."

Hasta el proximo <3

www.ingramcontent.com/pod-product-compliance
Lightning Source LLC
LaVergne TN
LVHW041107080826
845145LV00007B/1711

* 9 7 8 1 9 7 2 1 2 5 0 1 4 *